MURDER SUSPENDED

MURDER SUSPENDED

JOSEPH LEVALLEY

BookPress
publishing

Any requests or questions for the author should be submitted to him directly at Joe@JosephLeValley.com.

Published in Des Moines, Iowa, by:

Bookpress Publishing
P.O. Box 71532
Des Moines, IA 50325
www.BookpressPublishing.com

Publisher's Cataloging-in-Publication Data

Names: LeValley, Joseph, author.
Title: Murder Suspended / Joseph LeValley.
Series: Tony Harrington Series
Description: Des Moines, IA: BookPress Publishing, 2025.
Identifiers: LCCN: 2025909579 | ISBNs: 9781960259417 (Hardback) 9781960259509 (Paperback)
Subjects: LCSH Murder--Investigation--Fiction. | Organized crime--Fiction. | Beara Peninsula (Ireland) --Fiction. | Mystery fiction. | BISAC FICTION / Mystery | FICTION / Thrillers / Crime
Classification: LCC PS3612.E92311 M87 2025 | DDC 813.6--dc23

First Edition

Printed in the United States of America

10 9 8 7 6 5 4 3 2 1

For Catherine McAuley
and the extraordinary women
who followed in her footsteps.

Ireland, sir, for good or evil, is like no other place under heaven, and no man can touch its sod or breathe its air without becoming better, or worse.

— *George Bernard Shaw (1856-1950)*

Irish Terminology / Slang

Boyo – male juvenile, beginner

Cac – feces

Craic – fun, good, or fun activities, also gossip

Feck – alternative for the cruder term spelled with a "u." The same for "feckin'," "feck-all," etc.

Feek – attractive

Garda Síochána or Gardai – Irish national police force

Glunterpeck – stupid person

Gobshite – contemptible, stupid, incompetent person; literally, a goblet of spittle

Hallion – worthless person

Jagging – sexual intercourse

Jammy – lucky

Langer – penis

Maith go leor – very good, excellent

Manky – unpleasant, nasty

Minus craic – the opposite of fun or good

Peeler – police officer

Pure – intense, extreme

Scut – a stupid and/or worthless person

Seafoid – nonsense, BS

Slag – prostitute

Slagging – playful teasing

Sleeveen – a con artist, a rogue.

Stone – a measurement of weight, about 14 pounds

Chapter 1

Saturday, May 23

Allihies, Beara Peninsula, County Cork, Ireland

Like many colossally bad ideas, it began with a group of young people in a pub, drinking shots of Jameson and chasers of Guinness. Unlike most, it ended with two corpses and a baffling puzzle.

O'Connell's Bar was busy on Saturday night. University students were back in town for the weekend, enjoying the excuse to party before third term began on Monday. Their presence drew other young people from throughout the Beara Peninsula—farmers, fishermen, and even a handful of secondary school students who'd reached the legal age of eighteen.

Four of the university students—Dylan, Michael, Niamh, and Lauren—were lifelong friends, reunited in their hometown for the first time since Christmas break. They attended three different schools, but all had grown up in Allihies, a village on the southwest coast of Ireland. They were excited to be sharing drinks and laughs in their favorite hometown pub.

The four's relationships had been jumbles of ups and downs for two decades, but a million shared experiences in tiny schools and an equally tiny village had bonded them for life. Occasionally, their sharing involved romantic entanglements. At age seventeen, Dylan and Lauren had lost their virginity to each other in the tall grasses on the hill overlooking Ballydonegan Bay. It had been predictably awkward and clumsy, and wonderful. They had made a mess of a beautiful woolen blanket, a favorite of Dylan's mother. Later, when she had noticed it missing, Dylan had tried to claim it had been stolen from the back of the family's Opel Astra. She hadn't been fooled.

To Dylan's dismay, the encounter with Lauren was never repeated. She was terrified of getting pregnant, and no promised precautions could put her mind at ease. Now, three years later, he attended Trinity College, and she the Dublin Business School. They met for coffee occasionally, but Lauren's interest appeared limited to friendship.

Seated across the long, wooden table from Dylan and Lauren were Michael and Niamh. Michael was two years older, a senior at Cork Institute of Technology. He clearly considered himself the leader of the group. Nothing new there. Niamh was in her second year at the same institute. She had followed Michael there, not out of friendship or romantic pursuit, but due to a genuine interest in science and technology. She was the brains of the foursome, sometimes expressing surprise that the others didn't spend at least a portion of their free time each day studying the latest spectrographic data from space-based telescopes, or learning a new language, or memorizing the dictionary.

By 1 a.m., the crowd thinned, but the beer and the laughs remained in abundance.

"They did it on a waterslide?" Niamh was more than skeptical.

"I swear," Dylan said. "She mounted 'im on the platform at the top, and they did it all the way down to the pool."

Lauren, equally skeptical: "At the Dublin Community Pool, in broad daylight?"

Dylan, laughing: "No, no, no. In the dark. Like at midnight."

Michael: "Seafoid! The pool's not open at night. Even if it was, it'd be dark. How'd ya see it? They coulda told ya anything. Feckin' moron."

Dylan: "It's true, I swear. Yer right. 'Course the pool was closed. Eight or nine of us climbed the fence and swam bare-ass naked. I wasn't surprised to see some hooking up, but when I saw them two climbing up onto the slide, I told 'em to wait till I got the water turned on. Woulda served 'em right to get some burns tryin' it dry, but I din' want the night spoiled by a trip to hospital."

Michael: "And you knew how to do that? Turn on the water, I mean. Not hook up."

Dylan, ignoring the dig, said, "You forget. I worked at the north pool during my first summer in Dublin. A simple valve controls the flow. Even you coulda done it. Once the water was on, I climbed the ladder to make sure the chute was wet. I *saw* her mount his langer, just 'fore they disappeared over the edge."

Michael: "Well, now you've at least seen someone havin' a go. Maybe you'll know what to do when your time comes."

It took all of Dylan's strength to avoid looking at Lauren. He kept his smile focused on Michael as the others had a chuckle at his expense.

"Mind if I join you?"

They looked up to see the waitress, Moira, pulling up a chair with one hand. In her other, she held a tall Guinness. She said, "You're the last group here. I figure I've earned a pint before I call it a night."

"G'wan, absolutely," Michael said, leering at the young woman and waving her closer.

Perhaps in her mid-twenties, Moira was new to O'Connell's. She was lean, with a triangle face, dimples, and long, auburn hair pulled back into a ponytail.

As if noticing her for the first time, Dylan also stared, but with more curiosity than lust. "You two related?" he asked, nodding toward Lauren, also a slender brunette, albeit missing the prominent dimples.

Moira smiled and held out her hand. "Nope. I'm Moira Blake. Just moved here a couple of weeks ago." Lauren shook the hand, then introduced herself and the others.

Moira said, "Before you ask, I'm sorta hiding out. Bad breakup. Boyfriend wasn't ready to let go."

"Ye picked a damn fair place for it," Michael said. "Hard to get farther from civilization than the coast o' Beara."

"So far, I like it," she said. "I've got a view of the sea from my window and pay half what it cost in Dublin for a flat. I even found a job." She held up the pub's electronic order pad and nodded toward David O'Connell, known as Connie to his friends, standing behind the bar.

"Cheers to that!" Michael proclaimed, and they all raised a glass.

The door at the front opened, and a stocky man stepped in. He had dark, curly hair and bushy eyebrows. His blue jeans and Shamrock Rovers sweatshirt were both faded to pale gray. He glanced around, brow furrowed.

Moira stood. "Help you?"

"Uh, ya. A pint?"

"Sure. Come in," she said, turning toward the bar.

From behind it, Connie said, "Relax. I got it."

As Moira returned to her seat, the man approached. Gesturing toward the group, he said, "Sit? Okay?"

Glances around the mostly empty room and then at each other, ended in nods.

"Suit yerself," Michael said. "Maybe we'll let you buy a round."

The man grabbed a chair, turned it, and sat, straddling the seat and crossing his arms across the back. "I'm Rob," he said in a deep voice with a distinct Slavic accent. Holding up a palm in greeting, he didn't attempt to shake everyone's hands. "I do electrical, and some plumbing and other odd jobs, over in Castletownbere."

"Castletown? Bit of a drive this time o' night," Michael said, trying to sound friendly but not really succeeding.

"Nah, not so far. Made it in less than thirty," Rob said, referencing the minutes he spent driving southwest across the peninsula, from the harbor town on the east coast. Castletownbere was the only community of any size in the region, hosting a supermarket, hospital, and large port for fishing boats. Despite these things, it still fell short of a thousand permanent residents. Rob continued, "I'm doing some work at the cable car station in the morning, so I'm gonna sleep there tonight."

"In the ticket booth?" Niamh said. "How do you manage that?"

"Got a bedroll in my truck." He pointed a thumb toward the door. "If the booth's too small, I can always sleep inside the car."

"I hope you mean your truck, and not the cable car," Lauren said. "You don't wanna be sharing the floor with sheep droppings."

Dylan shook his head and said, "That's no worry. They don't allow sheep in the cable car anymore. Not since they rebuilt it a few years ago."

"Just because it's forbidden doesn't mean people don't do it," Lauren said. "It's still the fastest and cheapest way to get livestock on and off the island."

No one could argue with that, so they all took swallows of beer.

They were referencing the Dursey Island Cable Car which connected the southwest tip of the Beara Peninsula to the island. Stretching up to and over two steel towers at nearly a thousand feet in the air, it was the only cable car in Europe that traversed open seawater. Built in 1969, the cable car primarily transported tourists and lodgers to and from the three tiny villages on the island.

"Wherever I land, I'll be fine," Rob said. "I did almost two years against the Russians, so I've slept in worse."

"The Russians?"

"My mother's Ukrainian. When Putin invaded, I was in Kiev. I signed up like everyone else. I got a… uh, how you say… a free pass out when a shell fragment found its way to my lung." He tapped the right side of his chest to emphasize the point. "Better now, but don't ask me to run any races."

"So tell us about…" Dylan began, but a cold gaze from the newcomer stopped him.

After an uncomfortable pause, Michael said, "When you walked in, we were sharing stories about doing it."

"Jagging, ya mean."

"Yep. Tryin' to see who'd done it, or seen it done, in the weirdest places. Dylan, for example, was claiming a couple did it on a waterslide in Dublin. Feckin' lie, 'course."

"It's true, dammit!" Dylan snorted, followed by laughter all around.

"I'm guessing ya already talked about the car," Rob said, downing a shot and rubbing the back of his hand across his lips.

Niamh said, "The backseat of a car? That's not…"

"Nah, I mean the cable car, 'course."

Gasps escaped from more than one pair of lips.

"Nah, there's no chance," Michael said. "Unless you mean while it's shut down overnight. Only runs during the day. No one's getting laid over the sea in broad daylight."

Rob grinned. "I'm no expert, but I heard it was done. Was a thing back in the seventies. Free love and all that. Not in the day, though. At night."

"Seventies, huh?" Michael said. "That'd be our parents." He

looked at Dylan and grinned. “Ya, I could see your ma going at it up there.”

“Feck you,” Dylan said. “It’s all nonsense anyway.”

“True or not, I know it *can* be done,” Rob said.

“How’s that?” Michael said, more sneer than question.

The man reached into his front pocket and extracted a chrome ring. Dangling from it were shiny, finely honed pieces of stainless steel. He grinned and said, “I have the keys to the controls.”

Eyes widened as the group fell silent.

“Anyone care to have a go?” Rob asked, swinging the keys in front of each face.

Michael took the final drink of his Guinness and set the glass on the table. “Would be somethin’, up there in the stars, making those cables dance.” He peered at each woman, his question unspoken.

Niamh said, “We’d get arrested. You’re talkin’ real trouble.”

“For what?” Michael asked. “Our friend Rob has every right to be there. He has the keys. We’d be his guests. We’d not be trespassing and, far as I know, there’s no law against having a good score in a cable car.”

Niamh wasn’t convinced. “Even so, that farmer up the road would be all over us. Probably would call the Gardai. We’d be in the middle of a big mess before anyone even got started.”

“Not a problem.” This time the voice was Dylan’s. “Farmer’s gone. He hired my brother to tend his sheep for the weekend while he went to Dublin for a niece’s graduation or weddin’ or somethin’.”

“There ya go,” Rob said. “Yer all invited to the Dursey Cable Car for a right savage night you’ll never forget.”

No one moved.

“If you’re too chicken, that’s okay. Keep your clothes on. That don’t mean ya can’t join me there for a drink. I’ll buy a bottle of—What’re you havin’?—Jameson, and we can sit on the bluff and tell more lies. Then, if someone decides they want a ride, no problem."

"I'm game," Moira said. "I'm new here. I've never even seen the place. Could be fun."

"That settles it," Michael said. "We can't let our favorite waitress go out there in the middle of the night with a total stranger. We all go."

Lauren and Niamh looked at each other and shrugged.

Moments later, Rob held a full bottle of whiskey in one arm, and Moira in the other. The other four followed them out of the pub, in what seemed like natural pairs: Michael and Niamh, and Lauren and Dylan.

As the door closed, Connie called out to them from behind the bar. "Be careful out there!" No one noticed the anguish on his face.

***

Two vehicles made the twenty-minute trek out to Ballaghboy, a spot of rock and grass so remote it was hard to understand why it had a name. Once Rob's truck and Dylan's car were parked, and lights extinguished, the darkness was instantaneous and nearly complete. Through a handful of holes in the cloud cover, stars appeared to gather, like little swarms of fireflies.

Trudging up the hill from the vehicles to the cable car terminal, Dylan struggled to see the shapes of the friends walking ahead of him. He wondered what happened to the security light. A low-wattage bulb normally glowed above the station door. Tonight, nothing penetrated the shroud but the flashlight apps on their phones, activated occasionally to ensure their footing.

"It's lovely," Moira said, taking several strides up onto hillside next to the terminal building and lowering herself to the ground. Looking up at one of the patches of stars, she said, "You don't see that in Dublin."

"Breathtaking," Lauren agreed, joining her in the grass, sitting cross-legged.

Soon, all six were huddled together, passing the bottle and sharing a pair of blankets against the cool breeze wafting in from the Dursey Sound. Below and to the left, the cable car rested in its berth, just visible enough to beckon to those adequately aroused and adequately brave.

Eventually, and inevitably, Michael moved the conversation from sexual tension to overt decision-making. He said, "Can ye really run that thing?"

"Aye, to be sure," Rob said.

"C'mon then. Let's go see. Bound to be warmer down there anyway."

He stood and marched down the hill and across the parking lot. The other five followed. When they reached the door to the car, Michael slid it open and turned to the group. "Who's with me, then?"

Rob said, "Sorry to disappoint ya, but I'll be staying here to run the thing."

The others' laughter was quickly dampened by their nerves.

Rob said, "Gotta be Moira. She's the newcomer. Be a proper initiation to your group."

"That'd be right craic," Michael said, sidling to his right and putting his arm around Moira's shoulders. "She's the hottest of the lot 'o ye."

No one was fooled, knowing Michael would gladly take any one or more of the three women.

"Maybe," Moira said, squirming away from his grip. "Let me take a wee and think about it."

"Good idea," Lauren said. "I'm about to burst."

"There's a loo at the back of the building," Rob said. "Follow me."

The three women left with him. Michael and Dylan just walked to the edge of the station platform and relieved themselves over the side.

When finished, Dylan said, "I'm gonna take a look inside the station. Might be cool to see it."

"I'll be waiting here," Michael said. "See if our waitress wants the biggest tip of her life."

Dylan shook his head and walked the half-dozen paces to the building. In the dark, the building looked gray, but Dylan assumed it was still painted the pale-yellow color he'd seen in the past. As he went in, he caught a glimpse of the three women walking away from the loo behind the station.

The interior of the building was small and functional. As Dylan entered, he bumped into Rob, who was searching for a light switch. Once he found it and clicked it on, a glow filled the room from a single fixture in the ceiling. Most of the space was occupied by the large cable mechanism, with its electric motor, giant pulleys, and gears. A flat panel on one wall held a few simple control switches and sensor lights. A small TV screen mounted in the corner by the ceiling was shut off. Assuming it was connected to a closed-circuit camera for monitoring passengers in the cable car, Dylan thought it was good it wasn't operating tonight.

Another wall included a ticket sales window that opened to the sidewalk outside. Two simple wooden chairs and the narrow counter below the window were the only furnishings.

He and Rob looked around briefly, commenting about how simple it would be to operate the car, and speculating about what it would be like to work there. Rob said he wouldn't enjoy the remoteness of the location nor the repetitiveness of the tasks, but Dylan disagreed.

He said, "I'd be fascinated to see all the types of people who came and went. Some would be regulars, of course, like the farmers on the island. But many would be tourists. People of every type from every country." He paused and grinned. "And think about it. Some would look at those cables over the water and relish the idea of the ride, and some would be scared pure. What a hoot."

Rob seemed disinclined to argue and positioned himself in front of the controls. Dylan stepped back outside. As his eyes readjusted to the dark, he saw the backs of Michael and Moira as they entered the car.

"I'll be damned," he muttered, feeling a mix of awe, disgust, and jealousy. As he heard the machinery kick into gear and saw the cable car begin its climb up to the first suspension tower, he walked into the parking lot and sat on the hood of his car to wait.

Less than ten minutes later, the faint whirring of the winch fell silent. Dylan knew from experience that the cable car was now suspended above the sea, about halfway to the island.

"How long do I let them dangle?" Rob's voice erupted from the darkness.

"Shite! You scared me frantic."

"Sorry, mate."

Dylan turned back toward the sea and gazed up. He wasn't sure if he could make out the outline of the car, or if his imagination was creating the faint image among the clouds. Finally, he said, "What's in this for you? Why help two strangers do it up there?"

Rob laughed and reached up, gripping Dylan's shoulder. "We're makin' legends, my friend. It's glorious, don't ya think? More stories for your next reunion at the pub. Don't feel bad. Maybe you'll get to be next." He pulled his hand away.

The idea caused Dylan to stir. He turned to comment, but Rob was gone. Moments later, he heard the whirring resume, beckoning the cable car home.

***

Dylan slid down off the vehicle's hood and strolled toward the cable car berth. He didn't really want to be there when Michael and

Moira emerged, his friend all full of himself and ready to crow like some damn rooster. However, if he stayed away, it would look like he was pouting. That would be worse.

As he exited the parking lot and walked up the steps to the platform, he was surprised to hear Rob's truck engine roar to life. He turned to look as the truck drove away.

"Hey!" he shouted. *Why is he leaving? Where's he going?*

The truck's taillights quickly disappeared as it turned out of the lane and onto the road back to Allihies.

Dylan's thoughts quickly turned to the car's operation. *Will it stop itself when it arrives?* He spun and jogged the few steps to the station building. Rob had shown him the controls. They were simple. An on-off switch and an electrical breaker. He would not leave the car's safety to chance. He would hit the kill switch when the cable car arrived in berth, assuring it wouldn't be damaged. The station door was standing open and he rushed inside.

Everything went according to plan. The cable car arrived and, just before it touched the platform, Dylan hit the switch, causing it to halt in place, swinging front to back, inches above the platform. He stepped out of the building and turned to walk the short distance to the swinging car, ready to explain to the others that Rob had left.

He was stopped in his tracks by a pair of screams, then shouts and more screaming: "Oh my God! Oh my God!"

He ran the remaining steps. "What? What's wrong!"

His confusion was compounded by the fact that Niamh and Moira were stumbling off the platform. *Moira? Isn't Moira in the car?*

He grabbed Niamh's arm. "What is it? What's happened?"

She was shaking. Through sobs, she said, "Blood. There's blood everywhere. I think they're dead."

"Dead? Who's dead?"

"There. In the car." More sobs. "My God. Michael and Lauren."

She pulled away and fled toward his car, Moira by her side.

Lauren? Dylan felt his fingers and toes go numb. *No, no, no. Not Lauren.* The numbness reached his knees and he grabbed for the railing beside the walk to keep from falling. Taking several deep breaths to compose himself, he stood, pulled his phone from his pocket, and turned on the flashlight function.

As he approached the open door to the cable car, he stopped. Blood, bright red and still liquid, was oozing toward the door, then retreating, with each swing of the car. He swallowed hard to keep from retching and took two steps forward.

A scream of anguish erupted from his lungs. "Nooo!"

His beloved Lauren and that scutwad Michael lay on the floor, still naked, still entwined, but motionless. Blood and occasional bubbles of air seeped from gaping wounds on the sides of their necks.

Chapter 2

Ten Days Previously... Wednesday, May 13
County Cork, Ireland

Rurik Alekhin's ordeal had taken him past the tipping point—that point where a victim stops pleading to be spared and starts pleading to be killed. Still, he had given the Irish bastards nothing. He was a hard man, toughened by the cold plains of northeast Russia, and well trained by his handlers in the Bratva Medved, the Brotherhood of the Bear.

He screamed. He bled.

He had thought for a while that if he said nothing, his captors would kill him. He now realized that was foolish. If he wanted to end this agony, he would have to talk. He would have to give them something.

Just not the truth.

He screamed.

He would die neither a traitor nor a coward.

He swallowed a scream, then retched.

Give them something. But they seemed to know so much already. They knew the Bratva was planning retribution for the loss of one of its dealers at the hands of Foley's goons. They even knew, or had guessed, that Foley's niece was the target. Probably an educated guess. Everyone knew Ox Foley adored the girl.

He screamed. He spit. He spoke. A rasp of breath through broken teeth.

"Okay, okay." The words hurt in his throat. "You win."

The shadows receded and the pain ebbed. He realized the fear of its return was almost worse than the reality of it.

"Tell us. Now. No games."

Alekhin's mind raced. *Give them something.* "The girl. They've targeted the girl."

The voice, louder, harsher: "We coulda guessed that! Tell us more." The shadow loomed.

"They're sending an agent," Alekhin said quickly.

"Fer God's sake. It's hopeless. Give 'im more."

"Wait!" Alekhin tried to shout, but a raspy whine was all he was able to force from his exhausted lungs. *Give them something. Something close to the truth. Something close enough I can sell it.* "He's American."

"American?"

"He's FSB," Alekhin said, referring to the Russian intelligence service that replaced the KGB. "Russian, but embedded in the West. We borrowed him. Thought an American could get close."

"Clever, right 'nuff. Who? When?"

I've got them hooked. Don't make it too easy. "I can't. I can't." He squeezed his eyes shut.

The pain shot through him like a lightning bolt.

He screamed.

"Please," he whispered.

More pain, more screams.

"Okay, okay! Please, just stop."

"Who? When? Tell us now, and all this stops. We have a doctor waiting to care for your wounds. Dinner is waiting in your cell."

Alekhin knew it was all BS. He had known he was a dead man from the moment Foley's minions had dragged him into their van. Waking up chained to a steel table in this chamber of horrors had only confirmed his worst fears. He would die soon. He *wanted* to die soon. He just had to convince these bastards that they had retrieved what they needed. He said, "The guy—an assassin—he's on his way. I don't know which day exactly."

"A name!"

Alekhin almost smiled as an idea flitted into his consciousness. A brilliant idea. He knew the name of an American hated by a handful of people in the highest offices of the FSB, an American who had foiled a major Russian attack on American soil just five months previously. Because Alekhin had contacts in the FSB, and he paid attention to the daily dispatches, he also knew the American was traveling to Ireland. There had been a debate about whether or not to hit him there.

The FSB would relish the idea of Foley, a competitor to the Russians in Ireland, doing the dirty work for them. It was perfect. Alekhin could do one last thing for Mother Russia before he died.

He spoke.

"Tony Harrington. His name is Tony Harrington."

Chapter 3

Monday, May 18
Dublin, Ireland

His enemies might have gone unnoticed, at least at first, had their team not included a woman. He was, after all, on vacation. Just an American from the Midwest on his first trip to Ireland. Tony Harrington could not imagine any reason why someone in Dublin would be following him, but there she was for the third time, and not in a place where a coincidental meeting was likely.

Tony was thirty and in a committed relationship. Although he had no interest in cheating on the woman he loved, it was second nature for him to notice attractive young women, even the unusual ones—perhaps especially the unusual ones. So, earlier that morning, when he had first caught the woman looking at him, he'd looked back. She was standing in line at the airport baggage carousel. She had short, dark hair, a trim figure, and a pleasant, if not quite beautiful, face. She wore a denim jacket over a pale-gray tee. Without thinking, Tony smiled, but the woman just turned away.

She had a gothic vibe, but the only truly unusual thing about her was the fact she had been staring at Tony, who had never considered himself attractive to women. On the plus side, he was blessed with thick, black locks and dark eyes inherited from his Italian mother. The minus column was a longer list. He was too pale and too thin and lacked any athletic prowess. At five ten, he even fell short of achieving his father's height. Whenever he failed to attract the attention of a woman, his best friend, Doug Tenney, often reacted bluntly with comments such as, "You couldn't catch a cold in a kindergarten." In Tony's defense, his ineptitude was earned. While growing up, he had passed on most sports and had spent his time reading. His family had called him bookish, or intellectually curious. He had preferred it over "nerd."

So now, in Tony's mind, the woman's interest was a surprise, but her quick dismissal of him was not. She was yet another in a long line of attractive women who had looked, and decided to pass. He thought no more about it.

However, a few minutes later, he saw her outside the terminal, a few places behind him in the queue for a taxi. Curiosity pushed its way into his thoughts. She had no suitcase, just the tote that had hung from her shoulder at the carousel. *So why stand in line at baggage claim if you have no bag to retrieve? Lost luggage? Could she have given up on it so quickly?* He didn't dwell on the questions. Whatever she was doing, it was nothing to him. His thoughts soon turned to other things, things that mattered, like whether he would be able to check into his hotel at 9:15 a.m. He had slept on the plane from Chicago, but he wasn't ready to take on Dublin without a shower.

The next encounter awakened his sense of unease. It was noon, and he was strolling across St. Stephen's Green, a beautiful park filled with trees and flowers, located across the street from the

Fitzwilliam Hotel, where he was staying. He turned suddenly, after deciding to return to his room to fetch his visitor's guide, and saw the same woman again some distance behind him. She apparently didn't notice he had stopped, as she happened to be looking back over her shoulder. It seemed ridiculous to think she was tailing him, but he decided to wait for her and at least say hello.

From around a bend in the path behind the woman, a stocky, gray-haired man appeared and approached her. She nodded to the man, finished her pivot, and retreated, while the man continued ahead toward Tony. When the stranger realized Tony was looking at him, he awkwardly slowed and turned to examine a bed of bluebells beside the path.

Instantly, it was obvious Tony was being followed. And not just by the woman, but by some kind of team. He had caught the woman in the act of handing off her target to the person assigned to follow him next.

Goosebumps peppered Tony's forearms as he about-faced and resumed walking toward the park's western exit. He felt the pace of both his heart and his feet accelerate as he tried to fathom why anyone in Ireland would be interested in him. *A simple robbery? Not likely.* He'd never heard of muggers following their prey from the airport to the heart of the city and staying on the victim's trail for several hours. *Then what? A former foe?* Tony had worked as a news reporter for the past eight years. During that time, he had made a fair number of enemies—criminals he had helped to identify and convict, people angered by news coverage they had perceived to be unfair, and even a couple of members of organized crime families. But how does that translate to Ireland? *Why would anyone come for me here? I'm not even working!*

His need for an answer quickly overcame, or at least tempered, his fear. He had to know why these total strangers were interested in him, total strangers who weren't particularly good at surveillance. *Agent Tabors would give you yokels an F in spycraft*, Tony thought, referencing Anna Tabors, a friend in the FBI back in the US. However, he quickly retracted the thought. The truth was, if the group following him had not included an attractive female, he never would have caught on to them. They could have put the stocky gray-haired guy in the same taxi with him, and he wouldn't have noticed. He sighed, acknowledging that his over-appreciation of women had gotten him in trouble more than once. *Maybe this time it saved me*, he thought. *But from what?*

Tony decided to confront the man. He waited until the path through the trees opened to a broad lawn with a fountain at its center. A crowd of young people was gathered nearby, enjoying the warm May sun, perhaps on a noon break from work or college classes.

When he was certain he was in plain view of the crowd, Tony again stopped and checked his six o'clock. No one was behind him. He waited a full thirty seconds, then another thirty, but no one appeared on the path. Had he imagined it all? He knew he was feeling unusually vulnerable right now, alone in a foreign country, out of work for the first time in his life, and still recovering from injuries sustained the previous winter.

Okay, to be honest, "vulnerable" doesn't begin to cover it. You're a complete feckin mess, he thought, trying out the common Irish expression for the first time. *But no. I know what I saw. They were following me. Why?*

He was pretty sure he wouldn't find the answer in the middle of a Dublin park, so he turned and resumed his trek toward the café recommended by the hotel, a block west of the green. There, he hoped to enjoy some hot soup and a cold Guinness. He wasn't a big drinker, but he knew he wouldn't find Diet Dr Pepper in a Dublin restaurant. He didn't really mind. *When in Rome.*

His limp was barely perceptible as he walked. The frequent glances back over his shoulder were more noticeable.

Ironically, the trouble didn't come from behind. When he emerged from the green, three men stood on the sidewalk near the curb, facing him with hands folded at their belt buckles, feet shoulder-width apart. Behind them was a gray van, its open door mostly obscuring some kind of logo painted on the side. The man in the center was taller than Tony, with dark, wavy hair and a short-cropped beard. He wore jeans and a black windbreaker. The other two men were larger, younger, and wore coveralls.

Tony's muscles tensed and his head whipped left, then right.

"Don' e'en think it," the man in the center said, as each of the other two took a step forward, blocking the sidewalk on the left and right. "You'll be gettin' in now. You can go en healthy, or you can go en with a couple a broken bones. Yer call."

Despite the man's prohibition, Tony's mind was racing. *A kidnapping?* The thought was preposterous. *Assaulted here, in one of the busiest parts of Dublin?* It was beyond comprehension. Because the streets around the green were home to several government buildings and even a couple of foreign embassies, pedestrians were commonplace, and officers from the Garda Síochána, or national police service, were rarely far away.

Tony tried not to panic as he again stole glances in all directions. *Apparently, this was one of those times*, he groaned to himself.

His three options were obvious: flee, fight, or talk. He chose the latter. Through a forced smile, he said, "Guys, uh, I don't know what this… uh, who you are, but clearly you've made a mistake. I'm just a guy from America in Ireland for vacation. You can't possibly want me. Here, let me show you."

He reached for his wallet but stopped cold when the tall man said, "Harrington, right enough, yah?"

"Yes, but…"

He didn't have time to finish. The man in the windbreaker stepped forward, grabbed Tony's arm, and yanked him toward the van.

Tony didn't resist, for which the man was prepared, but rather pushed forward, amplifying the man's motion and causing him to stumble backwards. Tony kept pushing, harder with his second step, then his third. The man lost his footing at the curb and fell backward toward the open door of the van. His head made an ugly, wet "*thunk*" as it struck the edge of the van's threshold.

Tony didn't notice. He already was bending to the side, spinning on his left foot, and using his right leg to kick the feet out from under one of the men in coveralls. He heard someone shout "Awgh!" and realized it was his own voice, as pain shot up through his already weakened leg.

Taken by surprise, the man in coveralls fell to the concrete. Tony kicked him hard in the temple as he leapt over the body and tried to flee.

Coveralls number two was too quick. He caught the skull under Tony's right ear with what felt like a crowbar. Pain erupted throughout Tony's head. His eyes bulged and his ears roared. As his body twisted and fell back onto the sidewalk, Tony looked up in astonishment. His assailant held no weapon beyond the big, calloused fist that was recoiling in preparation for a second blow. Tony then noticed the fingers did bear a weapon of sorts. Beneath smears of blood were a series of steel rings—brass knuckles. Realizing the blood was not coming from the man's fingers, Tony reached back and pressed his hand to his scalp. His hair was wet and his hand came away smeared in red.

Tony didn't hesitate. He rolled back, in a reverse somersault, and pushed himself up onto his feet. Drenched in sweat and fighting intense pain and even greater fear, he desperately wanted to flee. However, he knew he would be even slower now. *If he strikes my head again, I'm finished*, he thought as he raised his hands and assumed a defensive stance. He had no illusions that he could win this fight. He simply hoped to ward off the worst until help arrived.

Coveralls number two sneered and glanced at his knuckles. Tony could imagine what the man was thinking, undoubtedly anxious to add more of Tony's blood to his fist.

Surprisingly, the man didn't attack. He suddenly seemed to remember he had two injured partners at his feet, on a busy and heavily patrolled Dublin street.

"Feck off then," the man growled, turning to lift the first man into the open door of the van. Without looking at Tony, he said, "Don' be thinkin' this be over. It ain't feckin' over."

Tony didn't hear him. He already was half a block away.

***

"What a feckin' mess," the stocky, gray-haired man said into his smart phone. Known to his team as Nixer, he continued, "You nah could manage a simple grab. Three of ye. Three!" His voice rose half an octave and shook. "For shish sakes, ye outweighed 'im by three stone each!"

There was no response from the caller, who apparently had no explanation for how the American had managed to best them.

"Well then, we at least learnt one thing, din' we?" Nixer said, not waiting for an answer. "Now we know fur sure it's 'im. You may be a right moron, but the others, they be savage. No boyo took down them two. This Harrington's fierce well trained. We'll be deadly ready for 'im next time."

Chapter 4

Monday, May 18

Bantry Bay, Beara Peninsula, Ireland

Sam Kilborgen had it all. He owned a fine boat, the *Jammy Lass*, and he was blessed with a loyal, hard-working crew. Unlike a lot of Irish fishermen, he had the advantage of owning land that reached the bay, which meant he owned his pier and saved a wee fortune on berthing fees. It was several kilometers from the marina where he purchased fuel and other supplies, which was inconvenient, but the savings and the privacy made it more than worth it.

Most important on Kilborgen's list of blessings was his affinity for the water. He had more than just the skills to succeed at sea. He possessed an almost magical ability to read the breezes and waves and currents the way others read charts and GPS displays. At over twenty metres, his beam trawler wasn't the biggest fishing vessel on the water, but it was bigger than many. To Kilborgen, it was the only part of the world that mattered. When at the helm, he was alive in a way he simply never felt on land. The satisfaction must be similar, he imagined, to how a conductor feels when a symphony orchestra responds to his every move. The *Jammy Lass* performed to Kilborgen's touch. He returned the favor by responding to every sight, sound, scent, and vibration she presented.

Sam Kilborgen belonged on the water, and he had no desire to be anywhere else. He was well aware he didn't own the sea; it owned him. He was a fifth-generation fisherman and was proud to acknowledge he had it all.

All, sadly, except one thing: fish. He shared this problem with every other Irish fisherman—there simply were not enough fish in the ocean. The supply had been depleted for decades by ever-larger trawlers, some boasting the ability to catch and process as much as seven thousand tons of fish before returning to shore. In addition to the larger boats was the challenge of increasing numbers of competitors. The Dutch and others from the continent were encroaching on Irish fishing waters in ever-greater numbers. The fishing industry, the government, indeed the world, watched helplessly from the sidelines as the problem grew worse year after year.

Academics described it as "the capacity to harvest exceeding the supply." Kilborgen had a simpler term for it. He was fecked. The income from his meager hauls no longer could pay the costs of salaries, fuel, insurance, maintenance, or the host of other inevitable expenses. Most of his life savings had been wiped out already, and if nothing changed, he would soon be bankrupt.

It was not in his nature to wring his hands and whine about his problems. Instead, he did what he always had done—indeed, what five generations of Kilborgens had done. He went to work to find a solution. *Feck the government and its regulations. Feck the Dutch, feck the fisheries, feck the world.*

And so, here he was, spending Monday morning in dock, making alterations to his boat instead of casting his nets. He didn't like it, but he knew it was necessary. The modifications, done well, might prevent him from being caught, and not getting caught was essential. He had no desire to live out the remaining years of his life in Cork Prison.

Chapter 5

Monday, May 18
Dublin, Ireland

"Three men, you say?"

"Yes," Tony answered tersely. "A big man with a beard in a black nylon jacket and two guys in coveralls. They looked like plumbers or electricians or something. The van…"

"And how did you know the jacket was nylon?"

"What?"

"You said the black jacket was nylon. How did you know that?"

Tony fought the urge to scream. Through gritted teeth, he said, "I didn't mean that literally. It was, you know, some kind of light-weight material, like nylon. What does that have to do with anything?"

"Nothing, I'm sure," the Garda investigator said. "I'm just trying the assess your, your…"

"You're trying to decide if I'm a damn liar," Tony said. "Please, just speak frankly, Inspector. Does this bandage on my head appear to you to be a lie?"

Inspector Colin Lynch and a young uniformed officer were interviewing him in a treatment room at St. James's Hospital on the west side of Dublin. They had arrived about thirty minutes after Tony had shown up in the Emergency Department seeking treatment for his skull, which seemed determined to continue seeping blood.

Tony assumed the nurses had called the police as a matter of routine, when an apparent victim of assault had shown up seeking medical care. He also assumed an inspector had been dispatched, and not a regular street cop, because Tony was a foreigner. This was not necessarily a good thing, as Inspector Lynch appeared to be ill-disposed toward tourists generally, and Tony specifically. The man had been dismissive and skeptical of his story from the beginning. They had been together for more than an hour, and Tony was relating the facts for the third time.

"Very well, Mr. Harrington. You asked me to speak frankly, so I will. I find it hard to believe almost everything you've said. You claim to be an ordinary tourist but say someone tried to kidnap you for no reason you can fathom. You say you were assaulted on the street by strangers, in an area of Dublin where street crime is almost nonexistent. And you describe your attackers as three men, all larger than you, but claim to have defeated them single-handedly. Let me ask you this, if a stranger walked into your newspaper office and shared this story with you, would you believe it?"

Tony couldn't help but smile. "Okay, I get it. I sound like I'm full of it. Unfortunately, it's the truth. I swear, I didn't come to Ireland looking for trouble. I just wanted to see my father's ancestral land, enjoy the beautiful scenery, and drink enough Guinness to forget my problems."

"Problems?"

"Poor choice of words. Not problems like getting assaulted or having enemies. I meant problems like being out of work and missing my girlfriend who's traveling for her job."

"You mean Miss Gillson, of course," the second officer said from the corner of the room, referencing the actress Darcy Gillson, with whom Tony shared a home and a life.

Tony and the inspector turned to look at him.

The officer held up a smartphone and said, "Yes, Mr. Harrington, we have the internet in Ireland too. While you've been talking, I've been doing a little homework. You not only have a famous girlfriend, you also have quite a history of causing trouble."

Tony felt his face flush hot as he said, "That's not true. I've had my share of finding trouble, and sometimes even stopping it, but I don't go around causing it. All that's over now, anyway. The newspaper is struggling financially and my boss was forced to let me go. I swear, I'm just here to sightsee."

The inspector seemed unconvinced and pressed on. "So with Gardai nearby, why didn't you report this to them right away?"

"I didn't see an officer anywhere, and I was *bleeding*," Tony said, emphasizing the word to communicate what was unsaid: *you ignorant twit*. "I grabbed the first taxi I saw and asked to be brought to the hospital."

"How did you manage it?"

"What? The taxi?"

The inspector quickly suppressed a grin. "No, no, not that. How did you manage to defeat three large men?"

"As I told you, I've had some training," Tony said. "Nothing fancy. No military service or anything. There's an old guy in the town where I live, Master Jun, who teaches a form of tae kwon do. Pretty basic stuff but focused on real-life street fighting. He would say practical and effective self-defense. I've been taking lessons weekly for almost three years. It's just about the only exercise I get, and the skills have come in handy a few times."

The cop in the corner grunted and held up his phone. "I'll say."

"That's enough, officer," the inspector said. To Tony, he said, "I think we're done here. I'll file the report as you've given it, but I'll feel compelled to include my doubts. I don't want my superiors thinking I bought all this."

"But…"

"I'm not finished. I'll ask my colleagues posted near the green to do some checking. See if anyone saw or heard anything. Maybe we can get a lead on the van. At the very least, maybe—and I mean maybe—we can find a witness to corroborate your story. I'll also see if I can free up someone to look at the traffic videos taken in the area. I can't justify an all-out camera search, but maybe a quick check of the obvious ones will turn up something."

"Thank you."

"Don't thank me yet, because if we find out you're lying, and that wound in your head came from some slag's stiletto, we're going to come down on you like an anvil on Roadrunner." He smiled. "Yes, we have cartoons in Ireland too." He nodded to the other officer, indicating they were leaving.

To be polite, Tony tried to rise, but immediately felt like he might faint. He sank back into the treatment recliner and held out his hand.

The inspector shook it, then handed him a business card. He said, "If your story is true, this is a very nasty business. You've described a brazen to attempt at an abduction on a busy city street in the middle of the day. Your attackers were either fearless, desperate, or stupid. Any of the three could make them very dangerous. Keep your eyes open and call for help if you see anything out of the ordinary."

Tony said he would, then the inspector added, "I should ask, will you head back home now?"

The hopeful tone in Lynch's voice wasn't lost on Tony. He said,

"I don't know. I need to be able to walk, or at least stand up, before I can worry about what's next. I'd like to continue with my plans to see Ireland, but I hate the thought of looking over my shoulder every minute. I'll have to think about it."

"Well, keep us posted, and I'll call you if we come up with anything on our end."

"Thanks again," Tony said.

As the two men exited the room, Tony leaned back farther in the chair and put his hands over his face. His fingers felt wet again and he pulled them away, realizing this time the cause was tears.

Chapter 6

Monday, May 18
Allihies, Beara Peninsula, Ireland

David O'Connell looked up from the keg he was wrestling into place behind the bar and watched Moira Blake as she bent to wipe off a table across the room. He couldn't help himself. The girl's jeans and sweater hugged her form like shrink wrap. O'Connell's mouth went dry and he looked away. He knew it had been a mistake to hire her. She was too pretty and too young. He also knew he shouldn't think of her as a girl. She was a woman, twenty-six years old, assuming she hadn't lied when he'd hired her. But her lean build, large brown eyes, and carefree manner belied her age. She wore her long, auburn hair in a ponytail, and had an easy smile punctuated by large dimples. He was captivated by her dimples. Every time they appeared, which was frequently throughout her afternoon and evening shifts, they pushed aside facts and political correctness, and shouted, "Girl!"

O'Connell, or Connie, as he was known to patrons of O'Connell's Bar, stole another glance at Blake and sighed. *A mistake. A big feckin' mistake.*

On the other hand, he argued with himself, she had been a godsend when she'd walked in his door looking for work. Two weeks ago, the pub's only waitress had quit without notice, moving to Cork to be closer to her musician boyfriend, a drummer in the next U2, to hear him tell it. Moira's appearance the next day had been as welcome as it was surprising. She had impressed O'Connell as smart, enthusiastic, and capable. Perhaps most importantly, she had been able and willing to start right away. O'Connell hadn't hesitated. He needed a waitress.

Historically, the May Bank Holiday wasn't a big deal for Irish pubs. However, in recent years, the observance had grown into a major event in Allihies, with locals taking advantage of the three-day weekend. They had turned the first weekend in May into an excuse to celebrate spring or, to put it more accurately, an excuse to drink. Saturday and Sunday were two of O'Connell's biggest days of the year. The Monday holiday itself was more reserved, with many of the regulars sleeping off hangovers, or at least slowing their consumption in anticipation of the coming workweek.

O'Connell had led the surge of interest in the spring celebration by offering three days of live music, food, beer, and whiskey. The weekend now accounted for more than 10 percent of his annual revenue. The thought of scaling back and watching half the people on the peninsula scurry up to Cork or Dublin in search of a better party was unthinkable. Moira's appearance had made it possible for him to "go big" at the pub for another year. As he had hoped, the days had been huge successes. Everyone had loved Moira and still did. Business was up, and O'Connell knew the girl's dimples deserved a lot of the credit.

He bent to twist the keg into place.

"Connie?"

He jumped, striking his head on the edge of the bar sink. "Shite!"

"Oh, sorry," Moira said. "I didn't mean to startle you."

O'Connell straightened and rubbed his head. "No apologies. Not your fault I'm a clumsy bastard. What's up?"

"One of the tables along the back wall is unsteady. I think it's missing a footy-thing on one of its legs. Got one I can use to fix it?"

O'Connell smiled. Another mark in the plus column on the Moira scorecard. How many waitresses would care about a wobbly table, or even notice it? More to the point, how many would offer to fix it?

"Don' ye worry," he said. "I'll take care of it. Thanks for tellin' me."

Blake smiled. "You're the best."

O'Connell just nodded and returned to tapping the keg. He didn't want the girl to see how desperately he wanted to jump across the bar and put his lips on those amazing dimples.

I'm fifty years old with a good woman at home. He sighed again. *A mistake. A big feckin' mistake.*

***

Dublin, Ireland

The spoon clattered onto the table, splattering fish and potato chowder across its surface. Tony silently unleashed a torrent of foul language and reached for his napkin. He wiped the soup from his chin as well as the table, returned the napkin to his lap, and took a deep breath. A slight tremor in his hand was making the simple act of eating chowder difficult and embarrassing.

He wondered if the attack had frightened him more than he realized, or if his trembling was driven by anger. He might be unsure of his fear, but his anger wasn't hiding. It burned in him like magma, ready to erupt at any moment.

Another breath. *Why so angry?* He unclenched his fingers, took a bite of bread, and actually pondered the question. He decided his ire was justified, which made him feel marginally better. He made a mental list. First, of course, was the loss of his job. He had loved reporting and had hated to walk away. Sadly, he had had no choice. Ben Smalley, editor and publisher of the *Orney Town Crier*, was out of money. Tony was his highest-paid reporter. If he hadn't left, Ben would have been forced to lay off someone else, perhaps more than one. Tony was no saint, but he had known what he had to do. Doug and Alison and others at the paper needed their jobs. Tony didn't. He was fortunate to come from a family with money, and to have a significant other who made millions. So, he resigned. Doing the right thing did not make it easier. Without his job, who was he? What would he do? He hated that feeling of relying on others or, even worse, living as some kind of gigolo beholden to Darcy.

Of course, Darcy didn't mind, and she certainly could afford to support them both. She was a film idol. Smart, talented, and beautiful, she was riding a tsunami of success and banking more money than a news reporter would earn in a hundred lifetimes. Living off her generous nature was distasteful for all the obvious male-ego-at-risk reasons. It was not made any easier by the fact he loved her to his core. He wanted her to be proud of him. Hell, she *had* been proud of him when his reporting had made a difference to the paper and to the community. How long could she sustain her admiration while living with an out-of-work journalist? Would his charmed life begin to erode, the mountain of success he'd built reduced to a mound of prairie dirt? He would do almost anything to prevent that. He loved his life in Iowa and loved sharing a home with Darcy, when she wasn't off filming romantic encounters with some famous stud.

Which brought up reason number two for his anger. Darcy *was* off making a movie. She currently was shooting at Pinewood Studios in England. In actual distance, it wasn't far from where he was now, but it might as well have been on the Moon in terms of separating her from him. In their most recent call, she'd said she would be tied up for another three weeks. At least this time, she was working for Disney, so it was unlikely she would be entwined in any steamy love scenes.

Reason number three was the death of Aunt Hill. Despite his anger and sorrow, Tony smiled at the thought of his great aunt. Her real name was Hilary Harrington. A lifelong teacher and administrator, she was a member of the Religious Sisters of Mercy, a Catholic order of women. Her professed name was Sister Mary Hilary. A tiny woman of Irish descent, she had effused energy and good humor throughout her life. She had insisted that Tony and his sister, Rita, call her "Aunt Hill," thinking the play on words was hilarious.

Aunt Hill was a second-generation American who lived and worked in Michigan for most of her life. However, her religious order had been founded in the early 1800s in Dublin. She had visited the original House of Mercy on Baggot Street twice in her life, and had promised to accompany Tony, Darcy, and Rita on a journey there someday. Tony had been making plans for that trip when he had gotten the telephone call. His dad, Charles Harrington, had informed him that Aunt Hill's heart had decided a third trip to Ireland wasn't necessary. Now she was gone and Tony was visiting Dublin without her.

That brought him to reason number four, which he considered the epitome of "piling on." Strangers were following him, forcing him to watch his back and wonder what they possibly could want. Almost as bad as the implied threat, their presence detracted from his ability to relax, explore, and absorb the beauty and culture of the Harrington family's homeland. *Why are they doing this to me?*

Suddenly, Tony realized what was truly fueling his anger. The way he had phrased the question made everything clear. For more than a month, he had been playing the role of victim. Victim to the financial woes of daily newspapers, victim to Darcy's success, victim to the natural passing of someone whose time had come, victim to his aches and pains. And now, victim to mysterious strangers.

He sat up straight, grabbed his spoon, and slurped down some soup. *I may have legitimate reasons to be asking who I am, but I know who I'm not. I'm not a victim.*

Putting on his best Irish brogue, he said quietly, "Feck the lot 'o them. From the plough to the stars, I'll be takin' charge of me own destiny then."

He laughed aloud, realizing his accent was terrible, less like a legitimate brogue and more like the Lucky Charms leprechaun. Nevertheless, he knew the truth of the revelation and felt the strength of his resolve. Tomorrow would be a better day.

Chapter 7

Monday, May 18
Lubyanka Square, Moscow, Russia

"The Brotherhood lost a good man to the Irish dogs. Rurik Alekhin led their operation in Ireland for years."

"Hmph." This simple grunt clearly communicated the FSB director's disgust as well as his acknowledgment. The fingers of his right hand lightly tapped a rhythm in three-quarters time on the highly polished ironwood desk at which he sat.

"They're going to retaliate. You know they will. Someone else will die. Then what? Another Russian head? Maybe worse?"

"Hmph." Tap, tap, tap. Tap, tap, tap.

"This is getting out of hand. The Bear's greed is going to bring the entire nest of wasps down on our heads."

"Hmph." Tap, tap, tap. Tap, tap, tap.

"We need to intervene. We must act before this escalates into an all-out war."

The tapping stopped. The director lifted his gaze to look at his lieutenant. Surely the man knew the greed didn't stop with the Brotherhood of the Bear. The profits from its criminal enterprises fed a lot of hungry bears, including some in this building and, more importantly, some in the Kremlin, less than one thousand meters south of where they sat.

He tried to keep the sarcasm from his voice but failed. "What do you propose? Shall I invite Polshkov to tea and suggest he forgive the Ox for murdering his friend?" The director's question referenced two ruthless and powerful leaders of rival drug cartels—Darius Polshkov, who held the top post at the Brotherhood of the Bear, based in Russia, and Lennox "Ox" Foley, longtime head of an Irish crime family most commonly called, simply, the Foley Gang.

Beads of sweat formed on the lieutenant's upper lip and forehead, but to the man's credit, he stood his ground. "Yes, director, I think a conversation is necessary. But even more urgently, I believe we must prevent the next killing. Or, it occurs to me now, two killings."

"Two?" The director had thought of this, but he wanted to hear his aide's reasoning.

"Polshkov will move swiftly to avenge Alekhin's torture and death. The two men were close, and Alekhin's body was almost unrecognizable when Polshkov's men found it. In addition, we must remember that Alekhin was tortured for a reason. The Ox was determined to get information, desperate for it. That usually means a target."

"Perhaps," the director said, his fingers resuming their waltz on the desktop. "Do you have intel on who or why?"

"Not the who. Not yet. As to the why, it appears the Ox started all this when he objected to the Brotherhood's incursion into his territory. His men caught a couple of the Bear's distributors in County Cork and worked them over badly. One was carved up like an Ivan Vitali sculpture. The Ox didn't stop there. He found the Brotherhood's boat in the bay off Bere Island and sank it." The lieutenant was careful to lay the blame at the Irish dog's feet. He was unsure how his boss, or his boss's boss, would react to the truth. However, the director wasn't fooled. His quick grasp of the situation demonstrated why he sat in the chair behind the desk.

"Cork? Bere? That's way the hell down south! What's the Brotherhood doing down there?" His face grew red, and his knuckles white as he continued, "I don't know shit about Ireland, and even I know they're not supposed to be selling in Cork. What you're saying is that Polshkov started this. He pushed the Brotherhood into territory that has been controlled by Ox Foley's syndicate for twenty years, and Foley struck back. What did Polshkov think the Ox would do? Damn fool."

"Yes, sir. It's no surprise Foley sank their boat. It's even less of a surprise that the Brotherhood struck back quickly. The two men suspected of sinking the Brotherhood's boat were found three days later, dead in their apartment in Cork. The Gardai are calling it a murder-suicide. We know better, of course."

"So then Foley, in an act of revenge for the killing of his two men, tortured and killed Polshkov's man, Alekhin."

"Yes, sir."

"Now you want us—me—to prevent a strike from Polshkov, because, of course, Polshkov is planning to take a pound of flesh in retaliation for his friend."

The young man nodded. "That's our belief. We've got a team of analysts and operatives watching this closely. Everyone agrees it's about to explode."

"And when it does, we all lose." The director sighed. "The Gardai, the Coast Guard, and everyone else will get involved, and our flow of cash from Ireland will turn to dust, at least for a while."

"Yes, sir. As the Irish say, it's a feckin' mess."

The director stared into the young man's eyes for a long moment. "You did well to bring this to me, to speak honestly about it, to have a team on it early. In our business, these things are difficult and often risky. Your foresight and your courage are why you sit in the office closest to mine. Do you understand?"

"Yes, sir."

"Very well. I will talk to Polshkov and try to get him to stand down. If I fail, we'll have to deal with it. In the meantime, you need to put someone on Foley. Find out what he's planning and make sure it doesn't happen."

"Yes, sir. I understand."

"And keep our fingerprints off it. The only thing worse than a meltdown in Ireland would be its fallout coming to rest on Lubyanka Square or, God forbid, the Kremlin. Use somebody clean. Somebody so clean his skin squeaks."

"I know just the man. I'll call him today."

Chapter 8

Tuesday, May 19
Dublin, Ireland

Ryan Stenford glanced up at the arch over the exit from Dublin Airport. The welcome sign announced, "Lovely Day for a Visit." He grimaced. It was a nice sentiment, but somehow he doubted it was true in his case.

Receiving the order to drop everything and travel to Dublin irritated him. After living for years in deep cover, he enjoyed his life in Chicago as an American musician and graduate student. Now, for the second time in less than six months, Moscow was sending him into the field, this time to a foreign country. It wasn't easy to explain to friends, employers, and professors why he suddenly had to take leave from his commitments.

The call from his handler at the FSB also unnerved him. He was inexperienced as a field operative and, if he was being honest, frightened to be jumping into a complex and potentially volatile situation without proper preparation. It didn't help that his orders were vague. By all accounts, Ox Foley was a powerful and ruthless crime boss, well protected by an army of loyal enforcers. *And I'm supposed to watch him, prevent him from doing... something? Bloody hell.*

The only good news in all this was the result of a colossal coincidence. His girlfriend, Rita Harrington, was only hours behind him, on her way to Dublin to meet her brother. Ryan didn't like the idea of putting Rita at risk, but the fact was, her presence would provide valuable cover. He would be far less conspicuous as a young man vacationing with his lover, than as a lone stranger suddenly appearing on the scene.

He took out his phone and speed-dialed her number. As expected, he got her voicemail. She probably was asleep in an airliner somewhere over the Atlantic. He waited for the beep, then said, "Hey, Babe! Good news..."

Chapter 9

Wednesday, May 20
Dublin, Ireland

The man called Nixer entered the hotel lobby first. He smiled at the bellman stationed near the elevators and walked toward the check-in desk. A few moments later, the young woman with short, dark hair entered the lobby. She looked very different from the previous day—less gothic and more society queen, overtly alluring in a short black skirt, a low-cut cotton top, and heels. Just past the main doors, she stumbled and cried out as she landed hard, the contents of her shoulder bag spilling out in all directions across the floor.

The bellman was at her side in an instant, asking if she was okay and helping the woman to her feet. The woman smiled, red-faced, and expressed her thanks as the bellman assisted her in gathering her things and returning them to the bag.

"I'm sorry," the woman said, "I'm so clumsy. I should learn to wear sensible shoes instead of trying to make these legs look longer."

"I... I think your legs look just fine," the bellman stammered, appreciating the excuse to stare at how much was exposed by the tiny skirt.

"Well, you're very sweet to say so, but I can tell at least one of them is going to be wearing a bruise from my fall." She adjusted her top and brushed her fingers through her hair. "Is the rest of me put together okay?" She grinned up at the man, inviting him to check her out.

The bellman was happy to oblige. His confidence grew as he realized the woman was braless, and wanted him to know it. She was enjoying his attention. "I think you look lovely, Mrs…?"

"It's miss, and you can call me Lila. What's your name?"

It didn't occur to the bellman that his name was on the tag on his sport coat, or that Lila might be trying to keep him talking.

As the pair continued flirting, Nixer quietly found his way to a door in the far corner of the lobby, slipped through, and made his way up the staircase to the third floor. He didn't know how his boss had found out the American was staying in Room 309 at the Fitzwilliam. He had learned long ago not to ask, and to trust the boss's sources.

From the stairwell, Nixer eased open the door to the corridor. As expected, no one was in sight. It was two in the afternoon, so most guests were out for the day, or had checked out of the hotel. Maid service would be concluded by now, and check-in wasn't until four. Despite this, he eased a ski mask over his head. He knew there could be cameras, or an unexpected visit from a maintenance worker or housekeeper.

He stepped quickly down the hall, pausing in front of 309 only long enough to use a hotel master key to activate the electronic lock and step through the door. Again, he marveled at the resources his boss could muster as needed. Inside the room, he was disappointed but not surprised to see the lights were off and the bed was empty. He had expected the man called Harrington to be out but had hoped to catch him resting or reading or something. It would have been faster, more certain, and less messy, to put a bullet in the man's head than to leave behind the letter bomb he carried in his coat. However, either path was better than a kidnapping.

Nixer had actually been relieved when the order had come down to kill the American. Apparently, the incident outside St. Stephen's Green had been enough to convince the boss they had identified the right man. It was a shame Harrington's room was vacant. The only good news was that it was clean, so he needn't worry about a maid finding the package by mistake.

Before placing the bomb on the desk, he hesitated, realizing something was amiss. He looked around the room a second time, then darted into the bathroom.

"Ah, feck me," Nixer growled softly, staring at an empty countertop. He stepped back into the room and opened the armoire. Empty. It was obvious his target wasn't just out for the day. He had checked out. Two things occurred to the assassin. First, this mission had failed. The boss would be extremely unhappy. Scoring two failures in three days was beyond unacceptable. Second, the intel from his boss had been wrong. Nixer had been told Harrington would be at the Fitzwilliam for two more days. He was surprised at how good it felt to know the boss could make a mistake.

***

Tony didn't realize Catherine McAuley had just saved his life. Of course, Mother McAuley didn't realize it either, as she had been dead for nearly two centuries.

As Nixer left the Fitzwilliam Hotel, Tony sat on a bench in a flower garden nearly a mile away, chatting with the woman who had founded the Religious Sisters of Mercy in Ireland in 1831. Oddly, the fact she was a bronze statue didn't diminish the experience. The statue had been crafted in a sitting position, on a garden bench, for just this purpose. People from all over the world came to this garden, at the Mercy International Center on Baggot Street, to visit Catherine's grave, to pay their respects to the remarkable woman who had devoted her life to teaching and healing, and to open their hearts to her presence. Catherine's spirit seemed to infuse every molecule of air, sharing the breeze with the scents from the rose bushes. As Tony absorbed it all, he realized why Aunt Hill had wanted so badly for Rita and him to experience this place. It touched him, invigorated him to a magnitude far beyond the proportions of this tiny garden.

It was a quiet day. Tony was grateful to be the only visitor. The woman at the front desk had been gracious, allowing him to leave his suitcase and shoulder bag in a corner of her office. She also had been generous with her time, giving Tony a personal tour of the original House of Mercy that formed the core of the center.

The house was built by Catherine two centuries before, in a monumental effort to help the poor, sick, and uneducated girls living on the streets of Dublin during one of the most challenging periods in the city's history. Catherine's story was a testament to how much good can be accomplished by one person with a big heart, a determined spirit, and a remarkable sense of humor. In this house, thousands of girls were rescued from poverty and abuse. Furthermore, Catherine didn't stop in Dublin. She founded similar houses in other towns and cities. During this time, she took her vows, became a nun, and converted the ministry to a religious order, believing this was the best way to ensure the work would continue after she was gone. She was right. From Baggot Street in Dublin grew a worldwide order that helped millions of people from all walks of life through its schools, hospitals, and other ministries. Today, the Sisters of Mercy continued their work on five continents. Tony's Aunt Hill had been excited and happy, truly fulfilled, to be a part of it.

Tony rose from the garden bench and approached Catherine's grave. He knelt on one knee and said a brief prayer. He stood, noticing the moment had sparked goosebumps on his arms. It wasn't the first time since arriving at the House of Mercy. However, he would have sported them for a far different reason if he had known that, while he enjoyed an afternoon of solitude and meditation in Mother McAuley's house, a manhunt was underway for him in Dublin.

He glanced at his watch and headed back into the house. It was time to retrieve his bags and go. Rita and her … what? … were waiting at Heuston Station. Tony didn't know what to call Ryan Stenford. "Boyfriend" seemed silly—both he and Rita were in their late twenties. "Significant other" was too formal and cumbersome. "Lover" made him cringe, and "weasel" was too revealing of how Tony felt about him.

Tony chastised himself, even before the thought completed its sprint through his brain. He knew it was completely unfair and probably wrong. Ryan seemed to be a genuinely nice guy. He treated Rita well and was polite and respectful toward Tony and his parents. According to Rita, who had met Ryan at the University of Chicago where they both studied music, her… beau, maybe? was a good student and a talented musician. He was also gorgeous. There was no disputing it. The guy was just over six feet tall and fit, with curly, blond hair and a wide smile that stretched his slender face. Tony hoped his distaste for Ryan wasn't simple jealousy.

Tony tried to push all these thoughts aside, reminding himself that Rita obviously adored Ryan. He knew his sister was not one to jump quickly nor easily into a relationship. A beauty herself, with looks inherited from their Italian mother, she could choose carefully.

She had chosen, and Tony had no alternative but to trust his sister's instincts and be supportive.

These noble thoughts did nothing, however, to ease his irritation about Ryan joining them on this trip. Tony and Rita had agreed to travel together in Ireland, and to the House of Mercy, to honor Aunt Hill's longstanding wish that they see it together. Rita's call, announcing that Ryan was joining the pilgrimage, was a big surprise, and a bigger disappointment. It was why Tony had come to Baggot Street a day early, and alone. He didn't want a near stranger interfering with his first experience of it.

Ryan had agreed to meet Rita at the airport, help her find a place to freshen up, and treat her to lunch. It had been decided the two of them would get their tour of the Baggot Street landmark on the return leg of the trip, so it worked out okay for everyone.

Today they were all headed south to County Cork, to explore the places that had been home to the Harrington ancestors. Even Ryan Stenford's presence couldn't mute Tony's excitement to see more of this beautiful country.

Chapter 10

Wednesday, May 20
Pinewood Studios, Iver Heath, England

"I heard your boyfriend got fired."

The forkful of Cobb salad stopped before reaching Darcy Gillson's mouth, then slowly descended back into the porcelain bowl perched on the gleaming hardwood table. A dozen retorts raced through her mind, but she refused to display the anger she felt. She swallowed hard, took a deep breath, and said, "That's nonsense, of course. May I ask where you heard it?"

Kurt Rowsmith, a fellow actor and her current lunch companion, said, "Oh, I dunno. One of the trades maybe, or an entertainment feed online."

Darcy could imagine the celebrity rags that Rowsmith monitored and had no trouble believing that one or more of them would be gloating over Tony's departure from the *Orney Town Crier*. From the beginning of Darcy and Tony's relationship, the gossip sheets' reactions had run the gamut from disbelief and dismissal to crude speculations and envy. Similarly, no one in or near the film industry seemed capable of understanding, let alone accepting, that a successful film star could be happy living with a news reporter in Iowa, someone who earned less in a year than she did in a day.

So far, she and Tony had weathered it all with good humor. He believed in the importance of the work he did, and she was proud of him for doing it. Now, however, with Tony out of work, she was terrified it would all come apart. Within days of Tony's resignation from the paper, she had seen the signs of a man less confident, less easygoing. She had worried Tony's difficulties would be compounded by the inevitable rumormongering. And now, here was Kurt effing Rowsmith confirming her worst fears.

She sat back and looked at him. Beneath his sandy hair and gray eyes, his lips formed a smirk. It took every ounce of Darcy's self-control not to reach across the table and slap him. Instead, she said, "If you would read some legitimate news on occasion, you'd know that Tony resigned from the paper. Like most local newspapers, it's struggling financially. Tony's boss was going to lay off someone else, and Tony volunteered to leave instead."

"Ah, of course. I forgot that Mr. Harrington is always the hero." Rowsmith's sarcasm was as thick as the gazpacho he was stirring.

"You should let go of your jealousy; it doesn't become you."

"Jealousy? Hardly," Rowsmith said, sounding offended. "Why would I be jealous of some out-of-work guy in Iowa? I have everything I ever dreamed of. I'm making seven figures a picture, I have a house in Bel Air and a condo in Aspen, and I'm having lunch with one of the most beautiful women in the world." Rowsmith took a bite of food and winked.

Darcy's face felt warm as she once again fought the urge to lash out. "Yes," she said. "I guess you're right. Poor Tony only won the

Pulitzer Prize and saved the world from disaster a few months ago. And no, he's not having lunch with us. On the other hand, he is the one who gets to climb under the sheets with me most nights." As she said it, she felt a mix of triumph and disgust with herself. She was letting a lowlife horndog like Rowsmith get to her.

He leered at her. "Yes, well, there is that. Of course, we can fix that any time you want to find out why women love me."

"Jesus, Kurt, give it a rest. We all know how proud you are of your body count. Despite that, I can assure you there are plenty of women who don't love you, including me. Don't think you're ever going to add my notch to your bedpost."

"Okay. I'm sorry. I…"

Darcy quit listening. She wasn't interested in forgiving him and making small talk. She wasn't even sure why she had agreed to have lunch with him. She'd known Rowsmith for a dozen years and had shared movie credits with him twice before. In all that time, the only things in which he'd ever shown an interest were his reviews and her cleavage. He was the opposite of Tony in every way, with little honor, less loyalty, and zero empathy for others. She'd only given him the time of day, she supposed, because they would be working closely together for the next three weeks. If she had declined, he would have taken it personally. She knew him well enough to know he was capable of blowing anything out of proportion, and having it become a rift between them. Things like that could show on film, despite an actor's best efforts. So here she was, having a spat anyway, and doing it with one of the hot, single stars of Hollywood. What would the paparazzi make of this? Fortunately, this was one place where celebrities could go and not worry about being seen except by other celebrities.

Darcy took a moment to study the surroundings. After she had agreed to lunch with him, Rowsmith had chosen The Bar at Pinewood Studios. He had justified the location, saying it was only a short walk from the soundstage where they were filming. For Darcy, the selection had raised a red flag as it was an intimate setting with just a few tables, subdued lighting, and a big fireplace. It was the kind of place where studio executives brought potential partners to woo them. She knew it was on her that she hadn't refused or hadn't at least insisted on an alternate venue. The vast studio complex featured at least a half dozen options for luncheon fare.

As she finished her salad, she heard Rowsmith say, "So are we good?"

She smiled warmly. She was, after all, an actress. "Yes, we're fine. Just please show a modicum of respect for me, whether I deserve it or not, and a healthy respect for Tony, who certainly does deserve it."

"Ten-four," he said, saluting her as they rose. "I'll get the bill."

She was tempted to argue, but knew he would turn it in on his expenses. In the end, one of the companies involved in the movie production would pay it.

"Thank you." She held out her hand, but he stepped forward and pulled her into a quick embrace.

As she pulled back, he said, "That was worth more than the cost of any meal."

Disappointed in and disgusted with her co-star, Darcy simply shook her head and excused herself. As she walked back to the makeup facility to prepare for her next scene, it occurred to her that in one important way, she owed Rowsmith a debt of gratitude. In just one hour, he had reinforced beyond measure Darcy's appreciation of Tony and her conviction that she was in love with the right man.

Oh, Tony. My loving, loyal, courageous man. I hope you're enjoying Ireland. I wish I could be there with you. Thoughts of him brought her fears rushing back. Would he regain his footing? Would he find meaningful work again? Would it be in Iowa, or would they have to leave their beautiful old house in the town of Orney and build a life in a larger city like Chicago, New York, or LA?

She attempted to quell her anxieties by reminding herself that for several months, she had been encouraging Tony to find other work. As a journalist, he had put himself in harm's way too many times. Just a few months ago, he had nearly been killed three times as he pursued a group a of domestic terrorists. *Whatever happens now, at least he's safe*.

Darcy Gillson had no idea how wrong she was.

Chapter 11

Wednesday, May 20
Dublin, Ireland

At Heuston Station, Tony walked within a dozen meters of one of Nixer's men, but wasn't spotted. His luck still holding, he was missed because Rita and Ryan were at his side. The goon was searching for an American traveling alone. Also, Tony had been careful to comb and spray his hair in place, to hide the scar on the back of his skull. The last thing he wanted was for Rita or Ryan to notice it and begin asking questions.

The three companions hurried up the steps into the first-class car of the 5 p.m. train to Cork. Tony wouldn't have bothered with first class on Iarnród Éireann, or Irish Rail, but it cost only a few Euros more, and he wanted to ensure Rita had a positive first experience in Ireland. She and Ryan had come almost directly from the airport to the train station in western Dublin. He hoped the two-and-a-half-hour trip would give them all a chance to enjoy the views of the Irish countryside.

The car was configured with facing seats separated by a small table. It was a perfect arrangement for chatting and enjoying the chocolates and other snacks Tony had brought in his bag. Rita nearly squealed when she saw them.

"I knew I loved you for a reason," she said, choosing a bag of raisins and a granola bar. Tony and Ryan glanced at each other, grinning. "What?"

"Nothing," Tony said. "I knew you'd want a snack during the trip. Our dinner reservations aren't until eight." He removed the foil from a large block of chocolate, a brand he didn't recognize but thought looked Swiss, and took a bite off the corner. Ryan chose a package of mixed nuts.

The three settled into small talk about their respective trips, their activities in Chicago and in Iowa, the news of the day, and other topics typical of siblings and friends who've been separated for a while. Tony was mildly surprised when Rita broached the subject of his current jobless status. She reached across the table and squeezed his forearm when she asked, "Are you doing okay?"

"I'm fine, really," Tony said. "It feels good to not wake up every day facing a backlog of assignments and looming deadlines. I also enjoy traveling without feeling guilty about missing work, and I finally have time to work on updates to our house."

Tony and Darcy lived in a century-old two-story home on a large property in Orney. It had been built by the town's banker and willed to his daughter, who became a writer for the *Orney Town Crier*. She had been elderly and semiretired when Tony had known her. He had been shocked when Evelyn Crowder had given the house to him in her will.

While everything Tony had just told Rita was technically true, he had been putting on a brave face for his sister and her beau. Most of what he was feeling—the uncertainty, the anxiety, the sense of loss—was left unspoken. At its core, Tony's "I'm fine" comment was BS, and Tony knew that Rita knew it was BS. He hoped she understood why he was unwilling to have a serious discussion about his current emotions in front of Ryan.

The bright May sun warmed the interior of the coach, and the nearly imperceptible dance of shadows on the table marked its gentle rocking. As the conversation ebbed, Tony noticed Rita's posture slacken and eyelids droop. She leaned left, placing her head on Ryan's shoulder, and soon was asleep. Ryan glanced down and kissed the top of her head.

Tony looked away, choosing to concentrate on the lush green fields parading past the window.

***

Allihies, Beara Peninsula, Ireland

Sam Kilborgen drained the last of his Guinness and waved the mug. Moira Blake quickly materialized next to his booth in the back corner of O'Connell's Pub.

"Another, Sam?"

"Nah, two's company but three's an argument at home."

Moira smiled. "I'll get your bill."

Kilborgen lowered his voice. "See that you're the one who collects it. I'll be leavin' somethin' with it for your uncle."

Moira's features flickered but the smile returned. "Of course. I'll be sure."

With the bar bill in front of him, secured to a simple plexiglass clipboard, Kilborgen took some cash from his wallet and placed it on top, then removed a folded sheet of paper from his coat pocket and slid it underneath. He rose, nodded at Blake, and strolled out of the bar.

Ox Foley will think I've lost my mind, Kilborgen thought. *But if he does exactly what I've instructed, his worries with the Coast Guard will be over for good.* He was proud to be clever enough to figure it out, and proud to be capable enough to make the modifications necessary for it to work. On the other hand, he wasn't proud to be a criminal, and he was disgusted with himself every time he thought about what the influx of cocaine and other illicit drugs were doing to his beloved country. So, he chose not to think about it. *I'm doing what I must to survive*, he told himself. *It's what I have to do.*

Chapter 12

Thursday, May 21
Cork, Ireland

"What's an Allihies?" Tony asked, poking at his shepherd's pie, waiting for it to cool. The three were seated in a second-story dining room of a restaurant in downtown Cork. The room was crowded with locals as well as tourists, enjoying the establishment's large menu and wine list. At 8 p.m., the light outside the large windows had a muted hue, the sun less of a cheerful companion and more of an old man waiting for a last train.

"It's a town," Ryan said, smiling warmly. "A village, really. Just a few hundred people. It's on the coast of the Beara Peninsula. Very remote. Very beautiful."

"We just got here. I haven't even been to the church or the cemetery yet." Tony was trying hard not to whine. He was failing. He glanced at Rita, who was glowing with excitement and approval of her beau's suggestion. Knowing the fight was lost, Tony said, "How'd you even hear of it?"

"Colin Ferrell said it's the most beautiful spot in the world. You can view the clip on YouTube. You know Colin Ferrell, the actor?"

"Yes, I know who he is," Tony said, his irritation growing.

"Well, he said the views of the ocean are magnificent, and the people are great. It's the far southwest tip of Ireland. From that spot, you can be the last person in Europe to see the sunset. That's what the locals claim. They even have a beach."

"A beach?" Rita's smile widened, if that was possible.

"Allihies once was home to one of the biggest copper mines in the world. The quartz dust from the mine was used to create a wonderful beach."

So people can sunbathe on the four days a year the sun shines on the coast of Ireland, Tony thought, unhappy that Ryan was altering their plans, and even more irritated with himself for being a poor sport about it.

"It sounds wonderful," Rita said. "What do you say, Tony? You okay if we take a side trip?"

He looked at Ryan. "How do we get there? Is there a train?"

Ryan shook his head. "No train. Far too remote for that. We'll rent a car."

"That means driving on the left side of the road."

"Not a problem," Ryan said. "I've done it before."

Who is this guy?

Rita said, "Then it's settled. While Ryan finds us a car, I'll go online and see about lodging. Tony, maybe you could talk to the inn here in Cork about cutting short our stay. I mean, if it's okay, we'll go first thing in the morning."

Ryan looked about to speak, then sat back and nodded.

Was he going to object? Tony looked down and took a bite of potatoes to hide his surprise. *Ryan couldn't want to go tonight, could he? What's up with the sudden passion for All-hees, or whatever this place is called?*

Aloud, Tony said, "Sounds like a plan. Can't object to a chance to see the coast, and who am I to argue with Colin Ferrell? My visits to the church and cemetery can wait until the return trip."

"Thanks, Tony," Ryan said. "You won't regret it."

Tony had a feeling he would but pushed his reservations to the back of his mind. Between bites of food, he opened his phone and began researching the Beara Peninsula. He learned Ryan was right. Many posts and reviews included positive comments claiming it was Ireland's best-kept secret and a "must-see" for people interested in the country's history, culture, and natural beauty. In addition, he learned that the Harrington name was prominent on the peninsula. Some families who shared his name had roots there going back centuries. By the end of the meal, he was convinced. While he didn't understand Ryan's desire to get there quickly, nor did he share Rita's enthusiasm, he at least agreed it was worth the more than two-hour drive to check it out.

Someone's phone buzzed. Ryan reached into a front pants pocket and withdrew his. He glanced at the screen, wrote a quick response, and returned it to his pocket. He said, "Sorry about that. I know it's rude."

"No worries," Tony said. "We all do it."

"My dad," Ryan said, apparently feeling the need to explain.

"Oh?" Tony couldn't help himself. Realizing he knew nothing about Ryan's family or background, he wanted more.

Rita answered on Ryan's behalf. "He's an art dealer in London. Has clients all over Europe, both private collectors and art galleries. Isn't that cool?"

Tony nodded in agreement. It sounded glamorous, even though he knew it might not be. Success or failure in the art world depended on many things, including a measure of luck. But if the man was successful, it certainly could be an enviable lifestyle.

"That's why I joined you here in Ireland at the last minute," Ryan said. "Dad has a client in Dublin who wants to sell a Mainie Jellett abstract. Dad's tied up in a big auction in Barcelona, so he asked me to take care of it. The finances can all flow electronically, of course, but the transportation of the art itself requires a courier."

"So you came all the way from the US to carry a painting from Dublin to London?" As soon as the words escaped his mouth, Tony realized how snarky he sounded. "Sorry. I just mean…"

Ryan smiled, "It's okay. I get it. It annoys me, too, when I get these assignments, which isn't very often, thank God. Understand, it's not only that he trusts me to deliver the painting safely. He shows the client a measure of respect by sending a member of the family to complete the deal."

"Makes sense," Tony said, appreciating that Ryan had let him off the hook so easily. "So you must be close, you and your dad."

Ryan snorted. "I wouldn't go that far. Let's just say he makes a better boss than he does a father."

"And your mother?"

"I never knew her. She died when I was just a baby. I was mostly raised by extended family. While my dad traveled the world, I was shipped off to the States. I lived in a half dozen different places, but primarily in New York and Chicago."

"I'm sorry," Tony said. "That must've been hard."

"Nothing to be sorry about. I never knew any other life, so it was fine."

Tony grew quiet as he thought about the huge role his parents played in his life. His father, Charles, was a successful novelist and screenwriter. In recent years, he had been teaching and directing the writers' program at the University of Iowa. His mother, Carlotta, or

Carla to her friends, was a homemaker, a serial volunteer, and if he was honest with himself, a helicopter parent. A first-generation Italian immigrant, two things topped her list of priorities: family and food.

He couldn't imagine growing up without the steadfast love and support of two parents like he and Rita had experienced. Trying to envision a life as dramatically different as Ryan's was like peering into a fog. Glimpses of occasional shapes allowed you to imagine what was out there, but not with any confidence. His appreciation of Ryan inched up a notch, and he resolved to treat him with more respect.

Chapter 13

Sunday, May 24

Allihies, Beara Peninsula, County Cork, Ireland

Tony was struggling to zip closed his roller bag when he was interrupted by three loud raps on the door. The knocks were too loud to be Rita and too early to be the hotel staff. He had risen at sunrise to enjoy a walk on the beach before breakfast. Later today, he, Rita, and Ryan would be traveling back to Cork.

He had thoroughly enjoyed the past two days in Allihies. He and the others had explored the local shops as well as the abandoned mine. They had driven miles of narrow roads outside the town, through rocky terrain and lush, green pastures, stopping to enjoy breathtaking views of the sea. They had seen a sprinkling of farmhouses and other abodes ranging from tiny bungalows to large, modern houses. They had even spotted one truly massive estate off in the distance, perched on a bluff above the water. The mansion was old and in disrepair, but that didn't diminish the impressive spectacle of its size, combined with a baroque architectural style reminiscent of the seventeenth century. When they had asked about it later, while enjoying a pint in a local pub, the bartender had told them the house had been built by one of the copper barons and had been abandoned after the mine had closed. Since that time, a series of owners had tried to restore it. Each had given up and walked away due to its difficulty and cost.

"Talk is, somebody's at it again," the host had said. "There be lots 'o activity up there. Sad to say, ne'er a soul been down to spend money with me, so I don' know much more. 'Course I wish 'em luck. Shame to see the place crumble, to be sure."

Late that afternoon, Tony, Rita, and Ryan walked a portion of the Beara Way, a miles-long path through the peninsula's natural beauty, with more spectacular views of both the land and the water.

Whether driving or walking, everywhere they stopped for refreshments featured wonderful food and plenty of drink. And true to Colin Ferrell's word, the people they encountered were welcoming, good-natured, and generous.

Their hotel in Allihies was a rather plain, flat-faced building painted light green. However, it was clean, comfortable, and in a perfect location on the main street through town, with a pub next door and a second one across the street. Now, at 5:41 a.m., a surprising knock on the hotel room's door was interrupting Tony's musings, as well as his packing.

He stepped over to the door and opened it. He was surprised to see a woman in uniform. The Gardai had no full-time presence in Allihies. Locals said it was rare to see them even drive through town on patrol.

"Tony Harrington?"

Tony nodded. "Yes. Can I help you?"

"If it's not too much trouble, I'd like you to come with me," the woman said.

"I'm sorry, officer, but are you sure you have the right Harrington? It's a common name around here. I…"

"From America? Tony Harrington from…" She paused to look at the screen on her phone. "Orney, Iowa?"

"Well, yes. That's me. Can I ask what this is about?"

"There's been some trouble. The inspector would like to talk to you."

Tony felt his pulse jump. He said, "At five-thirty in the morning? Can't this wait?"

"Perhaps, but he asked me to tell you he'd rather it didn't."

"Will I be long? I'm supposed to check out this morning."

"Leave your bag here. I'll have you back in an hour or two."

"Okay, but let me stop by my sister's room and tell her, so she won't worry."

***

After a twenty-minute drive along a narrow, twisting road through the countryside, the officer turned her patrol car into a parking lot and stopped short of a cluster of official vehicles. As Tony stepped out, the early morning sun, low on the horizon, was clawing away at a lingering haze that reached from the ground to about knee height. Above, the previous night's cloud cover had broken into patches of fluffy, white cauliflower florets. It was going to be a beautiful day.

Redirecting his attention, Tony examined his surroundings. Although he had not been there before, he immediately knew where they were. Not far away was a thousand-foot-high steel tower, from which cables extended in both directions. This was the station for the Dursey Island Cable Car, one of the peninsula's most famous attractions. He followed the officer up the hill, ducking under a *DO*

NOT CROSS tape, and approached a group of people near the station's ticket booth. As they neared, a man in jeans and a yellow-and-gray Gardai jacket stepped away from the group and down the hill to meet them.

Tony's breath caught. "Inspector Lynch. I didn't expect to see you today. What's…"

"I could say the same, Mr. Harrington. Come with me."

The inspector led Tony to a small police van. They climbed into the front seats and shut the doors. The inspector immediately took his phone from his pocket and propped it on the dashboard. "I'm recording this."

"Why…" Tony began, but was interrupted.

"Don't give me any feckin' trouble. Just answer my questions."

Tony swallowed and nodded.

The inspector said, "Why are you here?"

"An officer came to my door this morning. She said…"

An exasperated grunt escaped from the inspector's lips. "Not that. Why are you down here on the coast? Why Allihies?"

"I'm traveling with my sister and her boyfriend. We heard it was beautiful here. We came to see it. Also, there's a lot of Harrington history in this area. Why are you asking me this? What's happened?"

The inspector didn't answer. After a long moment, he turned and looked squarely into Tony's eyes. "Tell me the feckin' truth. Why are you really here?"

Tony's nervousness quickly morphed into irritation. He said, "It sounds like you're accusing me of lying. I'm not lying. I've told you the truth. Now tell me what's going on or take me back to my hotel."

The inspector's eyes flashed, and his face grew red. "You want me to believe that you just happened to be nearby when two people were killed, in an area where there hasn't been a murder in fifty years? This, just days after you were attacked on a busy Dublin street where crime is almost nonexistent? I'm sorry, but I don't believe in coincidences. So yes, I find your whole story unbelievable."

"Killed? Who's been killed? You said murder?"

The inspector stared, unblinking, then reached into a leather satchel near his feet and extracted an iPad. As he opened the photos file, he said, "Two college students. Two lovely young people just beginning their lives."

Tony realized the inspector's red face was accented by tears forming in the corners of his eyes. Suddenly, the iPad was shoved into Tony's hands.

"Dear God."

On the screen was a photograph of two naked bodies, entwined on a wooden floor and covered in blood. From the angle of the photo, it was difficult to know how the woman had died, but the open wound on the young man's neck stared back at him like an evil grin.

Tony wanted to turn away, but he forced himself to examine the image closely. He might not get another chance to see it.

Seconds later, the inspector pulled the iPad from his hands. "I'm going to ask you again. What do you know about this?"

Tony took a deep breath and stared back at Lynch. He said, "I swear to you, I know nothing about it. We have enjoyed two wonderful days of sightseeing and hiking, and we're headed back to Cork today. This has nothing to do with me, or with us."

As he spoke, something dark flitted through his mind. He tried to capture it, save it for contemplation later, but it wouldn't come into focus. He shook it off.

"Do you have an alibi for last night?"

Tony's face curled in disgust. Clearly Lynch wasn't going to take his word for anything. He said, "Depends on the time. The three of us had dinner together and then had a few beers at the pub."

"Which pub?"

"Across the street. O'Connell's."

The inspector's body language shifted.

Tony said, "What?"

"These two were there last night."

"A lot of people were there. We talked and drank until about eleven, then went back to the hotel to sleep. My sister was with her boyfriend, but I have a separate room. No alibi after that. When did this happen?"

The inspector didn't answer. Instead, he touched the iPad's screen and turned it to show Tony. "Do you recognize her?"

Tony studied the picture of a young brunette cuddling a long-haired cat under her chin. She was smiling and looking to the right of the camera. It appeared to be a photo pulled from a social media posting. "I think so. There was a group of young people at one of the long wooden tables. She could have been one of them. They were still there when we left."

"And him?"

A tall, rail-thin man looked back at Tony from the screen. The man's hair was uncombed and stood up from his scalp, adding to his height. He had a large, slightly beaked nose, and a stern, confident expression. It was the same man with the knife wound in the evidence photo.

"Yes. He was there for sure. His hair was visible above the heads of everyone at his table, and he had a distinctive voice with a bit of a rattle. So who are they? What happened?"

"Two locals. Michael Reilly and Lauren O'Grady. Kids who grew up here. Everyone's known them for two decades. Now they're students—were students—in Cork and Dublin. As to what happened, that's a big feckin' mystery."

"Show me." Tony's blunt request sounded more like a command. It surprised the inspector. It surprised Tony even more.

"Show you? Why in the name of all that's holy would I do that?"

"Maybe I can help."

"I don't want your damn help. Not unless you have information about this you haven't shared."

"I don't," Tony said, sitting up on the edge of his seat for emphasis. "What I do have is some experience with investigating murders. Look, I get it that you see me as an intruder and a suspicious coincidence. But, as your officer pointed out back in Dublin, I've been involved in writing about, and sometimes solving, murder cases."

Lynch was shaking his head. "You're a suspect. I can't let you near there."

"You know as well as I do that I didn't kill those kids. If you need more than my word for it, I can give you a list of people in law enforcement, from local cops to the FBI, who will vouch for me. In the meantime, think about it. I'm already here at the scene. And I'm no longer with the paper, so you don't have to worry about the news angle. In fact, I promise you right now, I won't share a word about this with anyone without your prior approval."

The inspector didn't respond.

In a quieter voice, Tony looked away and said, "The bottom line is, I don't have anything else to do. At least nothing as important as this. Let me have a look. Please."

Lynch glared at him, shook his head, and slipped the iPad back into his satchel. He climbed out of the van and slammed the door.

Tony sighed and looked out the side window of the van, searching the lot for his ride back to Allihies. He opened the passenger door just as he heard Lynch cry out, "Are you comin' or not?"

He leaped out and jogged up the hill to join Lynch on the station platform.

***

Tony reeled a little as they neared the cable car. Knowing the actual scene would be far worse than the photographs didn't shield him from the brutality of it. People in white coveralls were preparing body bags. Tony glanced at his watch. Not yet 7 a.m. He noted the blood had darkened and the bodies had taken on the gray, pasty look of the dead.

"Time of death?" he asked quietly.

"One forty-five this morning, if you believe our witnesses."

"Witnesses?"

"That can wait. What do you see?"

Tony didn't respond right away. He maneuvered around the technicians to get a view from another angle. After a couple of minutes, he said, "I see two young people having intercourse on the floor of the cable car. He's on his back; she's straddled over him. In the heat of it, someone approaches from behind her. He, assuming it's a he, puts his left arm around her neck, reaches past her with his right, and slices the man's right carotid. Then, as the knife comes up, he brings it across her throat. In a couple of seconds, maybe less, two people are bleeding out on the floor with no hope of survival."

Tony turned and faced Lynch, who nodded.

Tony continued. "It might look like the work of a jealous boyfriend, or girlfriend, but I don't think so."

"Because?"

"Because it would take balls the size of Guinness kegs to attempt this. Even if you look past that—maybe you assume a jealous rage caused someone to ignore the risks—it would have to have been done quickly and precisely. A miss, or even a moment's hesitation, could give one of the victims the time to react. So, he's either a well-trained killer or an incredibly lucky, anger-fueled crazy person."

"Or an American news reporter with three years of martial arts training," Lynch deadpanned.

Tony glanced at him but returned his gaze to the scene. He said, "Prints?"

"It's a public conveyance. There are a thousand sets of prints in there."

"Of course, but you know what I mean. Did you get lucky and find anything in blood? Anything on the bodies in places that only would have been exposed after they disrobed?"

Lynch gave him a begrudging nod. "I have to admit, you ask the right questions."

"So…?"

"Nothing yet. As soon as the bodies are gone, the technicians will go over every inch of the car."

Tony nodded and said, "So you know how it was done. Now you just have to figure out who wanted two college kids killed. Maybe a drug deal gone bad? Maybe…"

"You're wrong," Lynch said.

"Sorry?"

"We don't know how it was done."

"But I thought you agreed with the scenario I just painted."

"I wish it were that simple," the inspector said. "The problem is we have three witnesses. Three friends of the victims. Three apparently sane, upstanding young people, two of whom also grew up here."

"You've lost me, Inspector."

Lynch said, "Our three witnesses swear that these two young people, Michael and Lauren, died out there."

"Out where?" Tony could see Lynch was looking past him, out toward the Dursey Sound. He turned and followed the inspector's gaze up along the cables stretching toward the distant island. "Out *there*? Over the water? How is that possible?"

"I'd say it isn't," Lynch said. "But they swear it. A healthy young couple got into the car. The car was sent out to the midpoint over the water. A few minutes later, it was returned. When it stopped at the platform…" He gestured toward the bloody corpses. "That was what they found."

"That's ridiculous," Tony said. "They must be covering for whoever did it. This is no murder-suicide. Nobody cuts their own throat. It's not even possible to do it to the extent you see in those wounds."

"I agree," Lynch said. "In fact, the knife isn't here. Whoever killed them didn't try to make it look like anything other than what it was—cold-blooded murder."

"So, what then?" Tony pondered. "Someone was in the car with them?" He looked again through the open door. The cable car was designed for perhaps six passengers. There was no place to hide.

Lynch said, "As you can see, that's not possible."

"Unless," Tony said, "they invited someone along. Maybe they thought it was going to be a threesome, or maybe they wanted to make a porno. Someone was with them to film it."

"You have a strange mind, Mr. Harrington. It took me a couple of hours to think of those scenarios. The problem is, it didn't happen. Three witnesses are adamant in saying only Michael and Lauren got into the car. And no one came out when it re-docked at the station."

"Somebody's lying. They have to be."

"Maybe," Lynch said, stepping off the station platform and leading Tony away from the crime scene. "But so far, they're sticking to their stories and sounding very believable as they do it."

Tony tried to imagine other answers but couldn't. He remained silent as they walked down the hill to the parking lot. When they reached the patrol car it occurred to him to ask, "By the way, why are you down here? The Gardai must have investigators closer than Dublin."

"I was in Castletownbere, enjoying a weekend with my family. My brother-in-law has a nice boat there. We took the kids fishing yesterday. Planned to go again today. When the local guard got the call from a hysterical woman screaming about dead friends, they came and rousted me. It ruined my weekend, but I appreciated being on the scene quickly. I had a chance to interview the victims' friends while they were still here. I talked to them separately, of course, and asked each of them to walk me through it. Their stories matched well, if not perfectly. In other words, they sounded like the truth."

Tony wished he could meet these witnesses. He also wished… "Inspector, when your team clears the cable car, would you call me so I could go in and take a look? You know, before anyone cleans it up?"

"Can't imagine why you'd want to. It's just a box hanging from a couple of cables."

"Humor me. I just want to see it from the point of view of the killer, and his victims."

"It will take a couple of days. I thought you were headed back to Cork today."

Not now, Tony thought. *There's a mystery to solve, and a murderer to catch. And besides, I've got nothing better to do.*

***

"If you're staying, we're staying," Ryan said.

Tony tried to object, but once again, Rita sided with her beau. "We'd be leaving you without a car, which you might need. Besides, we love it here. A few more days on the coast is fine with us."

"Okay, I give, but you have to promise me you'll stay away from this case. Whoever killed these kids is skilled, and brazen as hell. I don't want you mixed up in trying to find him."

Rita smiled and grabbed Ryan's arm, pulling him close. "No problem. We have better things to do."

Tony groaned and shook his head. "I'm sorry I mentioned it."

They were sitting in the tiny dining room on the hotel's main floor. Tony and Ryan were enjoying typical Irish breakfasts of eggs, baked beans, fried tomatoes, and sausages. Rita was having a muffin and a cup of fresh fruit.

"Does the inspector know you're staying?" Ryan asked.

"Yeah, I told him I want to get inside the car before they clean it up. He wasn't too happy about it, but I think he's going to arrange it. Probably tomorrow or Tuesday."

"And in the meantime?"

"Not sure. I'd love to talk to one or more of the people who witnessed this, but I don't even know their names."

"That won't be a problem," Rita said.

Tony nodded, knowing she was referring to the town's size. By the end of the day, everyone would know everything about what had happened.

At that moment, as if to put an exclamation point on the thought, the innkeeper walked up to the table with a pot of coffee. As the petite, gray-haired woman topped off their cups, she said, "One 'o them was that new girl, Moira. The waitress at O'Connell's. We rent her a flat 'bove our place down the street. She called ta say not to worry that she ne'er come home last night. I guess the peelers kept 'er for questioning."

The three looked up, surprised—but not too surprised—that their hostess had been listening to their conversation.

Tony said, "She doing okay? It must have been horrible."

"Ya, she sounded shook, right 'nuff. Exhausted too. Poor thing."

"She tell you much about it?" Tony asked, knowing he was pushing the boundaries of what was appropriate to ask.

The woman didn't seem to notice. "Nah, just that she'd been with a couple of locals when two bodies were found, so the guard wanted her to stick around. They took her over to Castletownbere.

Should be back later today. Poor thing."

"New girl?"

The voice was Ryan's, surprising Tony.

"Yeh, only been 'ere a couple 'o weeks. Lovely girl. Said she came south to get away from some glunterpeck."

"Sorry?" Tony said.

"I, uh…" The woman seemed at a loss.

Ryan said, "A dick."

The woman grinned. "Not just so, but like that. Some boyo makin' her life bad craic. Poor thing."

The woman left, and Tony pulled out his phone, adding Moira's name and workplace to his Notes app.

Ryan smiled and said, "I guess we know where we're drinking tonight."

Tony looked up. "Not we. Remember your promise. You two find another pub and leave Moira to me."

"Aye, Captain," Rita said, giving him a little salute. Ryan looked about to speak, then relaxed and reached for his coffee instead.

Tony found himself wondering once again what was going on behind those gray-blue eyes.

Chapter 14

Sunday, May 24
Castletownbere, Beara Peninsula, County Cork, Ireland

"What did you do with the knife?"

"Will you please just stop? I never saw a knife. I didn't have a knife. I didn't kill them."

Inspector Lynch was undeterred. He needed young Dylan Maloney to change his story. Without that, he had no way to explain how two people died in the cable car. He said, "We're going to find the knife. We have teams of volunteers searching the brush and divers in the Dursey Sound. When we do, we'll be able to trace where it came from, and then we'll be able to find the person who bought it. We've got you, Dylan, so why don't you just tell me the truth and get this off your chest?"

Red-faced, Dylan looked across the small, metal interview desk at the inspector. "Listen to me, you self-righteous prick. I did not kill them! I loved Lauren. I've loved her since I was ten years old. I would give my life to bring her back."

"Sorry, Dylan, but that only provides your motive. You loved Lauren? Okay. I believe you. So, when she got into that car, stripped off her clothes, and invited Michael to lie down, you lost it. I understand. I would've done the same. You reacted out of passion. It wasn't premeditated. The prosecutor will under..."

"*No!*" Dylan screamed. His right fist pounded the table in sync with his words, "No, no, no! It was someone else. I don't know who. I don't know how. But it was not me." He leaned forward, burying his face in his arms on the table, and began to weep.

Lynch decided the boy had had enough. He rose to go. As he reached the door, he heard Dylan's voice, muffled by his sleeves.

"Find the knife. Find the fucker who did this. Then I will gladly commit murder."

***

Lynch was exhausted. It was Sunday afternoon, and he already had been working the case for fourteen hours. It worried him that he was no closer to understanding what had happened than when he first arrived on the scene early that morning. It angered him to think the scut who had brutally killed Michael and Lauren was getting further from his grasp with each passing hour.

He pushed open the door to the Gardai chief's office and sat behind the desk. Seated in a straight-backed chair, facing him, was Niamh Deiriocht. Before he spoke, he reminded himself how to pronounce her name: *Neeve Dare-ee-ah.*

"Thank you for being patient, Niamh," he said. "I know it's been a horrible day for you."

"You made Dylan cry," she said tersely.

Lynch shifted in his chair. "Yes, well, I'm sorry if you heard any of that. I had to push him. I had to know what really happened."

"So why him? Why not push me?"

Lynch looked at her for a couple of beats and said, "Did you kill them?"

"No."

"There you have it."

"Dylan didn't kill them either."

"Somebody did."

"Yes, obviously. But it wasn't Dylan. I was there. Of the three of us, he was the last on the scene. He came running when he heard Moira and me screaming."

Lynch rubbed his eyes with the knuckles of his index fingers. "So what happened? Tell me again."

Niamh walked him through it, from the bar to the bloody corpses. She concluded by saying, "They were killed in the cable car while it was over the water. Period."

"But how?" Lynch said, his tone almost pleading. "They're a thousand feet in the air, dangling from cables, inside a closed box."

"It wasn't closed."

"What?" Lynch leaned forward. "What do you mean?"

"The cable car wasn't closed. It will operate with the door open. I mean, apparently it will, because it did. Rob suggested they leave it open. Said it would add to the thrill. Michael, of course, jumped on the idea."

Open or closed, Lynch couldn't imagine why it mattered, considering the other circumstances, but the mention of Rob turned his attention to the secondary mystery. He said, "You mentioned Rob again. Tell me more about him."

"I wish I could. I've already described everything he did and said. That's all I know."

"You'd never seen him before last night?"

"No, sir, and not much then. A few minutes in the pub, a few minutes on the hill overlooking the sound, and then he was gone."

"Niamh, I need your help here. So far, we've found no trace of this guy. I didn't even believe he was real until Connie at the pub confirmed what the three of you told me. So please try hard to remember anything he said, any little reference he made, that might help us track him down."

Lynch waited while the young woman pondered the request.

Eventually, she said, "I'm sorry, but there's nothing."

"Don't apologize. Just keep thinking, and let me know if something occurs to you."

She nodded and the inspector added, "Do you think he could have done it?"

Niamh's eyes widened. "I don't see how. As I told you, he was in the ticket booth with the controls when Michael and Lauren got into the car, and he drove away before they returned."

"Could he have somehow doubled back and, uh, done the deed when they returned, before you and Moira saw the bodies?"

"No, sir. We were right there on the platform. No one else was around. Dylan was closest, and he was out in the parking lot."

"Well damn all," Lynch muttered. Then louder, he said, "Gather your things and tell Dylan and Moira you're all free to go. I'll get an officer to drive you back to Allihies. Try to get some rest."

"Yes, sir. Thank you, sir."

As Lynch watched her exit the office, he debated what to do next. A nationwide alert had already been issued to find this man named Rob, as a material witness to the double homicide. So far, nothing. Lynch wasn't really surprised. The region was sparsely populated, and at one-thirty in the morning, almost none of the handful of residents would have been awake to see anything.

Niamh apparently had been the only one to notice any details about the man's truck. She said it was an Isuzu D-Max. It wasn't commonplace to see one in the area, but it wasn't unheard of either. If it had been seen, it probably wouldn't have attracted any special notice.

Of course, the vehicle was immaterial if the man was hiding out somewhere. The peninsula had ten thousand places to hide, from mountain passes, to remote farmsteads, to wooded valleys. Tucked under an outcropping of stone along one of the hundreds of rocky fingers reaching into the sea, the truck could sit for weeks without being seen.

The impossibility of the task was especially frustrating because Lynch knew the mysterious stranger was the key to solving the case. Niamh might be right, that Rob couldn't have killed Michael and Lauren, but he was there, and left right before the discovery of the bodies. The timing wasn't just suspicious, it was damning. *And besides, who ever heard of a Ukrainian named Rob?*

Chapter 15

Sunday, May 24

Allihies, Beara Peninsula, County Cork, Ireland

Tony looked up from the menu as the bartender known as Connie approached.

"No waitress tonight?" he asked, disappointed. He had been hoping to meet and maybe even chat with the young woman who had been at the murder scene.

"Nah. She had a manky morning, to be sure. Hoped she'd be in but nar too surprised she's not. What have ye?"

"Fish and chips, and a diet soft drink, if you've got one."

"I got a light beer."

Tony considered it, then said, "A regular Coca-Cola will be fine."

The man nodded and turned to go.

To his back, Tony said, "Have you talked to her?"

Connie stopped and turned. His eyes narrowed and fleshy cheeks turned down into a scowl. "Why ye be askin'?"

"Sorry," Tony said. "I don't mean to pry. It's just that I was out there this morning, and…"

"Out where?"

"The Gardai inspector called me out to the scene."

"Did he now? Why would he do that?"

"Well, we met in Dublin a few days ago. He knows I have some experience with crime, so he asked me to take a look." Tony knew he was fudging the truth a little, but assumed the risk of being discovered was small and the consequences even smaller.

"So what'd ye see then?" Connie asked, his confrontational tone easing just a little.

"I saw the horror of two young people, brutally murdered. I want to do anything I can to help the inspector find the person who did it."

"Very noble," the man scoffed. He held out his hand.

"What?"

"ID. Show me."

Tony extracted his wallet and handed over his driver's license.

"Harrington? Huh. My neighbor's a Harrington. So's his neighbor."

"Yeah, we've met a few since coming south."

Connie handed back the license, then pulled out his phone. He didn't say anything while he poked at the screen. He paused, reading, then said, "I found ye. Says here ye got a Pulitzer Prize. Kinda big deal."

Tony nodded but didn't comment, as he wondered where this was going.

Connie said, "So ye look legit. Ye need somethin' from me?"

"Just my food," Tony said, then quickly added, "and maybe one favor."

"Yeah? That being what?"

"Could you call your waitress, Moira, and ask her if she'd talk to me?"

The man seemed to consider the question. Finally, he said, "Maybe. But not till later. I'm hoping she be sleepin' now. Stop back in a couple a hours. I'll let ye know then if she be willin' ta see ye."

***

It was nearly seven when Tony heard footsteps approaching behind him. He was standing on the beach at the bottom of a long, gradual hill south of Allihies. He turned from his view of the Ballydonegan Bay and found himself looking into the face of a young woman with dark eyes and prominent dimples. Her hair was pulled back into a ponytail, and she wore blue jeans and a light-blue windbreaker. He held out his hand, and she stepped closer and grasped it.

She said, "I'm Moira Blake. Thank you for meeting me here. I tried to think of a place remote enough to be private, but not so remote that I needed to be afraid." She gestured in a wide circle, indicating the dozen or so people within eyesight, walking or sitting on the beach.

"This is perfect," Tony said. "Thanks for agreeing to see me." He pulled out his wallet and displayed his driver's license. "And please don't be afraid. We've got at least a couple hours of daylight left, and I'm about as dangerous as Barney the Dinosaur."

The woman smiled and said, "I'm not sure who Barney is, but it sounds like you're selling yourself short. Connie told me a little about you, and I looked online before agreeing to meet. You seem able to take care of yourself."

"A little luck and easy access to firearms, that's all," Tony said. "But enough of that. I want to say right up front how sorry I am about your friends, about what you went through this morning."

"Thanks, but, as you probably know, they weren't really my friends. I just met them last night. It was a total fluke that I was hanging out with them."

Knowing Moira was new to the area, Tony had guessed this might be the case. However, hearing her say it so bluntly piqued his curiosity. He suggested they walk, then said, "How did that happen? I mean, if you can stand to tell it again, could you walk me through it?"

She nodded, took a deep breath, and told the story of joining the group of college friends in the pub, welcoming the stranger named Rob, traveling together to the Dursey Cable Car station, watching Michael and Lauren get into the car, watching it leave and return, and finding their lifeless, bloody bodies. She spoke softly and tersely. Her only display of emotion came at the end, as she struggled to describe the murder scene.

Tony knew her multiple recountals of the events to the police had helped her hone the telling into a succinct story. He also knew this could be a problem. As she refined the tale into a neat package, she could easily omit details that might be important.

They reached the end of the beach and wordlessly turned around and started back in the other direction. The sun was mostly obscured by clouds, but hung surprisingly high above the western horizon.

Tony said, "Just so I'm clear, you're saying the whole idea of the trip to the Dursey Sound was Rob's?"

"Oh, yeah," she said, pursing her lips. "He literally dangled the key to the ticket booth in front of our faces. And he offered to buy the whiskey if we agreed to go."

"Huh."

"He told us that sex in the car had been done before, and with his help could be done again. Of course, once that tree was planted, there was no stopping Michael till it bore fruit."

"So why Michael?"

"Besides being a horn-dog, you mean?"

"I mean, it doesn't sound like Rob was trying to get in on the action. He's out there with three beautiful women—sorry, I hope you don't mind me saying so—and he's in control of the cable car. Why isn't he the one coupled with Lauren, or someone, in that car?"

"I suppose the obvious answer is that he needed to operate the mechanism. But I'm not sure that was it. He could've shown Dylan which buttons to push and then joined us on the platform. He might have even succeeded with one of us. He was attractive enough, in a rough, brutish way. But he just didn't send those signals. Didn't seem interested. Might be one of those types who gets off watching others do it more than doing it himself."

"Hmm… I wonder."

Moira slowed, turned and stared out at the water. Without looking at Tony, she said, "It could have been me."

"Of course," Tony said, "but…"

"No." She turned to face him. "You have no idea how close I came. Michael asked me to join him in the car. I was tempted. At the last possible moment, I got cold feet and Lauren jumped in. Her decision to go for it was every bit as spontaneous as my decision to back away. Honest to God, I don't know which is worse, bleeding to death on the floor, or living with the knowledge that Lauren died because I was a coward."

Tony reached out and placed a hand on her forearm. He said, "This is *not* your fault. Not in any way. You know that. Some evil bastard injured you all. You're a victim. Period."

She sighed. "It's nice of you to say, and I agree with you. Of course I do. But I still feel like cac."

As they resumed walking, Tony had another thought, which led to a question he was desperate to ask. However, considering the extent to which Moira was suffering, he willed himself to ignore it. Instead, he said, "It must be as obvious to Lynch as it is to me that Rob is a key to all this. Do you know if they've questioned him?"

"I don't think so. At least they hadn't by the time I left the Gardai station. The inspector pushed me hard for any ideas about who he was or where he might be."

"Were you able to help?"

"Not even a little. He seemed so…so *normal*. He was just a working-class glunterpeck buying booze for women in a pub. I've seen hundreds of guys like him. He said he did electrical work and a little plumbing. Nothing about his clothes or his truck or his mannerisms gave me any reason to think otherwise. Even the suggestion that we drive out to Dursey Sound in the middle of the night seemed completely reasonable, considering he had a job to do there the next day."

"I wonder if that was true."

Moira didn't seem surprised by the question. She said, "They're searching for him, so it's obvious he didn't show up to do any work there this morning."

Tony nodded, feeling a little surge of adrenaline as he thought it through. "It was all a lie," he said. "If he'd been hired to work on the cable car, Lynch would already know his name. He wouldn't be asking you to help him figure it out. Also, the fact he fled makes him a suspect."

"He's not a suspect in the murders, at least not in my mind. I was there, and I know he didn't kill them. Maybe he just freaked out. Didn't want to be tied to it in any way."

"Maybe," Tony said, "but remember, he left the scene before the bodies were found. He had some other reason to leave."

"Like what?"

Tony debated saying more and decided to forge ahead. He wanted Moira's thoughts. He said, "Like maybe he knew the murders were going to happen, or had already happened, up in the car."

Moira's breath caught. She said, "You're saying there were two of them."

"That seems obvious, regardless of whether Rob was involved. I mean, assuming you and your companions are telling the truth, then someone else killed Michael and Lauren. If it wasn't Rob, then there's another stranger in the mix somehow."

"If Rob was involved, you're talking about some kind of orchestrated crime. Like an assassination." She crossed her arms and hugged herself. "That's terrifying. Far worse than some crime of passion."

"I agree," Tony said, "and totally baffling. What possible motive could someone have to kill one or both of those young people?"

Moira bent and plucked a small piece of driftwood from the water's edge. As she turned it in her hands, she said, "Hard to imagine. Drugs maybe? Something they got involved in at school?"

"Maybe." Tony said it without conviction. This felt too big for that, too brutal. He thought about Lynch's comment that the killer didn't try to disguise the crime. He wanted people to know it was murder. Someone was sending a message. *But to whom, and why?*

The two of them continued to chat as they walked, allowing the conversation to flow to things other than the morning's horrors. Tony learned Moira was from Galway, a port city on the western shore of Ireland. She said her family owned a construction company that did concrete and asphalt work for commercial buildings. "My dad and brothers work hard and play harder," she said. "They're quick to laugh, and quicker to throw a punch. Violence at home is rare, to be sure, but it's always lurking around the corner. It feels like you're a frog, living in a nice, warm pond, but aware that the water could turn to boiling at any moment."

Tony tried to express some sympathy, but she dismissed it. "I had a good life there. My parents loved me, loved all of us, so I don't want to overstate the pall that sometimes enveloped the place. And we had money and opportunity, which was more than most of my friends had."

Tony remained silent as they reached the end of the beach and once again reversed direction.

"So now you're wondering why I'm a waitress."

"No, I… No, of course not."

She laughed. It was a deep, rich sound, emanating from a warm heart. "It's okay," she said. "Of course you're curious. If we had money, why didn't I go to university and become a doctor or something? The answer is simple: I did. I was a student at Trinity College in Dublin and was doing pretty well. Then I met a boy."

"Ahh."

"Ahh is right. I thought I was in love and ignored all the warning signs. Skipping past all the gory details, I'll just say that six months later, he was enjoying life as a drunkard and womanizer, while I was supporting him by working two jobs. When my grades failed, I finally woke up and told him enough was enough. It didn't go well. His abuse finally crossed that line, from mental to physical, so I left, or tried to. Finally, I had to run away. So here I am, hiding out in a village at the end of the Earth, working for Connie." She again turned the driftwood in her hands, picked some mud from a crack in its side, and said, "So how 'bout you?"

The abrupt change made both of them giggle. Tony liked the sound and fought not to stare at her. He was keenly aware he was enjoying himself too much, so he forged ahead quickly.

"I grew up in Chicago," he said. "My dad, Charles, is a successful writer. You may know him by his pen name, C.A. Harker. We lived in a high-rise with a view of Lake Michigan. It was a truly urban lifestyle. However, my mom's an immigrant from the coast of Italy. She was never really comfortable in the big city, or at least that's what I surmised later. When I was in the ninth grade, we moved to Iowa, a very rural state a couple hundred miles to the west, to a town called Iowa City, where the University of Iowa is located. My dad took a job there."

"That must have been hard, to make a move at that age."

"You're very perceptive," Tony said, smiling. "It's hard to describe the magnitude of the change, from one of the largest cities in America to a town of seventy-five thousand, from a high-rise apartment to a big, rambling two-story house on a bluff overlooking a river, from world-class museums and major league sports, to... well, other things."

She giggled again. "I'm sorry. I shouldn't laugh. Did you hate it?"

"That's the thing," Tony said. "I didn't. Well, I did for about two weeks. But I quickly learned to love it. I loved the house and the yard and the river. I loved the freedom of riding my bike wherever I wanted and, later, doing the same in my car. It was like being released from prison. Many of the constraints necessary in the city, or perceived as necessary by my parents, were gone. Mom worried less, which meant my sister Rita and I could do more."

Tony paused to consider if he should continue, or if he was becoming a bore. Moira appeared to be interested, so he added, "Because of his new job, my dad was home more, and my mother was the happiest I ever saw her. Rita and I quickly made new friends and became involved in all kinds of activities. Rita, especially, was active in music and theater. Now she's a professional cellist and pianist. She went back to Chicago to go to college, but I remained at home and attended the U of Iowa. I guess the fact I stayed is the best testament to how much I loved my new life."

Moira nodded and he continued, "After college, I got a job as a reporter at the smallest daily newspaper in Iowa, the *Orney Town Crier*. It was my dream job because Ben Smalley owns and edits the paper. He's a Pulitzer Prize-winning journalist and maybe the best person I've ever known." He stopped to take a breath, decided he'd said enough, and concluded, "I guess you know the story from there, or at least the highlights, from what you saw online."

"You're not still at the paper."

Tony couldn't tell if she knew what had happened or was asking the question. He said, "the *Crier's* experiencing the same financial challenges as all newspapers. Ben was forced to make cuts."

"Wikipedia says you resigned."

"Yeah, well, I don't need the money. Some of my colleagues do. So I stepped aside."

"You gave up what you loved in order to help your friends."

Tony smiled. "Don't go making me out to be all noble. I have money, a beautiful house, a great family, and a new Jeep. And I'm on a dream vacation to Ireland. Pretty hard to complain about anything."

"Hmm." Moira paused their walk and turned toward the sea. Tony caught a glimpse of her arm, as it pulled back to toss a stick into the ocean. He turned his head quickly, to avoid getting dirt in his eyes as it left her hand. As he did so, he caught a glimpse of someone on the hillside above them. The person quickly disappeared behind one of the clapboard buildings on the road into Allihies. It was just a wisp of light-colored hair and dark clothing. He knew it could be totally harmless, just a coincidence of timing, but that's not how it felt. *Someone is watching us. Connie looking out for his waitress?* Tony dismissed that thought. Connie was too big, and didn't have enough hair, to have been the person he saw.

"What are you looking at?" Moira asked, as Tony scanned the hillside.

"Nothing," he said. "Just admiring the town while you play fetch with an imaginary dog."

She laughed. The sound was truly enchanting.

Don't go there, Tony silently admonished himself. Aloud, he said, "I've kept you long enough. We should go."

"I'm fine, but whatever you want is okay with me."

Again, he thought, *don't go there*. He said, "It's been a long day for both of us, and I still need to catch up with my sister and her boyfriend so we can have dinner before turning in. You can join us if you want. I mean, if you'd rather not be alone." The invitation escaped his lips before he could stop it. Immediately, he realized how it could be construed.

"Really, I'm fine." Moira said. "I appreciate the offer, but as you pointed out, it's been a long day. I think I'll go home, have a glass of wine, and turn in."

Tony hoped his relief wasn't painted on his face. He said, "I'll walk you there. It's right on my way."

She looked at him for a long moment, then said, "Are you worried about me? Do you know something I should know?"

"Good grief, no," Tony said. "I'm concerned only in the sense that we all need to be worried about each other. Someone capable of committing murder was just a few miles from here this morning. Until he's caught, some basic precautions are in order."

Moira nodded and they started up the hill toward the town. "Fair enough," she said, "but when we get to my door, no funny stuff. Darcy wouldn't like it."

Tony turned and gaped at her.

She laughed again. "I told you I did my research. You and Darcy Gillson are practically married. I'm not getting in the middle of that, even if I was egotistical enough to think you'd be interested."

Tony swallowed hard. Knowing he shouldn't say it, he did anyway. "Moira, I think I already mentioned you're beautiful. You're also still smiling after being through an unimaginable nightmare. And, by all accounts, you're smart and brave. When combined with that laugh, you're nearly irresistible. If I wasn't committed to Darcy, you'd need a whole division of the Gardai to keep me away."

"I wouldn't need them, to be sure," she said. "I would welcome you." She quickened her pace and stared straight ahead. Tony wisely let the conversation end there.

When they reached her door, he said thanks and reached out to take her hand. She ignored it and put her arms around him, squeezing tightly. After a moment, he reciprocated.

To his chest, she said, "I'm glad you asked to see me. I'm glad you're working on this. Go find the scut who killed those two innocents. And if Darcy ever gives you the boot, come back and find me."

"Moira, I…" Before he could formulate a response, she was through the door.

***

Tony hadn't walked ten paces up the street toward the hotel when his phone began playing "Till There Was You," the ringtone for Darcy.

Who says this woman doesn't have radar?

Into the phone, he said, "Hey, gorgeous."

"Hey back. How's vacation?"

"It's fine. I just took a walk on the beach with a beautiful woman."

After a pause, Darcy said, "Well, if you've decided to move out of our house, I'm not helping with the piano."

Tony laughed. "No worries. It's strictly business, I promise. I miss you like…"

"Business? I thought you were on vacation."

"It's a long story. How's the shoot going?"

"It's great, actually. We just wrapped up for today, so I thought I'd catch you before bed."

"Your timing's perfect," he said. "I'm just going to meet Rita and Ryan for a late dinner."

"So tell me about the beach. What's her name, and is she more attractive than me?"

"No one's more attractive than you." Tony had no trouble saying this with conviction, as he believed it to be true. Darcy was five-foot-eight and blonde with an oval face, a sculpted chin and nose, and a dancer's physique. A savvy businesswoman as well as a talented actress, she currently was riding a huge wave of popularity with film-makers and audiences. Tony marveled every day that this goddess had somehow fallen for him.

She said, "Very smooth, Mr. Harrington, but I still want to hear about it."

Debating how to broach the subject, he chose to ask, "Have you seen the news?"

"No. What about it? We've been doing sixteen-hour days. I've only looked at my phone to check for messages from you. Has something happened?"

"Not a world war or anything, but a couple of college students were killed near here."

"Killed how? Not an accident, I presume."

"You presume correctly. Murdered in a brutal and some would say impossible way. The local police inspector invited me to take a look."

"Tony..."

The exasperation in her voice wasn't as pronounced as he had feared. He said, "Don't worry. I'm just poking around, sharing my two cents' worth with the cops. I'm not doing anything dangerous."

"As we both know, the extent of the danger depends on where you poke. So this beach beauty is part of it somehow?"

"She was one of the people at the scene when it happened. I was just asking her for details in case something jumped out that the cops missed in her formal interviews."

"And did it?"

"I don't think so, except maybe the fact she's lucky to be alive."

He heard Darcy sigh as the background noise in the call diminished. He could picture her stepping into her trailer, closing the door, and sitting in the padded armchair near the refrigerator. As if on cue, he heard the distinctive hiss of a cap leaving the top of a beer bottle.

She said, "Tell me about it."

Tony began at the beginning and walked her through everything he knew. When he finished, she said, "So this guy named Rob orchestrated it. And," she paused, "there had to be two of them, right? Rob had an accomplice."

He was impressed but not surprised that she had reached this conclusion quickly. She was even smarter than her two graduate degrees from Carnegie Mellon implied.

"Seems obvious to me," he said, "assuming the three witnesses are telling the truth."

"Any reason to think otherwise?"

"No, but to be fair, I've only met one of them. Anything's possible at this point."

"So what's next? For you, I mean."

"Not much. Tomorrow or Tuesday, I'll get a look inside the cable car. I don't expect to learn much there. I'll try to talk to the two students, Dylan and Niamh, but again, I'm not sure why. Then I'm probably done. The police are in a better position than me to find this Rob guy and maybe figure out what happened."

"I'd love to believe you, but somehow I doubt you'll walk away. At least not before you've solved the locked-room mystery."

Tony knew she was referring to the impossibility of the murder occurring in the cable car while suspended above the sea.

"I have to admit, I'd love to find the answer to that puzzle. I'd also like to know why someone went to so much trouble to kill two innocent kids."

Quietly, Darcy said, "Tony, promise me, please, that you'll be careful. For once in your life, don't jump into the shark tank without a cage."

"I promise," he said, trying to sound sincere but subconsciously rubbing the ridge on the back of his skull. He had not yet told her about the attempted kidnapping in Dublin. "I've got no dog in this hunt, just my curiosity. Besides, Rita, Ryan, and I have travel schedules to keep. I won't be able to cause much trouble in the next few days."

"See that you don't," she said. "I can't bear the thought of visiting another hospital, or worse."

"Can't argue with that. Love you, babe."

"Love you more," she said, and was gone.

Chapter 16

Sunday, May 24

Allihies, Beara Peninsula, County Cork, Ireland

Moira watched Tony from her window as he strode up the hill toward the center of town. He was talking on his phone. *Probably talking to Darcy.* She felt a wave of melancholy, wondering what it would be like to have a normal life. She set that aside. She had a call of her own to make.

"Everything okay?" It wasn't her uncle's normal greeting, but Moira understood he was on edge. Waging war with a Russian drug cartel tended to heighten one's anxieties.

"I'm fine."

"Maith go leor. So what then?"

"He's here," Moira said, cringing in expectation of the reaction her words would evoke. She wasn't disappointed.

"Shite! I knew it. The American? The Harrington boyo, ye mean? Course ye do. Ye be safe? Can ye hole up till my boys get there?"

Moira said, "Slow down, uncle. It's okay. It's not him."

"What d'ya mean, nah 'im?"

"It's not Tony Harrington. At least not *this* Tony Harrington."

"Feck that. We 'ave sources. Bloody good sources. It's 'im. Don' be saying nay-wise."

Moira sighed and made up her mind. If she didn't push back, someone would come to take care of her "Tony problem."

"Uncle Ox, please believe me. The Tony Harrington staying here in Allihies is not an assassin. Maybe the Brotherhood is sending someone else with that name. Lord knows the Harringtons are everywhere down here."

"How be ye so sure? There be good men sayin' otherwise."

She steeled herself. "I met him. I talked to him."

"Ye *what*? I told ye to…"

"Uncle, please. It was fine. He asked to see me, to ask about the murders in the cable car. It was in daylight in a public place."

"I don' care if it was noon at a peeler convention. I told ye to steer clear of 'im!"

"I know. I'm sorry. But I'm glad I said yes. We talked for more than an hour. I'm convinced this man is no killer, and he's certainly not working for the Russians."

"Don be so feckin' naive. He be well trained. 'Course he hides the truth." Ox Foley paused, then seemed to realize what his niece had said a moment earlier. "Why the murders, anyway?"

"He said the guard asked him to take a look. He has some experience with violent crimes."

"I'll bet he does."

"As a journalist. Look him up online. You'll see. There's no Russian connection there."

"Maybe he killed those two. Did ye ne'er e'en think of that? Maybe jest tryin' to see how much ye know."

A shiver went through her as the grisly scene reappeared in her mind. She said, "It wasn't like that. He's genuinely curious about how it was done. Why it was done. Please trust me on this. He's not the guy."

"Ye know I'm jest tryin' to keep ye whole. The Russian gobshites have targeted ye. I'm pure sorry for that. 'Tis my fault an they'll ne'er succeed on my watch. That's why I sent ye to feckin' Allihies in the first place."

"I know, Uncle Ox, and I love you for protecting me. But we have to look elsewhere. We can't miss a real threat because we're focused on the wrong guy."

Ox Foley appeared to be relenting, then sent a jolt through Moira when he suggested he should eliminate Tony regardless of who was right. "Then we don' need a fret 'bout it."

Knowing she had to be careful not to challenge him, Moira said, "That makes some sense, but I worry about the consequences. He's working with the guard, which will ensure some extra attention if he dies."

"We can deal with…"

Moira kept going, speaking over her uncle. "Not to mention his partner is one of the most famous women in America. His death will bring a ton of media attention. It'll be impossible for me to stay hidden in this tiny village if it's filled with reporters from a dozen different news outlets."

"Yeah, that be a fair point to be sure," her uncle said, his tone reflecting equal measures of resignation and irritation. "Okay, then. I'll tell the boys ta stand down for now. But ye do the same, ye hear? Ye steer clear of this Harrington, and ye call me if he makes any move toward ye 'gain. Ye promise?"

"I promise, Uncle Ox." She took a deep breath, then changed the subject. "Before you go, I want to be sure you got the fisherman's message."

"Fer sure, I did. The glunterpeck's crazier than a drunken squirrel, but if it works, it'll be right good craic for us."

"Anything you need from me?"

"For sure ye can tell 'im we'll give it a try. Tell 'im to be there when we discussed."

"Of course. I can do that."

"Then keep an eye on 'im. Don' get too mixed up in it, but call if ye see trouble."

"I understand."

"And ye call me if that Harrington boyo or anyone else causes ye to e'en flinch."

"I will," Moira said, while thinking the "flinch" she got from Tony was nothing like what her uncle was imaging.

***

"Where were you this morning?"

Ryan Stenford tensed and said, "Huh?" The word escaped from his mouth before he could stop it. Anger flashed through him. He knew the response was a dead giveaway signaling that he had something to hide. Innocent people didn't respond to a simple question with "Huh?" He hoped the darkness masked his irritation with himself.

He could feel Rita withdraw from him just a little and could tell she was trying to keep her tone light.

She said, "Early this morning. I woke up and you weren't here."

"Of course," he said, forcing his lips into a smile, hoping the expression would find its way into his voice. "I couldn't sleep, so I went for a walk. Made it all the way down to the beach and back. I'm sorry if I woke you."

He turned onto his side to face her. They were lying together on the double bed in their hotel room. Rita's skin glistened where tendrils of light from the street outside found their way through slits in the blinds. A film of sweat coated both of their bodies, the result of a room with no air conditioning and their recently concluded intense physical activities. He leaned down and kissed her. Rita remained impassive. A ball of lead dropped into his stomach as he realized he had missed the signs all evening. If he'd been more focused on his job, and less on his lust, he would've known something was bothering her. He would've been prepared for her question.

"Don't be sorry," she said. "When you can't sleep, I want you to wake me. I would've walked with you."

Uh-oh. Knowing he couldn't promise her that, he said, "It would never occur to me to wake you. Not intentionally. That would be rude."

"But if I want you..."

"Shhh," he said, putting his finger to her lips. "It's not worth discussing because it rarely happens. Why would I ever want to get out of bed when you're beside me?" He smiled, kissed her again, and reached across her torso, pulling her close. He hoped some tender attention and perhaps even another round of lovemaking would distract her. The idea aroused him, and he spent much of the next hour employing various forms of seduction, both verbal and physical.

Rita engaged in the chatter but clearly wasn't responding to his caresses. Eventually, he conceded defeat and fell asleep.

Rita did not.

Chapter 17

Tuesday, May 26
Beara Peninsula, County Cork, Ireland

As Tony approached the cable car, he pulled his cell from his pocket and dialed Inspector Lynch. As promised, Lynch answered immediately. Tony said, “Hold on one second.”

A lone garda stood near the station platform, eyeing Tony with suspicion. Tony stepped closer and introduced himself, then explained that Inspector Lynch was on the phone. The officer took the phone, exchanged a few words with the inspector, and ended the call.

“He said to let you pass, to let you examine the car. Be quick about it. These people have been without service for more than two days. We need to get the car cleaned and operational soon.”

“Thank you. I will,” Tony said. To himself, he thought, *That’s why I got out of bed at six effing a.m., you twit.*

The sun hovered above the sea to the east, but a stiff breeze off the water kept the temperature uncomfortably cool. Tony zipped up his jacket and stepped onto the platform. Removing his phone from a front pocket of his Levi's, he used it to take numerous photos of the car's exterior. If he was going to be hurried this morning, he wanted a visual record to study more closely later. When finished, he stepped inside the car, doing his best to avoid the dried blood on the floor and walls. A glance around confirmed what he already knew. There was no way a third person could have hidden inside the car. If the killer was with the couple on their excursion, they had to know he was there.

Tony took another series of photos, trying to capture every surface in at least one image. He used the camera's zoom feature to take close-up shots of some of the blood smears and spatters, hoping it would help him assemble a more detailed description of what had occurred early Sunday. He was finished and ready to depart when he stopped short of the doorframe. A dark smudge caught his eye. Of course, a little dirt in the car was unsurprising and unnoteworthy, at least in normal circumstances. However, these circumstances were anything but normal. Tony photographed the spot, then used the screen to look at an enlarged view.

It appeared to be oil or grease. Again, not of particular interest. It could have come from the door lock or hinges, which undoubtedly were greased as a matter of routine. However, the smudge abutted a small spot of blood on the frame. As Tony examined it, he became convinced the two stains were intermixed. This meant, in Tony's mind, that the smudge appeared on the frame while the blood was still wet.

He removed a tissue from his pocket and dabbed it against a tiny corner of the stain. The dried blood remained undisturbed, but a dot of grease or oil came away on his tissue. He carefully folded and placed it in an inside pocket of his coat. He then began looking for a source. The door mechanisms were recessed and relatively clean. He didn't believe the grease came from there. Stumped, he gave up and stepped out of the car. He took two strides toward the edge of the platform, suddenly stopped, and turned around. He was staring at the car when he heard the garda's voice.

"Finished, sir?"

"Almost," Tony said. He turned to the guard. "Do you think there's a ladder in the station house?"

"Don't know, sir. Probably. There be regular maintenance to do on the cable mounts, to be sure."

"Could you ask for me?"

"Am I now your assistant?" the guard asked, clearly irritated.

"Sorry. I'll go check."

"Ne'er mind. I'll do it," the man said.

Moments later, he was back with a standard eight-foot step ladder. When Tony propped it against the side of the car and took two steps up, he heard the guard say, "Careful, sir. I'm no sure you're to be doin' that."

"No worries. I'll just be a moment."

Tony crested the top and peered down. The roof of the car was mostly obscured by an array of wooden and metal beams that formed the mounting framework. Between the superstructure and the cables, there wasn't much room to maneuver. He bent forward, grabbed the nearest metal strut, and pulled himself onto the structure. He took a moment to steady himself as the car swayed slightly on its cables. Satisfied it wasn't going to pitch him off, he began examining as much of the array as he could manage from one viewpoint. He didn't want to move around. Not only was he nervous about falling or perhaps twisting an ankle, he also didn't want to disturb the roof if he was right.

When he spotted the glob of grease on one of the crossbars, he choked back a shout. It wasn't proof, but it convinced him he was on the right track. He reached back into his inside pocket, removed the tissue, and reached across the I beam to retrieve another dot of grease. After returning the tissue to his pocket and snapping another series of photos, he retreated down the ladder.

The guard began to ask again if he was finished, but Tony held up a hand. He opened his phone to recent calls and redialed Lynch.

"You finished?" the inspector asked, ignoring any pleasantries or greeting.

"That depends."

"Depends on what?"

"Depends on how much time your team spent on the roof of the car."

"The roof? I'm not sure. Why? You don't think…"

"Yes, I do," Tony said. "Can't be sure, but I'd bet my girlfriend's Mercedes that someone was up there. That's how they did it."

"You're outta yer feckin' mind. He'd be exposed up there. He could be seen."

"It was dark, and the structure on top of the car is extensive. No one would notice a dark shape among the struts and cables."

"He'd have to get from there to the inside of the car, while dangling over the sea."

"Not a problem. Plenty of struts to swing from. A special forces guy could do it, or even a competent gymnast."

"He couldn't unlatch the doors from up there. How could he know they'd be ope…?" Lynch stopped himself.

Tony smiled, knowing the inspector had just recalled that the man named Rob had suggested the two lovers leave the doors open.

"Jesus, Mary, and Joseph, you really think it's possible?"

"If the three witnesses are telling the truth, it's the only answer."

"But wait. They said no one was in the car when it returned. No one except the victims. Are you suggesting the killer somehow climbed back on top? Was there when the car returned to the station?"

"Maybe, but I doubt it," Tony said, "He would've had to risk climbing down from the roof while the others were nearby. It's more likely he left the car before it re-docked."

"How could he do that?" Lynch asked, clearly skeptical.

Tony said, "Maybe he jumped onto the north tower as the car passed it and climbed down to a waiting boat from there. Or maybe he did a BASE jump."

"A parachute? From a thousand feet above open ocean? That's insane. You've seen too many Bond films."

"Difficult and improbable doesn't necessarily mean insane," Tony replied. "We're already discussing a highly coordinated assassination by at least two well-trained operatives. Adding a parachute jump to the mix isn't much of a leap, if you'll forgive the pun."

"Is this all just a wild guess, or did you actually find something?"

Tony pulled the tissue from his pocket and looked at the two identical spots of grease. He said, "I found a spot of grease on the doorjamb of the car. Looks to me like it came from a glob on the car's roof."

"That could have happened anytime. You can't assume…"

"The grease overlaps the blood."

Tony heard the inspector suck in a sharp breath.

Lynch said, "Well, shite. Did you touch anything?"

"You'll find my hand prints on two struts I grabbed to get up onto the roof. Nothing else."

"Good. Get away from there and tell the guard I'll be calling him in two minutes. No one goes near there. I'll meet you at your hotel at three this afternoon."

"Three?"

"I'm back in my office in Dublin. You weren't supposed to find anything."

***

Tony decided to try the shepherd's pie. He set the menu on the table and took a long pull from his Guinness, disappointed to see Connie headed his way rather than Moira. He sighed, knowing it was a mistake to seek more time with the Irish beauty when it could only lead to trouble. Connie was the safer, more rational choice, but still…

After placing his order with the bar's owner, Tony reached down and retrieved a manila envelope from beside his thigh on the booth's vinyl seat. Opening the clasp, he pulled out a handful of photos and documents and began reviewing everything he had assembled so far regarding the cable car murders.

During their afternoon meeting, Inspector Lynch had given Tony copies of the crime scene photos, the initial police report, and the autopsy report. He had even allowed Tony to take notes as he described his interviews with the three witnesses, and the Gardai's futile efforts to find the mysterious man who called himself Rob. Lynch also had confessed his extreme frustration in searching for a motive. So far, investigators had found nothing in Michael or Lauren's lives that would warrant an elaborate plot, professionally implemented, to kill either of them.

Lynch's willingness to share everything had astounded Tony. He had been as grateful as he was surprised, and he had said so. Lynch had simply shrugged, saying Tony had proven himself to be a valuable ally by finding an important clue overlooked by the forensics team. Lynch also had threatened to lock him up for a hundred years if he failed to keep the materials confidential.

Tony discreetly returned the crime scene photos to the envelope. He didn't want to risk someone catching a glimpse when walking past his table. He focused his attention on the autopsy report. The official cause of death was listed as "exsanguination." Tony almost smiled at the term. He remembered it well as the cause of death in the first car accident he covered for the *Orney Town Crier*, in what seemed like a lifetime ago. The term was a fancy way of saying a person died from loss of blood. It stuck in Tony's memory mostly because, in writing about the accident, he had misspelled it. The next day, Ben printed the word in large letters on a white sheet of paper and slapped it down on Tony's desk. Tony was sure he would never misspell it again. However, Ben's second lesson was even more important. He reminded Tony that using simpler terms such as "bled to death" was always better in a news story.

Returning his thoughts to the current case, Tony muttered softly, "They bled to death. Tell me something I don't know."

He kept reading and came to the details regarding the wounds.

The report said, in part, "…incisions made left to right, as viewed from behind the victims, slicing the left carotid artery of the female victim, the right carotid artery of the male victim, and the anterior aspect of the trachea of each victim. The wounds' edges were clean and straight, indicating a weapon with a smooth, extremely sharp blade. While not certain, it is possible the weapon was a straight-edged razor or a professional-grade switchblade. The positions of the two bodies, as found post-mortem, indicate they were attacked in rapid succession, with neither having the opportunity to react before both were mortally wounded. The precision and similarity of the wounds, completed in rapid succession, indicate a skilled perpetrator."

Tony slid the report and other papers back into the envelope, sat back, and closed his eyes. He could imagine the scene, but just barely. As Lynch had said, the idea bordered on fantasy. Sometime late Saturday night, a trained assassin positioned himself on the roof of the cable car, hidden by the near-perfect darkness of a cloudy night and, undoubtedly, aided by dark clothing and a disabled exterior lamp on the nearby building. Sometime later, his accomplice talked two young people into riding the car out over the ocean, explicitly to have sexual intercourse. Once the couple was engaged in the act, the assassin swung down into the car, landed behind them, and cut both throats before either could react. *To call him a skilled perpetrator doesn't do him justice,* Tony thought, as a shudder rose from his toes to the base of his neck.

A shuffle of feet and the sensation of air movement caused Tony to open his eyes. Moira Blake stood before him, holding a plate with his steaming-hot pie.

Tony smiled as he pushed the envelope to the side, clearing a spot for his dinner. "Hey!" he said. "I was just thinking about you."

"Liar," she chuckled, placing the plate on the table. "You were thinking about murder victims, or violent felons, or missing Ukrainians, or something contained in an official-looking report. You were not thinking about me."

"Well, I was. Earlier, I mean." *I'm flirting,* Tony realized. *Why am I flirting?*

Moira snorted. "If you thought of me at all, it was only to wonder if I've been lying about what happened Sunday morning."

"No, no. Of course not," Tony said, alarmed.

"Relax," Moira said, chuckling again. "I'm just slagging ye. Enjoy your dinner."

As she turned to go, her long, auburn ponytail swept across her back, as if beckoning Tony to watch her retreat. He did. Then, as she reached another table across the room and turned again, Tony's appreciation moved from her hair to her profile. She was, quite simply, a beautiful young woman, with dark eyes, fair skin, a runner's body, and dimples that could be seen from orbit. Even more compelling was the energy that seemed to emit from every pore. She glowed, and it warmed him just to be in her presence.

He thought about the number of attractive and charming women he'd met during his few days in Ireland and wondered if it was something in the water, or perhaps in the Guinness. *Are they all so...?* The thought triggered a thunderclap in his brain. *Oh, shit. Could it be?* He pulled the manila envelope into his lap and slid out one of the photographs of Lauren O'Grady. It was a shot lifted from her Facebook page. She was standing on a city sidewalk in front of a pair of glass entry doors, smiling as she cradled a cup of hot coffee or tea in her hands. She wore a long coat and mittens. A wisp of steam could be seen emanating from the beverage. Tony guessed it had been taken the previous winter while she was at college in Dublin.

He studied the picture, glanced across the room to where Moira stood, and returned his eyes to the photograph. The resemblance was striking.

He laid it out in his mind. *It was dark. Only the four young people on the platform could actually see who got into the cable car. Rob had urged Moira to join Michael there. It would've been natural for him to assume she had. Moira, the newcomer. Moira, the one who's background is least known. Moira, who's hiding from a jilted lover. Moira... the intended victim.*

Once the thought occurred to Tony, it seemed so obvious he was embarrassed he hadn't thought of it sooner. So obvious that he assumed Lynch had thought of it long before now. Either way, the inspector would be looking into her background. She was a key witness. He would want to know about her. Suddenly, so did Tony.

He slipped the photograph and other materials back into the envelope and turned his attention to his food. He needed to talk to Moira, but not in a crowded pub. Especially not when she was working. It would have to wait.

***

"You killed the wrong girl." Darius Polshkov spoke quietly in his native Russian. The menace in the Bratva leader's voice had no trouble finding its way through the satellite signal to Arsendo Petrov's smartphone.

"Yes, but I did exactly as instructed." Petrov's voice was cool, restrained. Although he couldn't be seen, he raised his head and set his jaw to ensure none of his embarrassment nor irritation with himself would find its way into his voice. "Talk to…"

"No names!" Polshkov barked.

"Talk to the… other man. *Your* man. It was his job to get the girl into the car. How was I to know…?"

"Shut up."

Petrov grimaced and waited.

Polshkov said, "You disgust me. Both of you. I gave you a soft target. An unarmed woman. Any teenager with a kitchen knife could have done the job. Your assignment was clear. Hit Foley where it would hurt him the most. Leave him a clear message." His voice rose. "You failed. Foley got no message. Or if he did, the message was 'Look at how incompetent your enemies are.' In the end, we attracted the swarm of Gardai we feared the deaths would bring, but without the result we needed."

"I performed flawlessly," Petrov said. "Two kills without being seen, and no trace…"

"Shut up. You have one chance to save your hide. I mean that literally. If you fail again, I will be there to watch as your skin is peeled strip by strip from your worthless body. Do you understand?"

Careful, you pompous ass. Your throat is not immune to my blade. Aloud, Petrov simply said, "Yes, sir."

"Two things," the Bratva boss said. "Get the girl. Hold her for me. Use the house on the coast. Maybe the money I spent will finally prove to be worth it. Don't mess her up until I arrive. I want to be there to see it."

"Of course." Petrov didn't betray his disappointment. He wanted the kill, wanted to correct the mistake. His mouth watered at the thought. He *needed* to kill the girl. Waiting would be hard. "The other thing?"

"Foley has a shipment coming in tonight. Steal it."

"Sir?"

"Do you have a poor signal?" Polshkov sneered. "Is your hearing failing you?"

"No, sir, but theft isn't what I..."

"Just listen carefully and do what you're told. Our satellite images show a smuggling operation is underway now. A ship from South America and an Irish fishing trawler are nestled abeam about eighteen kilometers offshore. Once they've finished the transfer of cargo and the trawler heads for shore, we'll have good estimates for its arrival time and destination. We'll pass those to you so you can be there to meet it."

Petrov was astounded. The Bratva leader was expecting him to mount a major operation tonight. Knowing a little about boats, he guessed it would take the trawler an hour to travel eighteen kilometers. Maybe another hour to negotiate the bay or some remote port along the coast and get moored. Depending on the size of the cargo being transferred, and the method being used, he might be able to count on another thirty minutes. Two and a half hours to find some muscle and travel out into one of the most remote parts of Ireland, to engage in battle with an experienced and heavily armed drug cartel. Polshkov was out of his damn mind.

Petrov debated with himself. Saying *yes* would mean doing work he didn't want. High-risk work. Saying *no* would almost certainly mean forfeiting his fee and any future work for the Brotherhood. He said, "Yes, sir."

"Deliver your take to the house. Someone can finish the trip to Cork when we're sure the heat is off. Am I clear?"

"Yes, sir."

"I'll call you soon with the trawler's information. And one more thing."

"Yes, sir?"

"Don't fuck this up. I get bored hearing grown men scream for hours."

The call ended.

Chapter 18

Wednesday, May 27
Allihies, Beara Peninsula, County Cork, Ireland

Tony intended to catch Moira Blake as she left the pub at the end of her shift. However, he was delayed in leaving the hotel. Rita and Ryan were arguing in their room, loudly enough to be heard from the hall. Tony was surprised and a little concerned. He hung back to ensure the spat didn't escalate into anything serious. After a few minutes, the couple's voices diminished, and Tony assumed it was okay to slip away.

He walked across the street and into O'Connell's. A quick look around confirmed Moira was gone. Back outside, Tony headed east down the hill toward her apartment, hoping she would still be up. His watch said it was just after 1 a.m.

As he neared her building, he was surprised to see her exit the side door and move toward the rear. He was tempted to call out, but he held his tongue. He didn't want to frighten her or disturb her neighbors at this hour. He picked up his pace.

When he reached the corner across from her building, he looked to the left and saw her pushing a bicycle out of a small shed. She was dressed all in black—yoga pants, hooded sweatshirt, and sneakers. Something about her attire caused Tony to hesitate again, now curious about what she was doing. She pushed closed the shed door, climbed onto the bike, and headed southwest on the main road out of Allihies.

Tony waited a few beats, then jogged over to the shed. He was glad to see there was no lock, just a simple metal hasp. He pulled open the door and slipped inside. As he'd hoped, Moira hadn't taken the only bike. Three others were propped against the back wall. Tony quickly examined them, selected the one that appeared to be in the best shape, and rolled it out onto the street. Soon he was headed out of town, hoping to catch sight of his prey before she turned off the road.

As he pedaled, he was quickly reminded that one of his legs was not yet functioning at a hundred percent. He adjusted his cadence to pump harder with his good leg and ease the growing ache in his other, all while chastising himself for being there at all.

What the hell am I doing? Moira's life is none of my business. So what if she takes a bike ride at night? Maybe she enjoys some exercise after work. Maybe she has a boyfriend. He felt a pang of jealousy, then pushed it out of his mind. *Maybe she's going fishing or visiting a sick relative.*

Knowing this was all nonsense, Tony couldn't imagine why the waitress, a newcomer to the area, would be out on a bike in the middle of the night, dressed in black. So he bore down and kept going. He crested a hill just in time to catch her form in the darkness as she turned left. When he arrived at the spot, he saw it was a one-lane gravel road leading up into the hills to the east. He groaned, took a deep breath, and followed.

Riding on a rough road at night wasn't ideal, but the conditions helped. The sky was clear, allowing the three-quarters moon to provide just enough illumination. The cloudless sky also caused the temperature to drop. Tony barely broke a sweat as he pedaled. He paced her at a comfortable distance to avoid being seen or heard and twice thought he'd lost her. In both cases, she eventually reappeared when the path straightened.

After about fifteen minutes, the gravel path merged onto a paved road. Still very narrow and unlit, it at least provided for easier passage. Unfortunately, it didn't last for long. Moira soon turned right, back toward the south on another gravel road.

Despite his concentration on the path, and on the woman he was pursuing, Tony couldn't help but notice the beauty of the landscape. The grassy hills hosted a mixture of well-maintained farm fields and open pastures dotted with outcroppings of stone. Occasionally, they passed farm buildings and upscale private homes nearer the road. For a few minutes, he could see an abandoned stone tower of some kind in the distance, silhouetted against the sky. It occurred to Tony that he should repeat the ride in daylight, when he could more fully appreciate the lush colors and landmarks of the ancient land.

At the forty-minute mark, Tony could see the glint of moonlight off water in the distance. At fifty minutes, the Atlantic Ocean was clearly visible. Tony assumed it was the Atlantic, based on the fact they had traveled south and east on their journey. They had, quite simply, crossed the peninsula. Now the road was mostly downhill and winding toward the water. Tony's curiosity only grew.

Moira turned left again, stopped, and let the bike fall to her feet. Tony stopped in the shadow of some trees and watched as she dragged it into the tall grass and continued on foot. Tony waited until she disappeared from view, then proceeded to the same spot. The path she had taken was less a road and more a pair of ruts through rocky terrain. Tony left his bicycle a few meters beyond Moira's and began walking. As he neared the coastline, he could see that the trail dipped and wound down through a break in the high bluffs, forming a natural passage down to the water. He slowed, knowing Moira couldn't be far away. The high walls of stone on either side, and the bay before him, limited a person's options.

The path made a final turn and Tony stopped. The rock walls opened up to a rough, but relatively flat, patch of ground that extended to the water. It might be called a beach, but it was only about sixty meters wide, and the ground was covered in pebbles and rocks, some as large as his fist, rather than sand. He could see Moira's destination. A long, wooden dock reached out from the land into the deep water of the cove. Backed up to the dock, where it connected to the land, was a box truck. Moored at the other end was a large fishing trawler.

Ah, man. This isn't good, Tony thought, as he spotted people on the dock dragging long, dark bags from the boat to the truck. Tony didn't know anything about smuggling via the sea—Iowa didn't present many opportunities for maritime crime—but he had little doubt about what he was seeing. Neither the boat nor the truck sported any lights. Everyone was dressed in black and no one spoke, except to greet Moira as she reached the dock and walked out to the boat. *No one unloads legitimate cargo at 2 a.m. in an isolated cove without lighting.*

Tony backtracked along the path until he was out of sight of the dock. He stepped off the path and moved closer to the expanse of stone supporting the bluff above. He found a clump of rocks and weeds and knelt behind them. Fighting to stay calm, he tried to think clearly about what he should do. Three options seemed obvious. One, run away. Get back on the bicycle and forget he saw anything. Two, call the authorities. The smuggling of drugs into Ireland was a serious problem. If that's what this was, the Gardai would want to know. On the other hand, Tony didn't know if the locals could be trusted. If drugs were involved, so was big money. Bribes might be in play. Calling the police could be dangerous.

Tony also had to admit that he didn't like the idea of causing trouble for Moira. She seemed so nice. She had to be an innocent, unaware of what was going on, didn't she?

Don't be a putz, Tony. She led you here. She's a part of this somehow.

Tony ignored the thought but allowed himself to consider another fact. He had no real evidence. If he called in the Gardai, and this was something other than what it appeared, something perfectly legal, he would look like an idiot, and Moira might never forgive him.

Option three seemed the least problematic. *Gather some intel, and make sure you know the facts before calling in the cavalry.* He started back down the path toward the beach.

***

Tony knew he was relatively safe as he approached the dock. He couldn't be seen as long as he kept the truck between himself and the people loading it. This assumed, of course, that no one was in the truck's cab, and no lookouts were posted. Although his brain was telegraphing, *You're safe. If you're careful, you're safe,* the message didn't seem to be finding its way to his heart, which was pounding.

As he neared the front of the truck, he knelt and pulled his phone from his pocket. Huddling over the screen as best he could to hide its glow, he took a photo of the truck's license plate, then quickly shut off the phone and returned it to his pants pocket.

What now?

He listened carefully but heard nothing distinguishable. A few grunts and curses, presumably from the men dragging the bags he'd seen from a distance. Knowing it was too risky to walk around the truck, Tony leaned forward, flattened himself out on the ground and began to crawl underneath. The truck had a high profile, but that didn't make the task easy. The rough terrain proved painful as shins and forearms were dragged across the stones.

He stopped short of the tail end of the truck, where a ramp was attached from the open box to the dock, and took his bearings. The scuffling of boots on wood could now be heard above his head. The thought of being so close to a gang of likely smugglers made his skin turn to ice. He glanced to each side and toward his feet to reassure himself that he couldn't be seen.

Relax. Breathe. Listen, he told himself. All good advice, but none of it very helpful. He strained to hear something meaningful, but no one was conversing. If the men weren't going to speak loud enough or coherently enough to reveal what they were doing, and if it was too dangerous to get up on the dock to examine the bags himself, Tony knew he was taking all this risk for nothing. He decided to retreat.

As he twisted his body to turn around under the truck, his head protruded just a few inches into the open, behind the rear wheel on the left side. As it did so, Tony glanced up and spotted movement on top the bluff behind him. He froze. The outline of a man could be seen moving through the grass high above the beach. The man stopped walking, then disappeared into the vegetation. An instant later, a glint of moonlight sparkled from that position.

A crushing sensation of dread filled Tony's chest as he realized what he was seeing. He turned his head and looked up at the dock. Several men were there. In addition, about a dozen paces down the planks toward the trawler stood Moira, chatting with a large, older man.

Without thinking, Tony scrambled out from under the truck, stood, and simultaneously screamed, "Gun!"

Everyone on the dock froze, then turned toward Tony's voice. "Run!" he yelled. "Sniper! On the bluff!"

One man turned and looked up just as a bullet tore through his torso, followed an instant later by a deep *crack*, the sound of a high-powered round being fired from afar. The man spun a half-turn and plunged into the water.

Moira screamed but didn't move. Tony leapt up onto the dock and ran hard toward her. He didn't stop. He bent low and drove his shoulder into her abdomen. The force lifted her off her feet and flung her off the dock. Tony heard her splash into the water just as a second slug ripped through the sleeve of his sweatshirt and buried itself in the piling behind where Moira had been standing. A second *crack* shook the air.

Tony spun and ran toward the truck. The sound of a third discharge followed a shower of sparks as a slug ricocheted off the truck's steel ramp ten inches from Tony's feet. He jumped off the dock and into the shallow water beneath it, near the shore. His feet slipped and his knees came down hard on the rocks beneath the surface. He barely noticed the pain. The terror of a sniper with a high-powered rifle and scope, firing from a superior position, was overwhelming. On hands and knees, Tony backed away farther, allowing the ice-cold water to wash over his legs. His teeth began chattering from the cold. The importance of keeping his phone dry occurred to him, so he stopped moving, hoping the water hadn't reached his pants pocket. He groped for the phone, pulled it out, and slid it into a zippered pocket on the front of his jacket. Looking over his shoulder beneath the dock, he caught sight of Moira at the other end, climbing up a ladder onto the aft deck of the trawler.

Suddenly, a volley of shots came from much closer, causing Tony to jerk. He took a deep breath and tried to relax as he realized it was the men from the smuggling operation firing back toward the sniper's position. The next sounds he heard were generated by engines. The trawler's powerful twin diesels roared to life. Tony assumed, hoped, this meant Moira was escaping to safety. Soon after, the truck engine revved, followed by the sounds of slamming doors and grinding gears. The truck lurched away and gained speed as it crossed the beach. Before reaching the relative safety of the passage through the bluffs, Tony saw one of the truck's rear tires shred in a puff of smoke. A bullet from the sniper's rifle had found its mark. However, because the truck was equipped with dual wheels on the rear, the driver didn't even slow, and the truck disappeared up the path.

As the sounds of both vehicles faded, it became eerily quiet. Tony crawled out of the water and sat, remaining under the dock just in case the sniper was waiting for him to emerge into the open. After ten minutes or so, the quiet, the cold, and the boredom convinced him to venture out.

He stood and sloshed back into the water, toward the spot where the wounded man had landed. After several minutes of searching, he found him floating at the water's edge, about twenty paces north of the dock. He was dead.

"Well, shit," Tony said, grabbing the man's arms and pulling him up onto the rocky shore. A quick check revealed nothing in the man's pockets. Tony wasn't surprised. He was tempted to take the man's picture, but knew his phone saved all his photos to the cloud, where they lived forever. He decided it was better not to be so clearly linked to a dead body. He turned and walked away.

Wet, cold, and battered, his instincts were to call for help, or to at least seek shelter until morning. Instead, he trudged up the path to where the road plateaued, then turned right and climbed up through the grass onto the top of the bluff. He picked his way across the rough terrain to the edge, where he had a clear view of the bay and the dock stretching out into the water from the beach. He turned back to the left and walked parallel to the cliff, looking for signs of where the sniper had perched. He moved carefully, not wanting to trip on a stone or fall into the abyss through a break in the bluff's contour.

At the sight of a dark shape lying in the grass, Tony froze. It hadn't occurred to him that the killer might still be in place. He backpedaled as quietly as possible, then turned to flee. His haste proved his downfall. He stumbled and fell hard on his left side. A cry escaped his lips. He scrambled up to resume his flight but stopped. He turned and looked. The shape hadn't moved.

"Ah, man," he muttered, slowly approaching the lump of dark clothing, partially hidden by the vegetation. As he feared, it was a body. The man was large, well over six feet, and broad shouldered. Because he was lying face down and was dressed in black from neck to toe, Tony couldn't make out much else. The man's appearance was further masked by the fact the back of his head was crushed and still mostly obscured by a large boulder. Someone had picked up the stone—Tony guessed it to be thirty or forty pounds—and had thrust it down hard as the sniper lay prone on the bluff, facing the bay. At least half of the gunman's skull had been obliterated.

The sniper's right hand still gripped a rifle. In the darkness, Tony couldn't make out the brand or specific type, but he noted that, mounted on the weapon, was the largest scope he'd ever seen. Tony turned and retreated the way he had come. He didn't want to contaminate the crime scene any more than he already had.

It took almost no time for him to find and retrieve both bicycles from the grass beside the road. He debated what to do about Moira's bike and decided he couldn't leave it there. Unsure why he was determined to protect her, he knew if he left it behind, the Gardai would find it and trace it back to her. His solution wasn't ideal, but it worked.

He opened the quick-release mechanism on the front wheel of her bike. The wheel slid off the fork effortlessly. He then unthreaded the leather belt from his jeans and used it to strap the front fork of Moira's bike to the frame behind the seat of the bike he had borrowed. Securing the fork high on the frame allowed Moira's bike to just clear the rear wheel of his own. It created an odd sight, like the second bike was riding piggyback on the first. Tony didn't care, as long as he could get far enough away from the two dead bodies before anyone noticed him.

He picked up the extra wheel, hung it on the handlebars of his bike, and began pedaling. The extra weight and awkward configuration transformed the journey from difficult to nightmarish, but Tony persisted. After a few false turns in retracing the route, and more than a few stops for rest, Tony finally spotted Allihies on the hill above Ballydonegan Bay. The sun was just rising over the water when Tony returned the two bicycles to the shed and secured the door.

He was exhausted and craved a hot shower, but he knew he must complete one more task first. While still several blocks from his hotel, he located a lamppost covered in promotional flyers. He tore one down, not even noticing what it was selling, or what lost animal it was seeking. He turned it over, retrieved a pen from his pocket, and wrote on the back:

CALL GARDAI

TWO DEAD MEN

ONE NORTH OF DOCK. ONE ON BLUFF ABOVE.

NOT A PRANK. THIS IS REAL. PLEASE CALL NOW.

He followed this with a few directional notes to ensure the authorities would find the place. He then turned and walked back toward the hotel, sticking the note under the windshield wiper of the first car he encountered parked on the street. He hoped the person who found it would do as the note instructed. Before walking away, he used the sleeve of his sweatshirt to wipe off the note as best he could, to ensure he left no fingerprints or stray hairs behind.

Tony did all this because he knew he couldn't be the person to report what he'd seen. Inspector Lynch, or some other investigator, would ask him what he had been doing out there. He couldn't think of a convincing lie that didn't make him appear to be involved somehow, or perhaps even a murder suspect. The alternative would be to tell the truth about following Moira to the scene. He was unwilling to make trouble for her, at least until he'd had a chance to talk with her himself.

It occurred to him once again that his over-appreciation of attractive women was the source of much of the trouble in his life.

***

As he trudged back to his hotel room, he wondered how, or if, he would ever see Moira Blake again. He hoped he would. He hoped she would answer at least a few of the thousand questions dancing jigs in his brain. The prospect seemed remote, considering she had fled a gunfight aboard a boat capable of long-distance trips in ocean water.

He needn't have worried. When he turned the key and walked through the door into his room, he froze. The lovely Irish waitress was asleep on his bed.

What the…?

More questions. Big ones.

When he realized his entry hadn't awakened her, he decided all the questions could wait. He took out his phone and sent his sister a text message, explaining he had been up late and would be sleeping late. Then he crawled onto the bed, lay beside Moira, and fell asleep.

Chapter 19

Wednesday, May 27
Allihies, Beara Peninsula, County Cork, Ireland

Paul McCartney's voice, once again singing "Till There Was You," dragged Tony out of a nightmare about being chased by wolves riding bicycles. The ringtone was Darcy's. *Damn radar.* The bed beside him was empty. *Good news.* The shower, however, was not. He could hear it. *Bad news. Really bad news.*

He sat up and grabbed his phone off the nightstand. "Hey, gorgeous." He tried to sound upbeat, but the frog that had stolen his voice gave him away.

"Did I wake you? I'm sorry. It's almost noon. I thought…"

"Relax. It's okay. I didn't know it was so late. I'm glad to be up."

"Everything okay?"

Tony pondered how to answer the question. Finally, he said, "Well, yes and no."

"Meaning?"

Tony could hear the tension in Darcy's voice. He said, "Meaning two dead college students may be just the start of something bigger."

"Are you referencing the bodies the Irish police found this morning?"

Tony was shocked to hear her say it, but pleased to know his note on a stranger's car had produced results. He played dumb.

"What's that? What's happened?"

"Tony, don't bullshit me. You're there. I'll bet you know all about it."

"I've been sleeping. What's up?"

Darcy said the news had gone viral, at least for anyone paying attention to the news in Ireland. Reports were that a dead man was found on a beach on the south coast of the Beara Peninsula, apparently shot by a second man whose body was found on a nearby hill. "The police are asking for help from anyone who saw anything in that area last night or this morning."

Tony prayed no one had. He said, "Sounds like I need to get moving. The peninsula's not that big. If more people are dying near me, I'd like to know about it."

"Tony…"

"I'll be careful, I promise."

Darcy apparently wasn't buying it. She said, "Noon is late, even for you. Why don't you just tell me the truth about what happened?"

"I'll tell you everything," he said. "You know I will. But not over the phone." The sound of the shower stopped. He feared Darcy would notice the change in the background noise, and decided to hit it head-on. He said, "I'll even tell you why there's a woman using the shower in my hotel room."

Silence.

"You don't have to worry. It's not anything…"

"The girl you strolled with on the beach?" Darcy's words came out staccato, like bullets from a Gatling gun.

"Well, yes, but…"

"Tony, I'm not stupid." Her voice was half an octave higher in pitch.

Firmly, he said, "That's right, you're not. In fact, you may be the smartest person I know. Which is one of the reasons why I love you. Just one of the reasons. There's a long list of others. Which is why I don't, didn't, and won't cheat on you."

He heard Darcy suck in a deep breath. Finally, she said. "Okay. I trust you. Well, maybe I do. I'm trying. So I'm listening. Why's that girl in your room?"

"Someone tried to hurt her. She's hiding out. Nothing happened between us. Nothing will happen. Please, Darcy. It's so important that you trust me." He could feel tears forming in his eyes.

Darcy already had shifted gears from jealousy to fear. "Who wants to hurt her? What did you get yourself into? You told me you'd be safe."

"I am safe. No one knows she's here. I need to ask her some questions, and then she'll be on her way, probably back to her family in Galway."

"I'm sorry to be this way, but you always seem to worm your way into the apple with the rottenest core. What is it this time?"

Darcy's words were obliterated as the door to Tony's room exploded inward. Two large men rushed in. Tony jumped up, threw his phone aside, and screamed, "Moira! Lock the door!" It made no difference. The first man charged into the door to the bathroom, splintering the wood and swatting it aside. As Moira screamed, the second man delivered a savage punch to Tony's abdomen. He doubled over and fell to his knees, unable to breathe. Moira screamed again.

He turned and dropped to his side on the floor. Looking up, he saw the first man pin Moira to the wall and whisper into her ear. She fell silent and nodded. The attacker bound her hands behind her back with duct tape, then dropped a black hood over her head. He pushed her toward the door out of the room.

Tony knew he had to stop him. Struggling to resume breathing, he rolled and forced himself onto his hands and knees. He reached up for the bed with his right hand, trying to find leverage to stand. From the corner of his eye, he caught the rush of a boot. It struck the side of his head and everything went black.

Chapter 20

Thursday, May 28

Castletownbere, Beara Peninsula, County Cork, Ireland

Tony knew where he was without opening his eyes. The sounds and smells of a hospital were unmistakable. He heard Rita's voice. Then Darcy's.

Ah, shit. If Darcy was here, then he'd been unconscious for a while. He forced his eyes open and turned his head.

"Hey, gorgeous," he croaked.

"Tony!" Darcy rushed to his side, threw an arm around him, and buried her face in his chest.

"Hey, easy."

"Sorry, but no." Her voice was muffled by his hospital gown and sheets. "I'm never letting go."

Tony smiled, but his face instantly morphed into a picture of agony as he remembered. He said, "Moira? They took her. Is Moira okay?"

Darcy looked up, her face stony. She stood and backed away.

From behind her, Rita said, "Whoever took her still has her. They got away."

Tony tried to sit up. "We have to find…" He collapsed back onto the bed.

Rita came closer. "Everyone's looking. The guard has a couple dozen officers here, and every village has been alerted. Even Ryan's been out knocking on farmhouse doors, trying to find someone who knows something. Your job, for now, is to get well. You got a nasty blow to your temple."

"I'll be fine. I've been kicked in the head before."

"Yes, you have, and each time increases your risk of serious consequences."

Tony looked at Darcy. "I'm surprised to see you. Aren't you supposed to be working?"

She nodded. "Yes. I am. Now that you're awake, maybe I should get back. They weren't happy when I left."

It occurred to Tony to ask, "What time is it? What day is it?"

Rita said, "It's Thursday afternoon. You were out for over twenty-four hours. You're in the hospital in Castletownbere. Darcy came immediately. She heard the commotion over the phone and called the guard from Pinewood. She was here almost as fast as they were."

Something in Rita's voice was trying to get Tony's attention, but he ignored it. He was tired and his head hurt. Any brother-sister secret messages could wait.

Darcy stepped forward, leaned down, and kissed him on the cheek. "Goodbye, Tony. I hope you're feeling better soon." She turned and left.

Silence hung in the room for several beats too many. Finally, Tony looked at Rita and said, "What?"

She said, "You are such an effing moron."

Irritated, Tony snapped. "So nice of you to stop by to cheer me up."

"Stop pouting and listen to me."

"Okay, okay. What did I do?"

"Think about it. The love of your life ran out of a movie studio, halting production on a multi-million-dollar film, and traveled to the remotest corner of Ireland to be by your side, and all you could do was ask about another woman."

"But Moira's been taken by…by those brutes. She could be raped, or tortured, or even murdered. I'd be a cold-hearted bastard if I wasn't concerned about her."

"Of course," Rita said, the strain in her voice telegraphing her frustration, "but that doesn't have to be the first thing you say to Darcy. You could've said, 'I love you for coming,' or 'It's wonderful to see you,' or 'I'm *sorry*.' But no, you have to ask about the beautiful Irish lass who just happened to spend the night with you."

"Now wait a minute," Tony said, forcing himself to sit up in the bed. "I explained that to Darcy. It was nothing."

Rita shook her head. "You said what every man says when he's caught with a woman. Darcy wants to believe you, but the idea of it shook her. She rushed here out of concern for you, but also needing reassurance. She needed to feel your affection, your loving arms confirming your devotion to her. Instead, you slapped her in the face. Didn't you see how she was when she left?"

Tony thought about that. Recalling Darcy's cursory kiss and quick departure, he felt a pit growing in his stomach.

"Well, hell. You're right. I'm a moron. So what do I do about it?"

Rita held out her phone. "Call her. Get her back here. Make it right."

Tony looked at the device in her hand. "With your phone?"

"I'm not sure she'll answer yours."

"Ah, man."

A nurse stepped into the room and stopped. "Was ye ever plannin' to tell me ma patient was awake then?"

"Yes," Rita said. "Sorry."

The stocky, middle-aged woman said, "Put down yer phone then, and let's have a look at ye."

"Not just yet," Tony said. "I have something to do first."

"Somethin' more important than getting' well then?"

"Yes," Tony and Rita said in unison.

***

They were alone. Apologies made and accepted. Professions of love exchanged. Fears expressed and reassurances made.

Darcy was snuggled beside him on the bed, a practice normally frowned upon by the hospital staff. Once again, her celebrity status granted her some extra consideration.

She said, "So tell me everything."

"Me first," said a man's voice.

They turned their heads and saw him standing in the doorway.

Tony said, "Darcy, meet Inspector Colin Lynch. Inspector, meet my partner, Darcy Gillson."

The inspector walked to the bed and held out his hand. "A pleasure to meet you, Ms. Gillson. I'm a fan."

Darcy reached up and shook the hand, saying, "Thank you, but forgive me if I don't get up. And call me Darcy, please."

Still looking at Darcy, Lynch said, "I'm sorry, but I need to talk with Mr. Harrington. You can wait in the hallway. I won't be long."

Tony said, "Inspector, we're the ones who're sorry because no, Darcy's not leaving. I'll tell you everything, but only if she's here. She's going to hear it all anyway, so save me the trouble of saying it twice. Besides, she's smarter than either of us, so she might be able to help."

Lynch sighed, pulled a chair from the corner of the room to the bedside, and sat. To Darcy, he said, “Is he always a pain in the ass?”

Tony and Darcy looked at each other.

Darcy grinned and said, “Not always, but often enough that it’s not worth keeping track.”

Lynch returned the smile, then grew serious. “So what happened?”

Tony began by describing his meal at O’Connell’s and his realization that Moira was probably the target of the assassin in the cable car. He watched Lynch’s face, and as expected, it registered no surprise. *He’s way ahead of me.*

Tony continued, explaining his decision to question Moira and how that had led him to follow her on a bicycle across the peninsula early Wednesday morning.

“She led you directly to that cove on the south coast?”

Tony said yes, then described what he’d seen there.

“You draw a conclusion from all this?” the inspector asked.

“I couldn’t be sure,” Tony said, “but I’m not totally clueless. It occurred to me that I might be seeing a smuggling operation. The hour of the morning, the lack of lights, the dark clothing, the bags being dragged from the boat to the truck. The whole thing stank, and not from the dead fish on the shore.”

“Why didn’t you call us?”

Tony explained that he wasn’t certain what he was seeing, and didn’t want to cause trouble if it was something innocent. Hearing it aloud, it sounded weak, even to him. However, he didn’t want to offend Lynch by mentioning his fears about the local Gardai, and he didn’t want to admit in front of Darcy that he’d been trying to protect Moira.

Lynch looked skeptical and was about to speak, when Darcy interjected, “He’s a crusader.”

“What’s that?” Lynch turned to her.

She said, “Tony’s a crusader. He lives to be the hero. They could have been roasting people alive on that beach, and Tony wouldn't have called. He would've run down there and attacked them with a pointed stick."

Tony wanted to protest, but he knew Darcy's comment served his purposes. Accepting her criticism was better than having Lynch ask him to explain further.

The inspector nodded and said, "So what *did* you do?"

Tony grinned and said, "I charged down there, but without a pointed stick."

Darcy punched him in the arm.

Tony ignored the jab and explained his actions on the beach. "Which reminds me," he said. "I have the truck's license plate number. It's on my phone."

Lynch looked around. "Where is it?"

Darcy said, "The hospital has it in a locker with his clothes. I asked about it earlier, knowing he'd want it when he woke up."

Lynch reached down and pushed the call button beside Tony's hand on the bed. "Jesus, you could've told me sooner. This could be important."

"Sorry, but I've only been awake for a couple of hours, and I've had other things to cope with." He looked at Darcy. "Like a lousy sense of priorities."

She smiled and hugged him tighter.

When Tony described crawling under the truck, trying to see or hear something important, he could feel Darcy tense beside him. It was exactly the kind of foolishness he undertook too often. Incidents like these stoked her fears and resentments and were the only things about which they ever argued.

However, Tony didn't falter. Moira was a captive, or worse. He knew Lynch needed to know everything, so he continued his story.

"A sniper? You're sure?" The inspector didn't look up as he took notes.

Tony nodded. "No question. I saw the guy's silhouette up on the bluff, then saw the glint of moonlight off the scope. I scrambled out from under the truck and screamed at everyone to run. That's when the first shot hit the man on the dock."

"You risked your life to save some smugglers?"

"I just reacted," Tony said, "I didn't…"

"No, Inspector." It was Darcy. She looked at Tony as a mixture of anger, sadness, and exhaustion crossed her face. "He risked his life to save the girl. That woman, Moira, was on the dock. Tony ran into the path of a damn sniper to save her."

Lynch looked from Darcy to Tony.

Tony shrugged. "I can't deny it. I viewed her as an innocent. Couldn't believe, still can't believe, she's mixed up in something illegal. So yes, I tried to save her. Thought I'd succeeded. She fled from the gunfire aboard the fishing trawler. I really thought I'd never see her again and was glad of it."

Darcy snorted. Tony ignored her and continued describing the remaining events, including the truck's departure and its tire being shot.

The nurse appeared in the doorway. "Did ye need somethin', Mr. Harrington?"

Lynch said, "That was me. Sorry to bother you, but please fetch Mr. Harrington's clothes and belongings from wherever they're stored."

"Of course." The nurse departed.

Tony resumed by describing his search for the man shot on the dock, how he'd located the body, and his confirmation the man was dead. "I dragged him up on the beach so he could be found. Then I walked away."

The inspector said, "The note you left reported both bodies. Tell me about the second one. Every detail."

Tony related his climb to the top of the bluff to look for the sniper's firing position.

"To what end?" Lynch asked.

"I've no idea," Tony said. "It just seemed like an obvious thing to do. If I'd ridden away without looking, I'd wonder later what I'd missed."

"So that's when you found him? The sniper, I mean."

Tony nodded. "It never occurred to me he might still be up there. Scared the shit out of me."

"Is that why you killed him?"

"What?" Tony and Darcy reacted almost in unison.

"Come now, Mr. Harrington, this one is obvious. Don't waste my time by denying it."

"But I didn't…"

"You don't even *need* to deny it. The man was a killer. You were in danger. It was self-defense."

"Inspector," Tony cleared his throat and stared into Lynch's eyes. "I swear to you I did not kill that man. The way your officers found him is how I found him, lying face down with his skull crushed."

"You were the only other person up there," Lynch persisted.

"Obviously, I wasn't." Saying this out loud gave Tony pause.

"What?"

"Nothing. Well, I mean, I haven't thought about that. Again, I just woke up. But who was out there, and why?"

"You're the obvious candidate," Lynch said. "The smugglers were on the beach. A member of a rival gang, or perhaps a killer after our mysterious waitress, was up on the bluff. There's no evidence of anyone else. Plus, you've proven in the past you have the capacity to kill when threatened, and you're strong enough to have lifted the boulder. And let's not forget you had plenty of motive."

"Such as?" Tony's face was red and his pulse was increasing.

"The man may have tried to kill Moira Blake. Just moments ago, you admitted you wanted to protect her. He probably had tried to kill you too."

Tony fought to slow his breathing and force some calm into his voice. He said, "It makes a tidy package for you. Too bad it's simply not true."

The nurse arrived carrying a large plastic bag tied with a drawstring. She said, "Everything's 'ere. It 'asn't been opened since it was stowed on his arrival."

"Very good," Lynch said, gesturing toward the end of the bed.

The nurse set the bag there and departed.

Lynch said, "Let's move on. What happened after you left the dead sniper?"

Tony explained his piggybacked bicycles and arduous journey back to Allihies, finding Moira in his room, and his decision to let her sleep.

"You never talked to her?"

"Unfortunately, no."

"So, later in the morning, when you awoke…"

"My phone woke me. Darcy called."

The inspector looked at her. "That must have been interesting."

Darcy nodded and said, "Tony told me immediately that Moira was there. That's the kind of person he is, Inspector. He's open and honest."

"Hmph. We'll see."

"Our conversation was just getting started when two men crashed through the door to my room," Tony said. "One came after me, and the other broke into the bathroom and took Moira."

Lynch pressed him for descriptions, but Tony was unable to provide much detail. "It all happened in seconds. I just caught glimpses. Moira was wearing black yoga pants and a sports bra. She hadn't finished dressing after her shower. Both men were big, muscular, dark.

One had a beard, neatly trimmed. They wore jeans and sweatshirts, hooded, no logos. I got the impression they were foreign, but I'm not sure why."

"Nothing else?"

Tony closed his eyes. "The boot. The one that struck my head. It had a logo on it."

"A brand you recognized?"

"No. Maybe that's what made me think he was foreign. It had a shield with a blue background. A kind of backward *F* was printed in white. It looked a little like the Facebook logo."

The inspector groaned, pulled out his phone and typed for a few moments. He paused and held the phone up for Tony to see the screen. He said, "Like this?"

"Yes! That's it. How did you…?"

"It's Russian."

"Russian?"

"We run into these boots sometimes when dealing with people from eastern Europe or western Asia. Vostock is one of the largest manufacturers of footwear in Russia."

Darcy spoke up, her voice strained. "Does this mean Tony's mixed up in some kind of Russian feud?"

"Not necessarily," Lynch said. "Anyone can buy and wear the boots. But when you combine the origin of the boot with Tony's description of the assailants, it seems possible."

"That guy named Rob told the students he was Ukrainian. Maybe he was one of them."

"Maybe," Lynch said, clearly distracted. He reached for the plastic bag at the foot of the bed and fished out Tony's phone. Handing it over, he said, "Send me the license plate picture, and add any details you remember about the truck."

Tony did so, then said, "Can I have my clothes? I gotta get out of here."

"Sorry, but no," Lynch said.

"But I'm feeling…"

"If you're as smart as you think you are, you know I have to keep the clothes. You were wearing them Wednesday morning. You're a suspect in a killing. They have to be checked for blood splatters and everything else."

Tony sank back into the bed and sighed. "Of course."

Darcy disengaged from him and sat up, swinging her legs over the side of the bed. She said, "No worries. I'll go shopping for you. Assuming I don't have to travel to Cork to find men's clothing, I'll be back soon."

She and Tony said their goodbyes, and Darcy departed.

Lynch surprised Tony by returning to his chair.

Tony said, "There's not much else."

"But there is something. You're a good liar, but I sensed when you cut things short. What is it you didn't want Ms. Gillson to hear?"

Tony closed his gaping mouth and said, "You're very good, Inspector Lynch. The only thing I skipped was what I heard when the men took Moira."

"Which was…?"

"When the second man crashed into the bathroom, Moira screamed. She screamed again as he turned her to face the wall and tried to secure her hands. She was fighting him, of course. Then he whispered in her ear, and she immediately grew quiet and complacent."

"Oh?"

"I couldn't hear everything, but I could tell he spoke with a thick accent, probably Slavic."

"Any idea what he said?"

"That's the part I didn't want to share in front of Darcy. I'm pretty sure he told her that if she shut up and went quietly, they would let me live. She did, and they did."

The inspector looked at Tony, then said, "There's more going on between you and Moira than you claimed."

"No, there's not," Tony said firmly. "I like her, yes. Of course I do. What's not to like? But I'm committed to Darcy, and I don't cheat. There's nothing between us beyond a friendly waitress and an admiring customer."

"Tony, don't be naive," Lynch said. "She was being assaulted and abducted. She had to know what surrendering to them might mean, what she faced in their hands. If she acquiesced to that to save you, that's not the action of a woman who's simply a friendly waitress."

"Well, dammit, I didn't ask her to do it!" Tony's voice rose in pitch and volume. "I didn't want her to." Now, nearly shouting, "I tried to *save* her!"

Lynch's tone softened. "Of course you did. I didn't mean to imply you did anything wrong."

Fighting tears, Tony tried to calm himself and said, "Why mysterious?"

"What?"

"Earlier you called her 'the mysterious waitress.' Why mysterious?"

Lynch tapped his notebook with his pen, apparently deliberating. Finally, he said, "Her name's not Moira Blake."

"What? Then who…?"

"We don't know. We've been digging into her background for the past three days or so. It was routine at the beginning. She was an important witness in one of the worst cases I've ever worked, so we checked her out. Almost immediately, I got reports back from my team that the name she gave her boss and landlady in Allihies was fake. That's when it dawned on me that she could've been the intended murder victim. I felt like an idiot for not thinking of it sooner."

"I know the feeling," Tony grumbled. "The resemblance of the two women was uncanny. Can you run her photo through facial recognition programs? You should be able to find her on social media, even if her official ID was fake."

"I could if I had her picture. I don't. We don't routinely photograph witnesses. So far, I've not found anyone who has it. You?"

Tony shook his head. "I had even less reason to take her picture than you did." Lynch nodded, and Tony continued. "She told me and others that she was here hiding from an ex-boyfriend who wasn't ready to separate. Of course that could've been a lie. I doubt an unhappy boyfriend sent Russian muscle to kidnap her."

It pained Tony to speak this aloud. It meant Moira had lied to his face. The thought drove a blade through his heart. The wound was bigger than it had any right to be.

Lynch said, "Depends on the boyfriend, I suppose. He could be someone rich, or powerful, or both."

"Or it could have been a convenient lie."

"More likely," the inspector agreed, "especially considering what you saw in that cove. This is about drugs."

"Ah, man."

"I get it, Tony. You don't want to believe it. She's nice. You were impressed with her. So was I, when I interviewed her. But nice people get mixed up in crimes every day. The facts are, she knew exactly when and where to go to find the smuggling op, and when she arrived, she was welcomed into the middle of it. At the very least, she knew those people."

Tony nodded, but said, "It doesn't matter. Either way, we have to find her. Whether innocent victim or criminal mastermind, we can't leave her in the hands of those brutes."

"Agreed." Lynch stood and returned his notepad to his satchel.

"What's next?" Tony asked.

"I've got plenty to do. Find the truck and try to trace it to the smugglers. Find the trawler and try to trace it to the people who helped her escape from the beach. Identify the girl. Find the bastards who took her. Rescue the girl and put everyone else in prison. Starting with you, if you're lying to me."

"I'm not."

"Good. I hope you feel better soon." The inspector turned to go.

To his back, Tony said, "I still want to help."

Lynch turned again. "Just concentrate on getting well. You have a sister and a girlfriend to consider."

"Moira was taken from my room. When she was scared and running, she came to me for help. I can't turn my back on that. I'm going to find her."

"I can still lock you up on suspicion of murder."

"Bullshit. Without me, you wouldn't have the license number for the truck, or a description of the trawler, or any clue about what happened on that dock Wednesday morning."

Lynch seemed to consider this. He said, "Fair enough, but there's nothing you can do that we're not already doing."

"Who are the Russians?"

"What do you mean?"

"I think you know, or at least fear, what you're up against. I think you're trying to protect me."

Lynch inhaled deeply and blew it out through parted lips. He walked back to the edge of the hospital bed. Quietly, he said, "There have been rumors of a Russian organization importing cocaine into Ireland. The country's been awash in the stuff for a few years now, and it's getting worse."

"Organization as in state sponsored, or private?" Tony asked.

"Who knows? In Russia, I'm not sure there's a difference. Military and political leaders have their fingers in everything. More to the point, there are signs of a war brewing. The Irish drug trade has been controlled for years by a couple of large, powerful cartels. They can't be happy about the Russians encroaching on their business."

"So the sniper Wednesday morning?"

"Could have been the Russians hijacking, or attempting to hijack, an Irish cartel's shipment. Or it could've been the opposite. When we identify the dead men, or at least get DNA tests back, we'll have a hint about that. Unfortunately, yesterday morning wasn't the first volley. Six weeks ago, a Russian ship exploded and sank in the bay just south of here. A few days later, two known associates of the Foley Gang were found dead in an apartment in Cork."

"The Foley Gang?"

"One of those powerful cartels I mentioned. All of this is hearsay and speculation, of course. But now you know why I'm worried, and why you should stay away from this. These are evil people who will happily remove your organs while you watch, then enjoy a nice meal while your corpse rots in the next room."

The thought made Tony wince but didn't stop him from saying, "So why would the Russians want Moira?"

"Your guess is as good as mine. If she's involved in one of the cartels, she's as good a target as any."

"It feels more substantial than that. More personal."

Lynch ran a hand through his hair. "Yeah, I think so too."

"None of that helps us find her."

"Right again."

Chapter 21

Thursday, May 28
Beara Peninsula, County Cork, Ireland

Moira thought of them as Thing One and Thing Two. Thing One had the beard. He was the one who'd kicked Tony in the head, so she had no illusions about his ability and willingness to injure. She also had no doubt that he would be the first to force himself on her. Lust burned in his eyes like the fires of Hell.

Last night, in the dark, she heard him behind her, smelled him, then felt his calloused hand sliding past her neck, down her chest, and inching beneath her bra. When he cupped her breast and began fondling her nipple with his thumb, she jerked and twisted, trying to resist. The straps that bound her to the chair held firm, and the tape around her head, covering her mouth, prevented her from crying out.

Then she sensed what he was doing with his other hand. *The pathetic, disgusting pig*. She nearly laughed, but was terrified to think what he might do if he realized she was amused by his desperation.

In the end, she calmed herself and let him finish, hoping it would satisfy him, at least for a while.

As horrifying as she found Thing One, his partner scared her more. Thing Two had a pretty-boy face, steel-gray eyes, and the cool, calculating manner of a true sociopath. Her uncle employed men like this, who killed without hesitation or guilt, and found pleasure in inflicting pain. She could imagine Thing Two coming into the room wearing a smile, announcing she was being released, removing her restraints, then slitting her throat before she could stand up. If Thing Two attacked her sexually, it would be with some horrible shop tool. The thought made her dizzy and brought tears to her eyes.

She fought the terror by stoking her anger and visualizing her revenge. She would begin with a knife. Thing One wouldn't be finding pleasure with his dick anymore; he wouldn't be finding his dick at all. Thing Two would die more quickly. Perhaps she could manage to slice a carotid artery too. Of course, these thoughts were probably moot. When Uncle Ox found these cretins, he would inflict horrors upon them far worse than anything Moira could imagine. Her job, she knew, was to survive until he arrived.

To that end, she considered her surroundings. Two high windows on one wall allowed her to track the sunlight across the floor. She knew it was late afternoon on the second day, Thursday. The windows faced north, she was pretty sure, because the shadows were muted. Sunlight through a south window would produce more distinct shadows. She was in a basement. They had dragged her down a set of stairs before securing her to the chair, an elaborate perch like a dentist's chair, but with restraints. The high windows, combined with the rough, damp, concrete floor and the musky smell confirmed the below-ground setting. The room was large, easily ten meters or more in each direction. If this was a house, it was a big one. She considered whether it could be the basement of a warehouse or an industrial building. The structure looming overhead said no. The joists for the floor above were exposed. She could see they were wooden and modest in size. A commercial building would be supported by stouter stuff. *So a large, old house not far from Allihies*. They had taken her in a panel van, and the ride had been short—thirty minutes at most.

She couldn't quite imagine it. The Beara Peninsula was home to farmers and fishermen, not the kind of people who built houses of this scale. *If it's old enough, maybe it dates back to the days of copper mining*. Even though she wasn't from the area, Moira knew the mine had once been big business. It made sense that big money had been involved.

In any case, she assumed the house was well concealed. In the weeks she'd lived and traveled around Allihies, she'd never seen it. The thought was not encouraging.

Her stomach grumbled, announcing to the empty room the extent of her hunger. She had heard somewhere that hunger was used to control the victims of sex trafficking and others held in captivity. She already understood why. She'd been given nothing but a little water since yesterday and now was at the point where she would do almost anything for a simple dumpling or piece of soda bread.

She heard the sound of the door behind her and was instantly filled with a mix of anticipation and dread.

***

Lubyanka Square, Moscow, Russia

The FSB leader's pencil was not tapping the desk. It was gripped too tightly in his fingers. To his lieutenant, he said, "You were right. The situation in Ireland is out of control."

"Yes, sir."

"I talked to Polshkov. He said he would stand down."

The lieutenant grunted.

"Exactly. The bastard lied. Now his goons have killed two innocent students and kidnapped some waitress."

"She's Ox Foley's niece."

"Fuck. He hurts her, there's going to be an all-out war down there. Where is she?"

"We're not sure. As far as we can tell, he's holding her somewhere in southern Ireland. We'd know if he'd taken her off the island."

"You have a man down there, as we discussed?"

"Yes, sir. He's been searching the countryside all day. Nothing yet."

The director broke the pencil into three pieces in his grip. He didn't seem to notice. He looked at his lieutenant and said, "Polshkov's men also put some American in the hospital. Do I understand that correctly?"

"Yes, sir. The girl was in his hotel room, so they put him down during their grab. The man's a former journalist. More importantly, he lives with Darcy Gillson, the American actress. If the press gets wind of this, from either the US or Great Britain, they'll be all over it."

"Fuck, fuck! That's it. Polshkov has to go. His greed and obstinance are intolerable. Can your man handle that?"

"It's a tall order," the lieutenant said. "Polshkov is the leader of the Brotherhood for a reason. He's well protected and would be no small threat even if he wasn't."

The director's anger reached his voice. He snapped. "I'm well aware of how dangerous he is. That's not what I asked. Can your man handle it?"

The lieutenant thought carefully about his answer, then decided to be honest. "He's pretty green, but yes, I'd give the assignment to him first. His cover's intact and he's already there, so he has the best chance of finding the girl without exposing us. Presumably, if he finds the girl, he finds Polshkov."

"Order it done. No fuckups."

"Yes, sir."

Chapter 22

Friday, May 29
Bantry Bay, Beara Peninsula, Ireland

The authorities arrived in a van. From the deck of the *Jammy Lass*, Sam Kilborgen spotted them instantly when they turned off the main road and began their descent down the hill, along the private lane to his dock. He assumed they were officers dispatched from Cork, or perhaps even Dublin. The guard station in Castletownbere didn't have a van as far as he was aware.

Keep yer wits about ye, he said to himself. He tried to adjust his face to show curiosity rather than fear. *They got nothin' on ye. They prolly be visitin' all the boats*. Somehow his internal reassurances weren't finding their way to his knuckles, which were white.

The van stopped on the patch of gravel in front of the pier. Two uniformed officers emerged and opened the back. A large, tan dog with a dark face and pointed ears hopped out. The presence of the dog explained the van. As the three visitors walked onto the pier,

Kilborgen put down the box of fruit he was about to store below and walked to the starboard side to greet them.

"Sam Kilborgen?" one of the officers asked.

"Aye," he said. "How can I help ye?"

"We'd like to come aboard and look around. We don't have a warrant, so you can decline. That's your right. But we're searching for a boat involved in that nasty business Wednesday morning on the coast west of here."

"Ye thinkin' I be involved there?"

"Not necessarily, sir. All the trawlers are being checked. A boat of about this size was seen there."

"Lot o' boats like mine."

"Yes, sir, we understand. We'll try to be quick and not disrupt your morning any longer than necessary. We'll certainly appreciate your cooperation."

"The dog too?" Kilborgen asked.

"Yes, sir, if that's alright."

"I'm stockin' provisions today. Boxes o' food stacked below."

The officer smiled and patted the dog. "She'll give you no problems. She's a Belgian Malinois, well trained to search for narcotics, not potatoes."

"Narcotics? Well, ye be wastin' yer time here, but come on if ye must." He beckoned them aboard.

The Gardai and the dog found nothing, of course. Kilborgen kept no drugs on the boat. Each of the two shipments he already had hauled had been picked up and unloaded on the same nights. More importantly, even while hauling the illegal cargo, it never touched the boat decks. He had worked hard to make sure his ingenious method of transporting the material could never leave a trace on his vessel.

The officers were thorough, checking every cabin, storage compartment, cabinet, and locker. They examined walls for hidden doors and access panels, and took swabs from common surfaces in the galley, head, and sleeping quarters, as well as on deck. When they finished, they appeared to be satisfied, neither surprised nor disappointed. This helped ease Kilborgen's nerves, as it indicated they had not suspected him before arriving.

As the officers prepared to leave, they thanked Kilborgen for his cooperation and apologized again for interrupting his work.

"Apologies no' be needed 'ere." he said, leaning down to pet the dog. "Have a grand day 'n be safe out there."

The officers nodded and exited down the gangplank.

As he watched them go, Kilborgen's parting thought was how lucky he was to have already finished repairing the bullet hole in the portside cabin wall inflicted by the sniper on Wednesday morning.

He had wondered from the beginning whether agreeing to work for Foley would be his undoing. Now, as he thought about the firefight in the cove and the search of his boat by the peelers, he knew it would. He took one long look out to sea, then went below to pour himself a whiskey.

Chapter 23

Friday, May 29

Beara Peninsula, County Cork, Ireland

Ninety-nine, one hundred.

Arsendo Petrov lay back, letting his sweat add to the puddle on the cool, hardwood floor beneath his shoulder blades. He stared at the ceiling, wondering what to do next. The cracks in the plaster held no answers, so he groaned and scrambled to his feet. It would have to be the jump rope he'd fashioned from lamp cords. He desperately wanted to go for a run, but knew it was a mistake to go outside. He would kill, literally, for a treadmill, or even a simple set of weights. The old house had plenty of space, but nothing inside to aid in his workout. By the end of the first day, he had grown bored with sit-ups, pushups, and jumping rope. He wished someone else in the house was skilled enough at hand-to-hand combat to provide even a moderate challenge as a sparring partner.

Grabbing the makeshift rope, he began his routine. The men

watching television downstairs wouldn't like it, but he didn't care. If they were more interested in gawking at some inane panel show than in preparing for battle, so be it.

His movements were second nature and required no conscious direction. He quickened his pace and began crossover moves with his hands. Against his better judgment, his thoughts turned to the girl downstairs. A young woman strapped to a dental chair, hungry and frightened. It was perfect, and yet forbidden. The frustration was overwhelming. *When is that bastard Polshkov coming?*

He wanted her, wanted to play with her, but not in the way dreamed about by the lowlifes all around him. His pleasure would come from the flick of his wrist, just a tiny nick with his Kizlyar blade, in just the right spot. He would watch the woman's life slowly drain away. It would be...*delicious*. He could think of no better word.

It would be so much more satisfying than the swift pair of killings in the cable car. Two sliced necks in less than two seconds had felt good, but fast was never as rewarding as slow. Here, he would be able to watch. After she bled for a while, perhaps he would bandage the cut. Watch the hope and pleading in her eyes. Then, with a grin and a shake of his head, the knife would reappear and... flick! She would sob and try to promise him things. He would watch. It would be...*delicious*.

His mouth was dry. His loins stirred. He dropped the lamp cords and bent over, hands on knees, breathing deeply. He knew the pleasure he derived from killing was not normal. He didn't care. What was normal to others was of no concern to him. The pleasure was real, and intense, and addictive. He was born to do this. The idea made him smile.

Born to it. This was literally true. His first kill was on the day of his birth. His mother had bled out before his father had come in from the field, before he had even known she was in labor. Petrov knew every detail of that day because his father had told him, and told him, and told him. Papa had wanted his son to know how his mother had died, and who was responsible.

Petrov had only known the man as a broken, grieving widower, an angry, short-tempered taskmaster. And there were plenty of tasks to be done. They lived on what was called a household farm, a single-family operation on one hectare of land, or about two and a half acres. They grew cabbages, sugar beets, and cucumbers. About a score of chickens and one dairy cow occupied the tiny, unpainted barn. Water came from a well in the yard, and one's business was done in a primitive outhouse, whether fighting flies and stifling heat, or four feet of snow and subfreezing temperatures.

The house was a simple, one-story wooden structure, painted brown with windows trimmed in what once had been yellow. Inside were three rooms, plus a small loft under the peaked roof. Its plot of land was walking distance from the village of Kirsnovo, on the western bank of the Belozevsky Canal in Vologda, perhaps a seven-hour drive east from St. Petersburg.

From the time Arsendo was old enough to walk, he was working. His father seemed determined to exact from his son every hour of effort lost to the death of his wife. When his father drank, which was often, he openly blamed his son for every obstacle the family encountered, every lonely moment. If Papa drank enough, Petrov felt the sting of his gnarled knuckles or his leather belt.

For as long as he could remember, Petrov had accepted that he had killed his mother. However, somewhere along the way—he had been nine or ten years old—he had begun to like the idea. He was glad he had caused pain for the miserable drunkard who demanded he work so hard, who often sent him to bed in pain and unfed. One night, as he lay on his tiny mattress in the loft, listening to his father sobbing below, he realized he was enjoying it. A few days later, when his father struck him again, Petrov decided who would be his second kill.

At age sixteen, when he knew he was old enough to run if necessary, he did it. His father was milking the cow one evening, bellowing his complaints that Arsendo hadn't finished his other chores in time to bring in the milk for dinner. Masked by his father's whining, and the accompanying noises of the animals, Petrov simply stepped up behind him and swung the blunt side of the axe as hard as he could into the side of his skull. His father toppled from the milking stool to the dirt floor and never moved again.

Petrov carefully washed and dried the axe, returning it to its perch near the woodpile. He then ran into the village, to the pub, where there was a telephone. He ran because he wanted to be out of breath and sweaty when he announced to the handful of patrons that the cow had kicked his father in the head.

The authorities didn't arrive until the next morning. Clearly skeptical of his story, they questioned Petrov at length. As they concluded the interview, they instructed him to remain at home until he heard from them again. When they left, his father's corpse went with them.

That night, Petrov stuffed his coat and a few other items of clothing into a sack. Before leaving, he searched his father's room until he found the cash under a loose floorboard. He was smart enough to take only half. It would be enough, and it would prevent the *politsiya* from thinking he had killed his father for the money.

When he left the house, he didn't look back. He walked to the village, then down the hill to the canal. A few simple motorboats and one rowboat were tied to a wooden dock that extended about ten meters into the waterway. He headed for the rowboat. Orlav wouldn't miss it. He was old. He hadn't used the boat even once since putting it in the water in the spring.

Walking quickly and quietly, Petrov approached the boat, but froze when he noticed a man sitting in the motorboat on the opposite side of the dock. Dressed in street clothes and what appeared to be an expensive leather jacket, the man was older, clean-shaven, and slender.

"Hard work, rowing all the way to…wherever," the man said. "You should take this one. The fuel tank is full and it looks like it gets used regularly. Probably will start right up."

Petrov didn't speak. He looked back over his shoulder, wanting to run, but unsure where he would go.

"Relax," the man said. "Arsendo, right?"

Petrov nodded.

"Sit, Arsendo. Please. You'll be glad you did."

Having no acceptable alternatives, Petrov sat.

"I'm sorry to hear about your father."

Petrov just stared.

"Are you grieving, Arsendo?"

Silence.

"No?" The man smiled wide enough to see the moonlight on his teeth. "I thought not."

"What?"

"Let me ask you an honest question, an important question. Do you regret killing him?"

"Now, wait…" Petrov began to get up.

"Sit!" the man barked.

Petrov dropped to the wooden planks. The abrupt change in tone and volume frightened him. He looked around to see if others had been alerted. The windows in the village remained dark.

"Perhaps most important of all, Arsendo, did you find it difficult?"

"I don't… I didn't…"

The man sighed and said, "Listen to me. It's important that you tell me the truth. Lie to everyone else. Lie to yourself if you like. But be honest with me. Was it difficult to swing that hammer, or axe, or whatever it was?"

With no idea why, Petrov looked the man in the eyes and said, "No. It wasn't difficult."

"Excellent. I'm not surprised. I hear he was an unpleasant man. Did you enjoy it?"

Petrov immediately understood that this was a completely different question.

"Enjoy it?" He found a smile coming to his lips. He said, "Yes, I believe I did… enjoy it."

"Outstanding." The man clapped his hands and stood, reaching out to the mooring post and stepping onto the dock.

"If you'll come with me, I'll teach you how to do it better, so strangers like me won't catch you, and I'll show you how to make a lot of money, doing what you…*enjoy*. Will you come?"

Petrov went.

***

The memory of that night still made Petrov smile. He felt his pulse slowing, a sense of calm returning. So much had happened since his recruitment. Years of training and apprenticeship, his first assigned hit, and his first narrow escape. Then, after his seventh successful kill, his decision to leave the protection of the FSB and strike out on his own. Soon he completed his first professional, private kill, followed soon after by his first six-figure contract, and that followed by multiple others.

Petrov relished each and every job. He often coaxed himself to sleep at night by reliving the details of particularly difficult or satisfying hits. He was proud of his abilities, gratified by his accumulated wealth, and excited by the prospects of what lay ahead.

Meanwhile, he would have to endure a few more hours, or perhaps days, in this old house, in the middle of nowhere, waiting for the opportunity to suck the life from poor little Moira. And what if Polshkov said no? What if the Brotherhood's boss wanted to keep her alive?

Petrov smiled. *I guess the torture will have to do.*

Chapter 24

Friday, May 29
Allihies, Beara Peninsula, Ireland

Tony, Darcy, and Rita huddled around Tony's laptop at a table in the rear corner of O'Connell's. It was 8 p.m. Friday.

Tony had been released from the hospital at noon and had gone back to the hotel to shower and try on the half dozen different outfits Darcy had purchased for him in Castletownbere. He'd spent the rest of the afternoon on his computer. They had convened at O'Connell's at seven for dinner. Their three bowls of beef stew sat at the far side of the table, mostly cold, and mostly uneaten.

The computer apparently offered better fare, as the three scrolled through social media sites and news media stories, looking for Moira Blake's image.

"This is like searching for a Honda Civic on a California freeway," Darcy said. "You can find a million of them, but finding a specific one is impossible."

Tony nodded. Women with long, dark hair were anything but rare in Ireland. "There!" he said, pointing at a crowd picture taken at an outdoor concert in Galway, and published online by the local newspaper.

Darcy reached over and zoomed in on the photo. "No dimples," she said simply. "You told me she has prominent dimples."

"Right." Tony returned to scrolling

Darcy sat back and closed her eyes. Eventually, she said, "We're going about this all wrong."

"How so?" Rita asked.

"We're looking at events and school activities and other materials from Galway."

"Because that's where she said she was from."

"Exactly," Darcy said, "but now we know she was lying. If the whole boyfriend story was fake, then she probably lied about her home as well."

"Maybe," Tony nodded, "but we can't search every town and city in Ireland."

"We need to focus on the drug cartels. If she was mixed up in that smuggling operation, then she must have ties to one of them."

"The only one we know about is the Foley Gang," Tony said. "I looked there first and found almost nothing. There's no Moira Foley, and no one I could find who fits the description of our missing waitress. Lennox Foley, the one they call the Ox, is the leader. He's extremely elusive for all the obvious reasons. He's been seen in public maybe a half dozen times in the past two decades and hasn't allowed his picture to be taken in more than forty years. There're plenty of articles about his suspected criminal activities, but little else."

"What does 'little else' mean?" Darcy asked. "Be specific."

Tony sat back and took a deep breath. "Well, he grew up in Galway, so that fits. But he's been gone from there for a long time. He's suspected of operating out of Dublin, but even that isn't known for certain. There have been reports of a female companion, but he's never married her, probably to avoid creating any kind of public record. No known children."

Tony continued, "He has one sister who's disowned him. She's still in Galway, but two different articles I read said she has no involvement in the Ox's enterprise. She's a widow who works as a church secretary. Married name is Kennington."

"What about the criminal stuff?" Rita asked. "Are they involved in things other than drugs?"

"Plenty," Tony said. "They started out in prostitution, then expanded into money laundering, lending, and protection rackets."

"Lending?" Rita asked.

"Loan sharks. They lend money to people who are desperate, charge exorbitant interest rates, and enforce collections with violence. Borrowers often are forced to resort to crime to pay their debts."

Darcy said, "So the drugs came later?"

"Apparently, yes. Inspector Lynch said the problem in Ireland has exploded in recent years. Once it became apparent the Irish have an appetite for cocaine, Foley's involvement came as no surprise. He had the cash to get started and had an established network of associates for distribution. Of course, he also had no conscience or moral objections standing in his way. With the help of his business sense, generous bribes, and occasional sheer brutality, the organization rapidly grew into a major player in the drug trade. Today, some believe the Foley Gang is responsible for half or more of all the cocaine sold in Ireland."

Everyone was quiet as they thought about that.

Darcy broke the silence, saying she needed to use the loo. Tony smiled at the reference. Clearly, his partner had been spending too much time in England. As soon as she was gone, Rita asked, "How's your head?"

"I'm okay. It throbs a little, but the Tylenol really helps. The bigger question is, are you okay?"

"What? Yes, of course." She tried to put a smile in her voice, but she wouldn't look her brother in the eye.

Tony asked, "Where's Ryan?"

Rita's lip quivered a little. "I… I'm not sure. Still out looking for Moira, I guess."

"I heard you fighting Tuesday night, or rather, Wednesday morning, early."

"Yeah, well, lovers argue sometimes. You and Darcy aren't perfect, you know."

"That's true," Tony said, "but we're not talking about Darcy and me. What's the issue?"

"I don't want to tell you, because you'll make too much of it."

"Rita, talk to me. Something's clearly bothering you. I promise to keep my head about it. Has he been abusive or something?"

Rita looked up, alarmed. "God, no. He's kind and gentle, and well, great, really."

"So?"

She sighed, "So, he's been going out at night."

"Going out? What do you mean? Like to the pub?"

She shook her head. "No. Later than that. After everything's closed and I'm asleep, or supposed to be. He leaves the room. Sometimes for hours. I don't know how he functions during the day, because he's not getting much rest."

"Have you asked him about it?"

She nodded. "He says he likes to walk at night by himself. It hurt my feelings at first, but now I worry that it's something else."

"Like what?" Tony asked.

"I don't have a clue. But remember, he's the one who pushed us to come down here, to Allihies. Maybe he's got another woman here." She brushed away a tear. "Maybe it's Moira. Why else would he be out searching the countryside for her? He seems almost desperate to find her."

Tony thought about that. It did seem odd, but it also seemed unlikely that Ryan and Moira were involved romantically. He realized it might just be his ego at work, but he still believed Moira had meant it when she'd expressed an interest in him at the end of their walk on the beach. Nothing in what she said or did hinted at being in a relationship beyond the one she was fleeing. *Of course that was all a total lie, so who knows?*

To Rita, he said, "I think your natural jealousy has led you down the wrong path. Just because Ryan's behavior is unusual doesn't mean he's cheating on you."

"Maybe, but I can tell he's not being honest. Why would late-night walks suddenly become a part of his routine here? He never does it in Chicago."

"A reasonable question," Tony said, "but don't let it ruin your relationship. Whatever he's doing is probably meaningless. He could be telling the truth about the walks, or he could be doing something he's embarrassed to have you know. He might even be doing something *for* you."

Rita's eyes widened. "Like what?"

"I don't know. Maybe he's going over to the men's shed and using the shop to build you something."

"Men's shed?"

"It's a building just up the hill from the town. The men go there to build things. It's like a social club, but with power tools instead of alcohol. Ryan could be going there."

"You think so?" The hope in Rita's voice was touching.

"Easy," Tony said. "It's just a thought. My point is that there are lots of possible explanations, and you should trust him until he gives you a reason not to."

"I suppose you're right."

Tony was succeeding in easing his sister's anxiety but was doing nothing for his own. Rita's boyfriend always had been a bit of a mystery. His unusual background, surprisingly long list of capabilities, and too-good-to-be-true looks, combined to make Tony suspicious. Learning that he was out every night, at a time when people were being murdered and drugs were being transported across the landscape, frightened Tony and further fueled his suspicions. In his heart, he knew Rita was asking the right questions. *Why did Ryan insist we come down here, and what in the hell is he doing every night?*

***

Thoughts of Ryan and everything else disappeared instantly when the front door opened and two men entered.

"Uh-oh," Tony said.

"What?"

In nearly a whisper, he told Rita, "Get out of here. Now. Go!"

Her confusion seemed to glue her to her seat.

In the lead, striding toward them, was the man who'd attacked Tony outside St. Stephen's Green in Dublin—the man who'd put a crease in the back of his skull. Behind him was a taller man with broad shoulders and neatly trimmed red hair and beard.

Tony scrambled to get out of the booth, but the second man shouted, "Sit!"

As he spoke, the first man drew a handgun from his jacket pocket and pointed it at Rita.

The red-haired man said, "You move, she dies."

Tony retreated back into his seat. Out of the corner of his eye, he saw Darcy emerge from the women's room. Hearing the man's command, she stopped short in the hallway and silently retreated back through a door at the rear. Tony hoped it was an exit, but thought it looked more like a door to a storeroom. He forced himself to keep his gaze on the two men.

The red-haired man turned to Connie, standing behind the bar.

"You the owner?"

Connie nodded.

"You know who I am?"

"I can guess," Connie said, sounding more irritated than afraid.

"Ox Foley. Anyone be in there?" He gestured toward the restrooms.

"No. I don't think so." The lie came effortlessly. Foley seemed to buy it.

Tony reminded himself to breathe.

Foley barked loudly, "This pub now be closed." He looked around the room to the dozen or so other patrons. "Ye want 'ta save yer skins, get out. But don' be sayin' nothin'. If anyone o' ye call the peelers, I'll know who and I'll be comin' for ye. Now git."

No one hesitated. In seconds, the crowd was gone.

To Connie, he said, "You, too. Go home 'n sit on yer hands. The peelers show here, and I'll burn the place to the ground, no slaggin'."

"I'd rather stay."

"Your feckin' ears plugged? Ye stay 'an we be cleanin' 'em out with Goblin's automatic. Go. Now. And take yer cook with ye."

Connie untied his apron, tossed it on the bar, and walked through the door into the kitchen. A few muffled words could be heard, followed by the sound of a door slamming.

Foley turned his attention to Tony. The man called Goblin kept his gun trained on Rita's head. Tony assumed his sister was feeling a mix of fear and defiance. She had faced serious threats before, and had kept her wits, so he wasn't overly concerned about her reaction. He was, however, nervous about a potential accident.

To Foley, he said, "I'm Tony Harrington. I assume you're looking for me."

"Brilliant. A feckin' genius, this one."

"The gun's not necessary. I welcome the chance to talk to you."

Foley sneered. "It is, and you shouldn't."

"But I…"

"Shut up! I 'ave one question. Give me an answer true, and maybe yer friend's brains don' make a manky mess on the wall behind ye."

"I'll tell you everything. Anything."

"Where is she?"

"You mean Moira?"

Foley charged up to the edge of the table and slapped Tony across the face. The blow nearly knocked him over. As he returned to sitting upright, he was seeing stars.

Foley hissed, "You know feckin' well I mean Moira. Where. Is. She?"

"We don't know. We're searching."

Foley turned to nod at the man he called Goblin.

Tony nearly shouted, "For God's sake, wait a minute! You're here, so you must've heard that they took her from me."

Foley turned back to him. "Who's they?"

"I can't be sure. They looked and sounded Slavic. One of them wore a Vostok boot. They drove off in a white panel van. You must know all this already."

"Why she be with you?"

"Again, I'm not sure. She was asleep in my hotel room when I got there yesterday morning. They took her before we had a chance to talk. I assume she was there because she thought she'd be safe."

"Feckin' load 'o good it did her."

Tony nodded. “I agree. I tried to help her, but they kicked my head in before I could react. I’m sorry.”

“Sorry don’ help.” Foley stepped back, seething and appearing to consider his next move. He turned to Rita. “Who ye be?”

Firmly, loudly, she said, “I’m Rita, Tony’s sister.”

Shit, Tony thought, wishing she hadn’t been honest, and hoping her defiance didn’t cross the line into belligerence. Clearly Foley’s brutality was on a trigger as sensitive as the one on Goblin’s pistol.

“A strong one, ye be then?” Foley said. “I admire a strong woman. An’ pretty too. Maybe ye be needing a good Irish jaggin’?”

Tony could feel his face growing hot. It took every ounce of strength he had to sound calm as he tried to redirect the conversation. “Do you know who they are?”

Foley appeared momentarily put off by the change of subject, then said, “The bastards what took ’er? Yah, I know. Don’ take a genius. Anyone knows anything ’bout what’s happenin’ ’ere can guess. I ’spose that don’ include some gobshite American who can’t e’en keep a job.”

The comment stung, even though Tony realized instantly how ridiculous it was to be worrying about his ego when his sister had a gun pointed at her head. To Foley, he said, “So why are you here? You know we don’t have her, and you know we don’t know where she is. Why all this?” He nodded toward the automatic in Goblin’s hand.

Foley leaned down, placed his elbows on the table, and pushed his face forward until his nose nearly touched Tony’s.

Through a barrage of bad breath and spittle, he said, “We be ’ere ’cause I don’ know where they be hidin.’ We be ’ere ’cause you gave her up. *You*.” His right hand came forward and gripped Tony by the throat. He said, “We be ‘ere to deliver a message. Ye find her. Ye find her safe, ’an healthy, ’an happy. If ye don’, we be comin’ back for the both of ye, and ye get to watch twenty ’o my biggest men have their way with Miss Rita, then she get to watch while we dismember ye piece by piece. I be clear then?"

Tony nodded. After several more seconds, Foley finally released his grip. Tony choked, sucked in a big breath, and reached up to massage his throat.

Foley reached in his pocket, pulled out a simple, white index card, and slapped it on the table. Printed on it was a phone number. "When ye find 'er, ye call. No be a hero. Ye call. I be clear then?"

Tony nodded again, and Foley gestured at Goblin. The pistol disappeared back into his coat. The two men turned to go.

To their backs, Tony said, "Why did they take her?"

Foley stopped, but didn't turn around. "They think they can bully me. Think I'll stand down an' let 'em destroy my business. They be wrong. *Dead* wrong."

Tony risked one more question. "It would help to know who they are."

Foley resumed walking but said, "Nae, it won'. They be Russians. You 'ave to find 'em here. If they took her back to Russia, it be too late for her, and too late for ye all."

***

After the door closed, Tony counted to five, then turned to Rita. Grasping her shoulders, he asked, "You okay?"

"I'm fine," she said, chin thrusted out and head held high. "The creeps."

Tony could feel a slight tremble go through her, but took her at her word and let go. He scrambled out of the booth in time to meet Darcy as she calmly walked out of the restroom hallway toward him. He put his arms around her and held her tightly. "Thank God you're okay," he said. "Good job staying out of sight."

"As they say, better to be lucky than good," Darcy said, grinning. "Did you hear any of that?"

She stepped back, and her smile widened. "I did better than that." She held up her phone. "I recorded it."

"You what?" Tony's eyes went wide. "Do you know what he would've done if he'd seen you?"

"I was careful," she said, "and the risk was worth it."

"Nothing is worth risking your life!"

"Says the man who stepped in front of a sniper. Think about it. The cops have complained for years that they haven't had a current photograph of Foley. Now they will."

Tony didn't know what else to say, so he pulled her back into his arms and kissed her. Finally, he said, "You're too amazing for words."

"It's a team effort," she said. "Let's get back to work."

***

The three returned to their table and finally ate their stew, still cold. There was no one in the building to ask to reheat it, but they didn't complain. They liked having the privacy of an otherwise empty room. The only foray onto Connie's turf was Tony's trip behind the bar to brew and pour them all fresh cups of coffee. It was likely to be a long night.

As they ate, their conversation returned to the case. First, they agreed to keep the video a secret for now. Tony pointed out how dangerous it would be for Darcy if Foley knew she had it.

He said, "We can't be sure who we can trust. Foley obviously has connections everywhere." Darcy and Rita nodded their agreement, and Tony added, "For example, it occurs to me that someone must have told him we were here. He and his goon didn't come in here asking about us. They knew. They stormed right up to our table."

He swallowed hard. The thought that someone nearby was in touch with Foley was chilling. "We need to be very careful about where and when we discuss things."

Rita instinctively looked around at the empty tables, then said, "So who is she?"

"You mean Moira," Darcy said, more statement than question.

"Yes. Why is Foley so desperate to find her, and why do the Russians think they can use her to coerce him into standing down?"

"Has to be a lover or a family member," Tony said.

"I'd say family," Darcy said. "He strikes me as the kind of guy who'd throw a girlfriend to the wolves without a moment's hesitation."

Tony nodded. "He's old enough to be her dad, so I tend to agree with you. The age difference doesn't rule out romantic ties, but the intensity of his anger argues for the family connection. He's not only protective of her, he's incensed that someone attacked his family."

Rita asked, "Wouldn't the guard know if Foley had a daughter? That'd be a hard thing to hide."

"Maybe."

"Wait a minute," Darcy said. "Let me see that." She indicated the laptop, and Tony slid it over in front of her.

As Darcy typed, she said, "You said Foley's sister had a married name, right? Kensington or something like that."

"Kennington," Tony said, spelling it for her. "It's a relatively rare surname in Ireland."

Darcy smiled, "Bingo!" She turned the screen to face Tony and Rita. On it was a photograph of Moira, posed in front of the entrance to the Dublin Zoo.

"I'll be damned," Tony said. "How did you...?"

"The instant I typed Moira Kennington into Facebook, her page came up. There are plenty of pictures to choose from. We'll be able to learn a lot about her life before she came to Allihies."

"You're amazing," Tony said. "So this means she's Foley's niece? That would explain a lot."

"Looks that way," Darcy said. "Foley's sister must be going out of her mind. No wonder he's desperate."

Tony sat back and said, "It also explains why she went to the coast early Wednesday. If that was her uncle's drug trafficking operation, maybe she felt obligated to be there. Maybe he insisted or called on her sense of loyalty to help with it."

With an edge in her voice, Darcy said, "Tony, you're still making excuses for her. Family or not, helping a gang smuggle drugs into the country is still a crime, still morally reprehensible."

Tony sighed, "You're right, of course, but it helps to answer the 'why' question. If she grew up in a crime family, it undoubtedly skewed her perspective. And family bonds are a powerful factor."

"Fine. If it makes you feel better…" Darcy's voice trailed off.

Rita said, "One mystery solved, and that's great, but we still have to find her. Photos from the past aren't going to help us figure out where a group of Russian thugs have hidden her."

Tony grimaced and said, "They could be anywhere." He looked at his watch. "They've had her for more than fifty hours. In that much time, they could've reached anywhere on the planet."

Darcy shook her head. "I don't think so. She's here. I mean, somewhere nearby."

"What makes you say that?" Rita asked, as both she and Tony turned to stare.

"They took her in broad daylight, at a time when everyone on the peninsula was on edge because of the murders in the cable car and the other two bodies found that morning on the coast. Plus, the area was crawling with police. The kidnappers had to have a place to take her that was fast and easy to access. They couldn't risk driving through the countryside in an easily identifiable vehicle. If their destination was farther away, they would've waited until after dark to take her."

"Logical," Tony said. "At least it gives us some hope of finding her."

"Still a needle in a bale of straw," Rita said. "There must be fifty remote farmsteads within an hour's drive of here."

"Probably not that many," Tony said, "and probably the Russians wouldn't have wanted to go that far. I bet the actual list of possibilities is pretty short." As he spoke, he was thinking about one large coastal property in particular where strangers were known to be living and working.

Picking up on Tony's comment about a short list, Rita said, "I wonder if Ryan had the same idea, and if that's why he's out knocking on farmstead doors."

"Maybe," Tony said, thinking, *He'd better hope he doesn't find them.*

Obviously, the same thought occurred to Rita. She said, "My God, what happens if he knocks on the right door? I never thought of that. We have to stop him."

"I agree," Tony said. "You should call him. Tell him at the very least, he shouldn't be out there alone. He should have me or one of the guard accompany him."

Rita took out her phone and dialed. After multiple rings, it went to voicemail. She said, "Honey, it's me. Please call. I'm worried about you."

When she ended the call, tears were blurring her eyes.

Tony said, "Don't worry. I'm sure he's fine. Probably talking with someone and doesn't want to be rude."

Rita nodded, but she was clearly unconvinced.

Darcy's phone buzzed, and she pulled it from her purse. Looking at the screen, she said, "Crap." She shut it off and returned it to her bag.

"What?" Tony asked.

"I have to go," she said. "Everyone back at Pinewood is fuming. I can get away with three days off set, but no more."

"Oh, Babe…"

"I know. I really want to stay, but I risk getting a reputation of being unreliable. More importantly, the cast and crew are working hard. They deserve to have me holding up my end of the deal."

"I understand," Tony said, and meant it. "What can I do to help? Can I drive you?"

"No," Darcy said. "A car is outside waiting. That's what the text was just now. It'll take me to Kerry, where a private King Air is waiting."

Tony knew she was referencing a large twin-engine prop plane. It would have her back in London in the blink of an eye. He shook his head. Even after two years, it was difficult to grasp how different Darcy's professional world was from his own. He winced as the thought reminded him that he no longer had a professional world of any kind. He pushed his chair back and stood.

"I'll walk you out," he said.

"I'll come too," Rita said. "We're done here anyway. I want to check our room to see if Ryan's there." She closed the laptop, gathered her things, and followed Darcy and Tony out the door.

Outside, Tony turned and checked the door lock. Then he turned back to Darcy. Wrapping his arms around her, he whispered in her ear, "You don't know what you're missing tonight." He flicked his tongue across her lobe.

She tensed, then chuckled, and said, "I do know what I'm missing, and I'm not happy about it. Save the thought. I'll be done in another couple of weeks, maybe less. Then I'll happily ride the Tony train to big-O land."

Tony could feel himself getting aroused. He pulled Darcy against him tighter so she could feel it too.

"You're sure you want to go?" he asked.

"I'm sure I don't. Sadly, I have a job to finish, and you need a good night's rest." She kissed him hungrily, then pulled back. "Stay out of trouble. Try to remember I love you."

"Love you more," Tony said, then sighed as she climbed into the back seat of the town car and drove away.

"Well, that sucks," Rita said.

Tony nodded and tried to maintain his sorrowful face. He didn't want Rita to know he was secretly relieved. He had a job to do tonight. If Darcy had stayed, she never would have allowed him to do it.

Chapter 25

Friday, May 29
Beara Peninsula, County Cork, Ireland

"Hello, Moira."

Moira squirmed in her chair, twisting her head left, then right, to see if she could see the man. It was a new voice, mellow and speaking perfect English. Its source remained out of sight, standing behind her.

"I'm sorry to keep you waiting for two days. It was unkind of me, but I had a long way to travel. My name is Darius Polshkov."

Suddenly, Thing One appeared at her side. He reached down and tore the tape from her mouth. She cried out briefly from the pain, then clamped her mouth shut. She was determined to show no weakness to these people.

The voice calling itself Polshkov said, "Do you know why I told you my name?"

Moira remained silent.

He said, "I want you to understand you will not survive this. It matters not what you hear or see. You will never have a chance to share it. You are alive now because it gives us some leverage with your uncle. When we no longer have need of you, I will allow my friends here to do what they wish to you. Then we will carve you up and leave your parts in a bag on his doorstep."

"You are a fool," Moira said, unable to contain herself. "When the Ox finds you, you'll beg for mercy like a wounded dog."

Polshkov laughed. "I like your style, but you are wrong. Do you know why I am called Darius?"

Again, Moira said nothing.

"I am named for Darius the Great. He was a god among men. Five hundred years before Christ walked the Earth, Darius ruled a vast empire from India to southern Russia. I am Darius because I, too, am a god among men. My enemies fall like leaves before me, to be crushed under my boots."

You're a pathetic, delusional egomaniac, Moira thought, but wisely kept quiet. She had no desire to fuel whatever horrors the man was planning for her. As if on cue, she heard a click behind her. She knew the sound. It was a cigarette lighter.

Polshkov said, "We're going to start small, just enough to get your uncle's cooperation, and the sizable shipment of cocaine he unloaded from the trawler Wednesday morning. His men escaped my sniper and took the drugs with them. You're going to help us retrieve what was lost."

Thing One was back, holding a smartphone and smirking. He stood at the foot of the chair, clearly preparing to create a video.

Moira shuddered and tears made tracks down her cheeks.

Polshkov came into view. Moira was surprised to see he was anything but imposing physically. She almost laughed. This 'god among men' was perhaps five-foot-seven and slender. He had gray hair and deep-set eyes. However, any temptation to laugh was quickly subdued when she saw his hands. In his right, he was carrying a simple metal rod, perhaps two feet long and the diameter of a pencil. In his other, he held a lit cigarette lighter, positioned under one end of the rod, where it glowed red.

"Dear God," Moira whispered.

Polshkov said, "Moira, listen carefully. When you feel the pain, I suggest you scream loudly and cry like a baby. Your uncle is being stubborn. If he doesn't respond to this video, we will have to come back and do something worse. Do you understand?"

Moira nodded, bracing herself.

Polshkov nodded to Thing One, who touched a button on the screen of his phone. Then, suddenly, the hot end of the rod was burrowing into the side of Moira's neck. She had no trouble screaming and sobbing.

***

Allihies, Beara Peninsula, Ireland

Once Rita was in her hotel room with plans to wait there for Ryan, Tony headed back across the street to the pub. It was after 10 p.m. and dark. Glancing around and seeing no one, he walked through the front door, and closed it behind him. When he had made a show of checking the lock earlier, he actually had made sure it was unsecured.

The lights were off inside, except for an under-counter fluorescent and a neon Guinness sign. It was all the illumination Tony needed. He walked around behind the bar and reached for a narrow shelf, tucked under the countertop. He withdrew a shotgun. A quick inspection under the light revealed it was a Webley & Scott double-barrel 12-gauge. It appeared to be beautifully crafted and meticulously maintained.

Firearms were relatively rare in Ireland, and required a permit, but Tony wasn't surprised that Connie kept one handy. Tony had spotted it earlier in the evening when he'd gone behind the bar to pour coffee.

He pushed the release and confirmed that shells occupied both barrels. He closed the gun and began digging around under the bar, looking for more cartridges. He stopped and looked up when he heard the door open.

"Didn't figure ye for a thief," Connie said as he strode across the room.

Tony stood. "I'm not. You'll get it back. I just need it for a couple of hours."

"Yeh, that be all it takes to rob some poor bloke in his roadside store."

"Don't be silly," Tony said, resuming his rummaging through bar towels, cleaning supplies, and a box of utensils.

"What it be then?" Connie asked, taking a seat at the bar.

Tony couldn't think of a reasonable lie, so he opted for the truth. "I have a hunch where Moira is."

"What!" Connie nearly leapt off his stool. "So call the guard, now. You don' be needin' my gun."

"No," Tony said. "First of all, it's just a hunch. I'm probably wrong. Secondly, if Moira's being held there and the Gardai come storming in, the Russians will kill her immediately. They won't want to leave her as a witness, and they won't want to take her along, slowing down their escape."

"Russians? That be who nipped 'er?"

"Yes," Tony said grimly. "I'm afraid so."

"Why?"

"It's a long story," Tony said.

"Give me the short version."

Tony considered, then said, “They’ve got a beef with her family.”

“An’ what ye be thinkin’ you’ll do?”

“I’m gonna try to find her—confirm if she’s there or not. If she is, I want to get the lay of the land, so I can give the guard good advice about how to get her out.”

“None o’ that requires my shotgun.”

“No, it’s not required. But I’ll sure as hell feel better if I have it with me.”

Connie sat again and ran his hand through his wisps of remaining hair. He said, “Ye know how te use that thing?”

Tony quickly demonstrated the opening lever, the manual safety, and the shell ejection mechanism. Regarding the latter, he smiled and said, “Apparently I won’t be needing that anyway”

“Yer feckin’ right ye won’t.”

Tony said, “By the way, I need your car too.”

“Feck that,” Connie said. “I’ll drive ye.”

“No,” Tony said. “Absolutely not. These people are ruthless. I can tell you from experience, they don’t hesitate to attack. I won’t let you risk it. Besides, if I’m alone, I’m less likely to be seen.”

Connie stared at him, then said, “Ye swear?”

“What?”

“Swear ye not be going somewhere to shoot those gobshites.”

“I swear,” Tony said, returning to his search under the bar. “Some quick reconnaissance, and I’ll be back.”

“By all that’s holy, what ye be doin’ back there?”

Tony stood. “I’m looking for more shells.”

“Ye be down on ye luck there, lad. I keep no cartridges here, ’cept what be in the gun. If I run into somethin’ needin’ more than two shells, I’ll be long gone.”

Tony smiled. “Understood. Where’s the car?”

***

Before he drove away, he decided to take one additional precaution. He looked at his watch. It was late afternoon back in Iowa. He took out his phone and sent a text to Doug Tenney, his best friend and former colleague at the *Orney Town Crier*.

If I go missing, contact Inspector Lynch with the Irish Gardai (police) in Dublin. Tell him 'copper mine baron estate.' That's all you need to know. Do NOT share this with anyone unless you're certain I'm in trouble. Thanks!

Thirty seconds later, he received a reply: *I thought you were on vacation! What have you gotten yourself mixed up in this time? I can't afford to come to Ireland to save your ass.*

Tony grinned and typed: *Understood. Smiling. Probably nothing. I'll tell you everything soon.*

Chapter 26

Friday, May 29
Beara Peninsula, County Cork, Ireland

Tony had little trouble returning to the spot on the main road from which they'd spotted the huge, baroque house on Saturday. However, finding a way to access the mansion proved challenging. Narrow, one-lane gravel roads branched off from the main road in several places, but it was impossible to discern which one might wander through the rocky hills and eventually get him closer to the estate. The darkness and lack of signage didn't help.

After two false starts, he decided to abandon the car and proceed on foot. It wouldn't be easy, but it would probably be safer. The occupants of the house might have the road monitored for traffic. He found a patch of grass next to the road just large enough to accommodate the car and parked. He removed the shotgun from the back seat, double-checked to ensure the safety was on, and began walking.

The trek was a combination of hiking and rock climbing. It took nearly an hour, but eventually, when he cleared an outcropping of stone, he spotted the house about a hundred yards away. Tony's approach was from the south. The house faced west, with a view of the ocean, so Tony was looking at a side entrance to the south wing. Even that had an expansive domed entryway with elaborate colonnades and other architectural detailing. Illuminated only by the moon, the monstrous structure looked ominous.

Tony crouched down and began picking his way closer to the house. Using boulders and occasional trees for cover, he felt reasonably certain he wouldn't be spotted. Logic said there would not be motion detectors on the grounds. The property wasn't fenced, which meant animals could roam the hills. Cameras might be in use, but they probably wouldn't be a factor until he was much closer. So unless they had guards with night-vision goggles, he was okay.

At twenty yards out, Tony dropped to his hands and knees. Tall grass obscured him from view. It also obstructed his view of the house. He considered it a fair trade. Being careful not to damage or even scratch Connie's gun, he crawled forward. About thirty feet from the house, the long grass gave way to a more traditional lawn. Tony paused and looked carefully in every direction.

He sucked in a breath and his pulse jumped when he spotted a man standing at the southwest corner of the mansion, staring out toward the sea.

Son of a bitch. I knew it!

The man was Ryan Stenford, Rita's boyfriend. Tony couldn't see his face, but he was certain. Taking another look around, he stood and moved silently forward and to his right. When he reached the house, he turned left and came up behind Ryan. He raised the shotgun and touched it to the back of his head.

Ryan jumped but didn't cry out.

Tony hissed, "If you make a sound, I will blow your fucking

head off."

"Tony?" Ryan whispered, turning to face him. "Put that down."

"I will not," Tony whispered back. "You're coming with me."

"What? Where?"

"We're going to make our way down the hill to an outcropping of stone about halfway to the water. Once behind there, you stop. We do this quickly and silently. If you shout or try to run, I'll blow out your knee. I swear I will."

"Jesus. Chill out. I'm going."

Ryan looked around, crouched, and began moving quickly down the hill. Tony followed suit, keeping the shotgun trained on Ryan's legs as they went.

When they arrived at the designated spot, Tony was confident they couldn't be seen or heard. In addition to the protection of the rock face, any sound was masked by the white noise of the ocean waves pounding the cliffs in the distance.

"Sit," Tony said, indicating a spot far enough away that Ryan couldn't try anything before Tony would be able to react.

Ryan sat.

Tony remained standing, with the shotgun pointed at Ryan's right kneecap.

"You're a part of this," Tony said.

Ryan said nothing.

His voice rising, Tony spat out, "You took her. You helped them."

"No, you're wrong. I…"

"You've been following her. I saw you. That day, on the hill above the beach. You've been stalking her. Rita told me you've been going out every night at the time Moira gets off work. You followed her to my room. You led them there!"

"No, Tony. No."

"Don't lie to me!" Tony clicked off the gun's safety.

Ryan's eyes grew wide. Then, unexpectedly, he broke into a grin and tried to suppress a laugh.

"You find this funny?" Tony barked. "Those bastards have her. Who knows what she's suffering because of you. I would kill you here and now, if not for Rita. But even that won't stop me if you don't tell the truth. Tell me why. What in the hell is your connection to a bunch of Russian thugs?"

Ryan seemed to contemplate what to say next.

Tony snapped, "Don't sit there trying to dream up a lie. Speak, or I swear…"

Ryan interrupted with a roar, "I've been *protecting* her! Put down the damn gun. I've been watching her to keep her safe."

"What?" Tony could feel the blood draining from his face. He felt faint and stepped back. *Could it be true?*

He reengaged the shotgun's safety, but kept it pointed at Ryan. He said, "Why would you do that?"

"I can't tell you that. I'm sorry."

"If you don't, an ambulance is going to haul a man with one leg off this hill."

"Tony, please. Just trust me."

"Sorry, but I don't trust you. I've never trusted you. Tell me. Now." Once again, he clicked off the gun's safety.

Ryan looked at the ground and shook his head. Quietly, he said, "Fuckin' cowboy."

"What?"

Ryan looked up. "I said you're a fucking cowboy. Riding in here with your shotgun, thinking you're going save the girl. You don't have a clue what you're up against. The men in that house are part of the Bratva Medved—the Brotherhood of the Bear. Their leader is a psychopath named Darius Polshkov, one of the most dangerous men in the world. If he catches you here, he will chop you into pieces small enough to mail home in envelopes."

"How do you know these things? Tell me everything. Now. Or I swear..." Tony stopped talking, took a step forward, and slipped his index finger inside the trigger guard.

Ryan sighed and said, "Because I'm Russian."

"What?"

Ryan looked up and nearly shouted, "Because I'm Russian! I was told to keep Moira safe because the FSB is trying to prevent a war. Polshkov is out of control. He's determined to take over the drug trade in southern Ireland, and he's using Moira to get what he wants."

Tony's brain wasn't keeping up. He said, "You're Russian? But you said..."

"It's called a cover, Tony. Yes, I lied. I've lied for twenty years. I would still be lying, but I must get you to put down the damn gun if I'm going to have any chance of saving Moira and killing Polshkov."

Tony's chin jerked upward, and he stared at Ryan, "Killing Polshkov? What are you? Some kind of assassin? A *spy*?"

"I'm a patriot," Ryan said. "I serve my country. I hope you can respect that. But for the moment, all that matters is that you understand our interests align. If we work together, maybe Moira has a chance."

It was too much to comprehend. Tony took his finger off the trigger, engaged the safety, and laid the shotgun in the grass at his feet.

Ryan instantly leapt up and produced an automatic pistol from behind his back. He pointed it at Tony's head and said, "I'll take the shotgun. Pick it up by the barrel and toss it over here."

"Ah, man..." Tony said. He picked up the gun and held it out. "I won't throw it. It's Connie's, and I don't want to scratch it."

Ryan leaned forward and snatched it out of his hands.

Tony said, "So what now?"

Ryan said, "I don't know. I should kill you. I *need* to kill you. You've heard enough to destroy me."

"So all that was true?"

"Yes. Especially the part about me being a patriot."

"And you kill people for Russia?"

"This is *not* normal," Ryan said. "The FSB almost never calls on me for anything. For years, I almost forgot I had ties there."

"But now?"

"Now, the leaders in Russia realize Polshkov must die. The alternative is to let southern Ireland run red with blood from two warring gangs. Bad for the Irish. Bad for the Russians."

"And Moira?"

"We have to get her out of there."

"If Polshkov dies, why would the Russians care? Why would you care?"

"Tony, try to understand this. I'm a good person. I don't want an innocent woman to suffer needlessly."

Suddenly, it dawned on Tony. "You killed the sniper."

"My God, do you have to know everything? You're just making this harder."

"Tell me."

"Okay, okay. You're right, of course. You weren't the only one who followed Moira across the peninsula to the shore Wednesday morning. You nearly spotted me when you stole…"

"Borrowed."

"Fine, *borrowed*, the bicycle. I arrived at the base of the bluff just behind you. I saw Polshkov's man up on the ridge, so I climbed up there and took care of him. Unfortunately, I was about one minute too late to prevent the shooting."

"Jesus."

Ryan said, "You've no right to point fingers. You've killed when you've known it was necessary."

Tony grimaced. He didn't like to be reminded how far he would go, did go, when circumstances were out of control.

"Okay, fine," Tony said. "We're both saints who just happen to kill people. So what do we do now?"

Ryan lowered his weapon and returned it to the small of his back. He said, "We work together. In any case, I can't shoot you."

"Because you need me?"

"Well, yes, but not that primarily. I can't kill you because I love your sister. I'm not sure she would recover if you died, and she would despise me for all eternity if she ever found out."

Tony wondered again if Ryan was being honest, but he was happy to accept it at face value, especially if it kept him alive. He said, "By the way, if all this is true, how do you know this is where Moira's being held?"

"I don't. I'm guessing. What about you? Do you have some intel that says she's here?"

"No," Tony said. "It just seemed likely. It's out of the way, has access to the water, and is big enough to hide whatever they're doing. The bartender's comment about the work being done up here made me think it's possible the Russians are using it."

A partial grin crossed his face and he added, "It would be ironic if we almost killed each other while prowling around the wrong estate."

"Ironic, but not very helpful to Moira or anyone else."

"Have you learned anything about the place so far?"

"No. I'd just arrived when some cowboy marched me down the hill at gunpoint."

"Very funny. So let's go. Maybe if we cover each other's backs, we'll get in and out of there alive."

Ryan nodded, handed the shotgun to Tony, and began walking back up the hill.

***

A dark, heavy blanket of fear enveloped Moira. It was slowly morphing into sheer terror. She was losing faith that Uncle Ox would find her, and she knew he would not bend to the Russians' demands. That meant they would be back, probably soon, to inflict more… She tried not to think about it.

The burn on her neck stung like an angry wasp unwilling to disengage, her muscles radiated pain from being strapped to the chair, and she was starving. The hunger was a tangible thing, like a fire burning in her abdomen.

She heard the door. Dread sucked the air from her lungs. Then she smelled food. *Dear God, food!* The aroma pierced her senses. *Is that beef? A stew? It smells like stew. And warm bread!* She could smell freshly baked bread. It bore through her nostrils, down her throat, and into her bowls, where it churned like an angry sea. *Oh please, food!*

Thing One appeared at her side. He looked down, smirked, and said, "Hello, Moira. Can you smell that?"

She nodded vigorously.

He said, "I have a deal for you. I have food, but I'm not going to give it to you. I want you to buy it."

Moira's eyes narrowed. She didn't know what he meant, didn't want to know. She didn't want to talk. She wanted to eat.

Thing One said, "So here's the price. I'm going to kiss you. If you kiss me back, if your kiss pleases me, I will let you eat."

Her eyes went wide. Her immediate thought was, *Yes! Yes, anything. I'll do anything*. Almost as soon as the thought erupted, a deeper part of her brain, or perhaps her heart, asserted itself. *This is just more torture. This is another way to break me. He wants to prove he owns me.*

Aloud, she forced herself to croak, "Feck off. I'd rather starve than please a piece of shite like you."

Thing One lashed out, striking her across the face.

Moira screamed in pain, followed it with a torrent of obscenities, and ended by calling him a coward. "You're not a man," she spat. "No real man beats on someone helpless."

Thing One reared back, as if to strike again, then relaxed. His brow furrowed, and he sneered as he grabbed her left breast. He barked, "You just wait. When the time comes, I'm gonna hurt you in ways you can't imagine. You're gonna regret talkin' to me like that."

Moira held her tongue.

Thing One said, "Darius told me to feed ya, but now I think I'll enjoy it myself. Try not to die by morning. We're gonna be making another movie."

When she heard the door close, she began sobbing uncontrollably.

Chapter 27

Saturday, May 30
Beara Peninsula, County Cork, Ireland

Am I really hanging out at midnight, in the middle of nowhere, with a Russian spy? Tony seriously wondered if he was dreaming. He often experienced long dream sequences filled with vivid details. As he and Ryan neared the house, they once again dropped to their hands and knees, proceeding cautiously. The rough terrain scraping Tony's forearms and shins convinced him it was all too real.

Just as they reached the lawn, a woman's scream ripped through the interior of the home. The two men looked at each other, then simultaneously stood and ran to the side of the structure. They crouched down in the darkness, partially obscured by a pair of colonnades near the south entrance.

Tony whispered, "Could you tell where it came from?"

"Not for sure, but I'd say from the east side and low."

"Basement?"

"Probably. That would be the easiest place to secure."

Tony nodded, then gestured toward the east. They scurried past the south entrance to the southeast corner of the mansion, being careful not to fall on the broken marble surface, nor to trip over pieces of stone and other obstacles that had accumulated on the once-grand courtyard.

Tony reached the corner of the house first and took a quick glance. He turned back to Ryan and whispered, "Can't see shit."

The three-quarters moon was nearly obscured by clouds. In addition, the east side was mostly in shadow.

"That may be good," Ryan said. "Let's go. Look for a basement access or windows and move carefully. A broken bone won't help us."

They spotted the narrow basement windows at the base of the foundation. Returning to all fours, they crept close to the first one. Tony was preparing to steal a quick glance inside, when both he and Ryan heard a man growl, "Darius told me to feed ya, but now I think I'll enjoy it myself. Try not to die before morning. We're gonna be making another movie." This was followed by a door slamming and the sounds of someone crying.

Tony risked a look, then pulled back and turned to Ryan.

"It's her. She's in some kind of reclining chair. Hard to see, but it looks like leather or nylon straps are holding her."

"I've got a knife," Ryan said.

"Of course you do," Tony said, sarcasm dripping off each whispered word. "Do you also have a rope we can use to climb in and out of there?"

"Sorry, but no. I thought the cowboy carried the rope."

Tony bit back a laugh. He had to admit, it was a pretty good comeback.

Ryan said, "Let me look."

They traded places, and a few seconds later, Ryan was facing him again.

Also speaking in whispers, he said, "We won't need a rope. It's not much of a drop. Eight feet at the most. As long as you stay up here, this will work. I'll drop down, cut her free and lift her up to you. Assuming she can raise her arms, you'll be able to grab her and get her out."

"And you?"

"I'll find a piece of furniture or a crate and use it to get up high enough for you to pull me out."

"What if you can't?"

"I'm Russian. I'm with the FSB. I'll have a decent chance of convincing them not to hurt me."

"Bullshit," Tony said. "If you're caught, you'll be dead before you can say 'Nyet!' Besides, I'm the one who has to go."

"You? Why?"

"Moira knows me. She trusts me. She'll respond better to me. If she's suspicious of you, it could cause her to hesitate. Any delay could be disastrous."

"Speaking of bullshit."

"Just give me your knife."

"No, I'm going."

"I'm going."

Ryan, exasperated, said, "This is ridiculous. How do we decide?"

"Rock, paper, scissors," Tony said.

"You're kidding."

"You got a better idea?"

"No."

Scissors won. Tony went.

The first step was to use Ryan's very sturdy, very exotic knife to chip away the caulk around the window. Once exposed, it was relatively easy to pry the old, rotting wood away from the glass pane. Tony then slipped the knife blade behind the glass and pulled it forward.

When a gap of three or four inches was achieved at the top of the pane, the two men worked together to pull it out and set it aside.

Tony quickly turned so his feet faced the opening. "Take my hands," he said, "and help lower me down."

"You're sure?"

"Just do it. We need to hurry."

Once inside, the final drop to the floor was just a couple of feet. Tony was proud to note he made it almost noiselessly, but not quite. In her chair, Moira began to squirm, apparently trying to turn to see what was happening behind her left shoulder.

Tony hurried to her side, bent to her ear, and spoke as quietly as he could.

"Moira, it's me, Tony."

She choked back a squeal.

"Shh. I'm going to get you out of here. Do you know, are you wired in any way? Any alarms or other devices?"

"I don't think so," she said hoarsely.

"Good. Great. Will the guard be back tonight? Is there a schedule?"

She shook her head, but said, "If he comes back, it'll be because he likes to touch me." Saying it aloud caused her tears to return.

Tony gently touched her face. "Moira, I am so sorry."

"How did you find me?"

"That can wait." Tony took the knife from his pocket. "I'll start with your arms, but try to lie still until I have all these straps cut."

She nodded.

Whatever material comprised the restraints, it was tough, and progress was slow. By the time he finished, Tony was sweating, both from exertion and from fear. He knew every moment inside the house risked discovery, and terrible consequences for all of them.

"Okay, easy now," he said, coaxing Moira into a sitting position.

She sniffled. "I don't think I can walk. I haven't eaten. I haven't been out of that chair. Just water twice a day."

Tony could tell from the stench, as well as from her gaunt appearance, that she hadn't been given even the most basic accommodations. *Damned barbarians*.

He didn't dwell on it. He bent over, leaned into Moira, and stood, draping her over his shoulder. He had no trouble carrying her to the wall under the open window where Ryan was waiting.

Tony said, "She's very weak. Reach down as far as you can." To Moira, he said, "I'm going to put your back up against the wall. A friend is above you. Try to lean back and raise your arms. He'll pull you out of here."

Moira mumbled. "Okay. Just give me a moment."

Tony could feel her swinging her arms back and forth behind his back, trying to get some feeling to return. He lifted her up, pressing her back as high as he could against the cold, rough wall, and said, "That's good. Whenever you're ready."

Suddenly, she reared up and Ryan grabbed her. Smartly, he spun her to face the wall, then pulled. In seconds, she was free and Tony was alone. He paused to listen, fearing the little noise they'd made would summon a threat. He heard nothing ominous, so he turned his attention to escaping. He scanned the room, looking for something to use to climb out. There was nothing.

He looked up at the open window and wondered if Ryan would leave him. It would solve the spy's very big problem. Five seconds ticked by. Then ten.

Tony had just decided he needed to try to exit out the door and take his chances in the house, when Ryan's face reappeared.

"Sorry," he said. "I had trouble finding a spot to set her down, out of sight and rubble-free."

"Explain later," Tony hissed. "A hand, please."

Ryan reached down as far as he could with his right arm. Tony jumped up, grabbed it with his right hand, and clawed at the cracks between the stones with his left. Ryan rolled back, pulling Tony with him. Soon he was out.

"Ouch," Ryan said. "I think you pulled my arm out of its socket."

"Small price to pay to save the hero," Tony said. "Since you're hurting, I'll take the first shift carrying Moira. Don't forget to bring the shotgun."

"Which way?"

Tony said, "The car I borrowed is all the way down the mountainside, just off the main road."

"Then we take the rental," Ryan said. "I drove it most of the way up here."

Ten minutes later, two young men and one emaciated young waitress, were in the rented Renault, headed into the night.

***

At the first opportunity, Ryan turned north.

"Any idea where to go?" Tony asked.

"No. Just away. Kerry is this way. It's big enough to have an inn we can access at 2 a.m."

Tony took out his cell, touched a redial button, and waited.

After eight rings, a groggy voice said, "Lynch."

"Inspector, it's me, Tony Harrington."

"Harrington? What the hell? Do you know what time it is?"

Tony ignored him. "We have her. We need your help."

"Have who? You mean Moira Blake? You found her?"

"Yes. We helped her escape. She was tied up in a basement. The Russians won't be far behind us. We need…"

Lynch cut him off. "Russians? You're saying I was right?"

"I'll explain everything, but first I need to know if you have someone in Kerry you trust. Or near Kerry. Someone you *really* trust. She needs food and perhaps some medical attention, but we don't dare go to a hospital or clinic. They'll be searching for her there."

"Let me think." After a few moments, he said, "Are you sure you're not being followed?"

Tony looked back at the dark road behind them.

"Positive. We got away clean. They may not even know she's gone yet. Plus, I can see the road for several miles back. We're the only car out here, at least for the moment."

"Okay," Lynch said. "I'm going to text you an address in Kenmare. It's closer than Kerry. A woman named Bridget will be waiting for you. Park on the patch of pavement to the right of the front door, near the garden. The trees will hide your car. She's a retired nurse. She'll know what to do."

"It sounds perfect," Tony said, "but are you sure you can trust her?"

"Pretty sure," Lynch said. "She's my mother."

"Your *mother*?"

"Yes. Now I'm going to get off the phone so I can call her."

"Wait!" Tony said. "One more thing. Ryan is here with me. Rita is alone in the inn back in Allihies. If the Russians have done their homework, and they probably have, they'll know she's there. They might try to grab her in retaliation, or to use as leverage. We need…"

"I get it," the inspector said. "I'll have a man outside her door in thirty minutes. Maybe less."

"Someone you trust!" Tony spouted, but the call had ended.

The address popped up in his text messages almost immediately. Tony plugged it into the GPS app on his phone, and turned on the speaker so Ryan could hear the automated voice as it gave routing directions. Less than twenty minutes later, they drove across a narrow bridge with arched trusses into Kenmare. Tony knew from the map on his screen that they had crossed the Kenmare River into County Kerry on the Iveragh Peninsula.

Even with the app to guide them, they made two errant turns as they tried to find their way through the narrow, tree-lined streets in the dark. Despite the frustrations of wayfinding, Tony's first impression of the town was overwhelmingly positive. Lush vegetation, well-kept houses, and tall, beautiful trees seemed to be everywhere.

Once on the correct street, Ryan slowed the car to a crawl. They scanned the houses for numbers or some indication of which one was their destination. Just as Ryan began to express his exasperation, Tony pointed ahead and to the right, and said, "Maybe it's the one with the old lady standing in the doorway."

The house was a modest-sized cottage, painted a light color that was difficult to discern in the dark. The exterior walls were smooth like stucco, and the peaked roof included a dormer with a window. Set back about thirty feet from the road, a well-trimmed lawn filled the space to the left of the door, and an asphalt drive to the right. On both sides, flower beds adorned narrow spaces beneath the windows.

Ryan smiled, turned the car through a gap in the fence onto the short patch of asphalt driveway, then turned right again and pulled up as close as he could to the garden.

Tony could see what the inspector had meant. A large tree, surrounded by a thick hedge, stood between the street and their parking spot. Their car would be invisible to anyone driving past on the road. Ryan jumped out of the driver's seat and opened the back door, reaching in for Moira, who was lying on her side in a fetal position.

Tony began to object, but Ryan said, "It's my turn to carry. You take care of greeting our hostess."

Tony grunted a begrudging approval, grabbed the shotgun from the car, and headed for the woman still waiting in the open door. Her build was slight and she had a stoop, but nothing about her seemed frail. Her hair shone white in the backlighting from inside the house. It was styled in curls that framed her face. Age spots dotted her arms, but her eyes shined brightly, even in the dim light.

Reaching the stoop, Tony said, “Mrs. Lynch?”

“You must be Tony.”

He nodded and switched the shotgun to his left hand, being careful to keep the barrels pointed at the ground. Mrs. Lynch took his right hand in hers. The grip was firm, but the fingers were attached at odd angles. *Arthritis*, he thought, forcing his gaze back to her face. She looked past him at Ryan, walking briskly toward them with Moira cradled in his arms.

She said, “Come in. Come in. Follow me.”

Tony stepped back to allow Ryan and Moira to pass and enter the house behind Mrs. Lynch. He followed, closing and locking the door behind him. He propped the gun against the wall, next to the door. When he joined the others, Ryan was placing Moira on a narrow bed in what appeared to be a guest room.

The woman turned to Tony and said, “I have soup on the stove. And there’s bread and tea ready on the table. Please finish preparing the tray and bring it in here.”

Moira’s eyes opened to slits. “Food?” she said hoarsely. “Thank you.”

When Tony arrived with the tray, their hostess said, “Thank you both for your help. Now please go to the kitchen and make yourselves at home. We women have some things we need to do.”

“Understood,” Tony said. “Let us know if you need anything at all.” They left the room, pulling closed the door.

As if on cue, Tony’s phone buzzed. It was Lynch.

“We made it,” he said, without any preamble.

“Thank God,” Lynch said. “Was she hurt?”

"Weak from starvation and from being strapped down for days, but I didn't see any actual injuries. No knife wounds or broken bones or anything."

Ryan said, in a voice loud enough for the inspector to hear, "She has a nasty burn on her neck." More quietly, to Tony, he said, "I saw it just now, as I carried her into the light."

"Bastards," Tony said. "Did you hear that?"

Lynch said he had, then added, "I'm on my way there now. I've been staying in Cork, so I'm only an hour away. Oh, shite."

"What?" Tony asked.

"I'm going to have hell to pay with my mother. She's going to ask me why I haven't been staying with her."

Tony smiled. He knew exactly what it was like to have a mother who wanted more of her son's time.

Chapter 28

Saturday, May 30
Kenmare, County Kerry, Ireland

As they waited for the inspector to arrive, and for Mrs. Lynch to finish tending to Moira, Tony and Ryan took a moment to recharge. They took turns using the tiny bathroom, fixed themselves a snack, and settled into a pair of deep-cushioned armchairs in the front room. Ryan was soon drooped over the right arm, fast asleep.

Tony, however, was too agitated, their rescue and escape churning in his mind. In addition, he had a white index card burning a hole in his wallet. He thought about Ox Foley's threats, especially as they related to his sister. Rita was at risk because her brother couldn't resist following Moira on Wednesday and getting mixed up in a smuggling war. The thought was almost too much to bear. He knew he had to call Ox Foley. It was Rita's only chance to return home safely, and to not spend the rest of her life looking over her shoulder.

Tony also knew that if he made the call, he risked Inspector

Lynch's ire, and perhaps worse. If he helped Foley in any way that advanced the gang's illegal activities, he could be criminally liable.

Damned if I do, damned if I don't. He continued to debate with himself, but through it all, he knew where it would end. He would make the call. Nothing was more important than Rita's safety and peace of mind. The only question was when…

He jumped at the sound of a rattle at the front door. Realizing he must have dozed off, Tony stood and rushed across the room. He picked up the shotgun and positioned himself on the blind side of the door, just as the handle turned and the heavy oak panel swung in.

Tony lifted the gun. It made it to the intruder's ankles before Tony recognized the familiar long coat and form of Inspector Lynch.

"Shit! You scared me," Tony said, lowering the gun.

The inspector spun at the sound of his voice. "Shite!" Lynch yelped. "Where in the feck did you get a firearm?"

"It's borrowed," Tony said. "I won't have it for long."

"See that you don't. It's not legal for you to have that." He glanced around. "Where's my mother?"

"With Moira," Tony gestured toward the small bedroom on the right, behind the kitchen. "She's helping her get cleaned up and fed."

Lynch's arrival woke Ryan. He stood and introduced himself.

Lynch said, "Rita's boyfriend, right? And you helped Tony find and rescue Moira?"

Ryan smiled. "Well, I'd say Tony helped me, but yes."

"Unbelievable. I guess I have to say good work, but I'm tempted to put you both in jail for criminal stupidity. Once you found her, why didn't you call me?"

Tony responded, "We heard her scream in pain and just acted. We couldn't leave her there and let those cretins beat on her."

Lynch didn't seem to know how to respond to that, so he said, "Did you two leave any Guinness in the icebox for me?"

"Might be one left," Tony said smiling, "but I don't think you'll find any of the leftover lamb chops."

"Pricks," Lynch said, heading into the kitchen.

He found beer, cheese, and bread, and settled into a chair at the table. "Sit," he commanded. "Tell me everything."

They sat.

***

Tony and Ryan described in great detail what they had learned about Moira, and what had transpired during Foley's visit to the pub in Allihies. They explained how they'd found and rescued Moira. However, they did not tell the inspector everything. As the two men shared stories and gibes, an unspoken understanding led them to avoid any mention of the conflict on the mountainside or of Ryan's true identity as a Russian agent.

From Tony's perspective, his silence was a matter of self-preservation. He needed Ryan's help. Outside the four walls of this cottage, two large, well-organized, and ruthless criminal gangs were going to war. Currently, they shared only one thing in common. They both wanted Tony's head. Secondly, his sister loved this man. If Tony turned him in, and he was arrested and tried as a spy, it would be devastating for her.

Tony had no idea what he was going to do about Ryan. He only knew he wasn't ready to divulge the secret to Lynch, or to anyone, just yet.

The inspector rescued him from his thoughts, asking, "What about the second car, the one you borrowed? Will it be spotted?"

"I called Connie as soon as we left in the other car. I told him where it was parked and encouraged him to get it out of there right away, so nothing would come back on him. I got an earful of colorful curses, but I'm sure he took care of it."

"Good. It would have been easy to overlook that one."

"By the way, I assume Rita's safe," Tony said, looking at the inspector.

At the mention of Rita's name, Ryan turned to the inspector as well, waiting for an answer.

"She's with two of our best," Lynch said. He turned to Tony. "One is the woman you met when she drove you to the cable car station."

"I remember. Good," Tony said.

Lynch continued. "They packed her things and moved her to the second officer's home. His wife owns a software company, so they have a big house with good security. It's near the Taiscumar Reservoir west of Cork. She'll be safe there."

"Not to sound like…"

"Yes, Tony, I trust them. She wouldn't be with them if I didn't."

"Sorry."

"In any case," the inspector said, "it was the best I could do at 2 a.m. I thought it was pretty good."

"You're right," Ryan said. "We appreciate it."

"So what's next?" Tony asked.

"I'm not sure," Lynch said. "I need to question Moira. See what she knows about Foley's gang, as well as what she learned about the Russians."

"They're members of the Brotherhood of the Bear," Ryan said. "The leader is a whack-job named Polshkov."

"How do you know that?" Lynch asked.

"Moira told me as I carried her," Ryan said.

The lie flowed effortlessly and credibly. Tony was impressed, and more than a little uneasy. In any case, he understood that Ryan couldn't tell Lynch the truth about how he'd come to know about Polshkov's organization.

The inspector said, "We've been worried it was them. When we heard the Russians were stepping up their efforts in Ireland, the Brotherhood seemed the most likely group to be behind it."

"Will you go after them? Obviously, we can point out where they were holding Moira. It's huge house. It could even be their primary base of operations in the south."

Lynch shook his head. "Surely they've cleared out, or will have by the time we mount an operation to take them on."

"Maybe not," Tony said. "In fact, I'd bet my Renault that they're not leaving."

Ryan snorted. "Don't get excited, Inspector. It's a rental."

Lynch grinned but quickly grew serious. "Why do you say they're staying?"

"They're going to think Foley took Moira, or somebody loyal to Foley. They know the guard wouldn't have pulled her out through a basement window. They sure as hell know your people wouldn't have left them unmolested and free to escape. So think about it. If they're confident it wasn't the guard, they're going to assume Foley's people will be coming to seek revenge."

"So they'll run," Lynch said. "Doesn't matter if it's us or the Foley Gang."

"It matters," Ryan said. "I spent a few minutes online reading about Polshkov. He thinks he's some kind of god. Thinks he's invincible. If Tony's right—and, as much as it pains me to say so, I think he is—Polshkov will keep his men in place. He'll see the coming fight as his chance to take control of everything in one fell swoop."

Tony added, "We know Polshkov is in the house. Moira saw him just a few hours ago."

"So if we mount an operation quickly, we could arrest them all," Lynch said.

"Exactly," Tony said, "as long as you can assemble enough

firepower."

"We have teams at the ready, waiting for an opportunity like this. Too bad Foley won't be there too."

"No?" Ryan said.

"Foley never gets involved personally. That's why he's been on top for thirty-five years. There's no way he'll show, especially now that Moira's free."

Tony sat up straighter in his chair. A wide smile stretched his cheeks and made its way to his eyes. "Think about this. He doesn't know Moira's free. She doesn't have a phone, and I'm pretty sure the Russians aren't going to tell him. Once Foley learns Moira's strapped to a chair and being tortured by Polshkov, he won't be able to resist. He'll come for her."

Lynch nodded slowly. "You may be right, but how will he hear the lie?"

Tony pulled the white index card from his pocket and set it on the table. "I'm going to tell him."

Lynch finally smiled. "Of course. I should've guessed the bastard left you a number to call. This could actually work."

The inspector's face fell again, and Tony said, "What?"

"I wish we had a decent picture of him… Foley, I mean. It would really help to show our teams who to watch for in the midst of a big, complex operation."

Tony's smile morphed into a chortle. He said, "Your wish is my command!" He pulled out his phone, typed a message, and pushed Send.

The inspector appeared unsure how to react. He simply said, "What?"

"Darcy has him on her phone. She filmed him in the pub."

"*What?* When were you…"

Tony interrupted. "Remember, it was just a few hours ago when

Foley assaulted us. We haven't exactly had an opportunity to chat. In any case, once Darcy wakes, she'll see my text and will send the video to you." He looked at the inspector, as if to ask if there was anything more. Lynch was silent.

"Okay," Tony said, "get your teams ready. With a lot of planning, and a little luck, you could strike a gigantic blow to the drug trade."

Lynch began making calls, rousting people from their sleep and setting things in motion. Tony excused himself from the table and collapsed onto the empty couch in the living room. He fell asleep with his hands folded in prayer, hoping to help with the luck.

Chapter 29

Saturday, May 30
Kenmare, County Kerry, Ireland

Muffled sounds, movement. Someone was nearby. Tony eased his eyes open just enough to see through tiny slits beneath his lashes. He was on the couch, where he'd been sleeping. The old quilt he'd borrowed for bedding was mostly on the floor, exposing his legs and boxer briefs. Sunlight streamed through the front window. He assumed he'd slept six or more hours, so it could be as late as 9 a.m.

He sensed the motion again, and turned his head up to look past the end of the couch nearest his head. Sitting on the neighboring armchair, rifling through his jeans, was Moira Kennington.

She jumped when he said, "I always knew you wanted to get in my pants."

She didn't laugh, or even smile. "I need your phone, Tony. Where's your phone?"

"You won't find it there," he said, reaching into the crack

between the couch cushions to retrieve it.

"Give it to me," she demanded.

"Where is everybody?"

"The inspector went to work. Ryan went for fresh rolls. Mrs. Lynch is in the shower. Now give it to me."

"Why so desperate, Moira?"

"I can't find a phone. The old lady doesn't have a landline, or she unplugged it and hid it somewhere. I have to call someone. I have to warn him."

"I'm sorry, Moira, but not yet."

"It can't wait," she said, reaching down beside the chair.

Even before he saw it, Tony knew she had the shotgun.

She pulled it up, aimed it at him, and said, "*Now*, Tony."

He turned and sat up, using his left hand to tug the quilt up over his legs and lap. He said, "If you hold the gun like that and pull the trigger, you'll break your shoulder."

"Dammit, Tony. Give me the phone. Please. I don't want to hurt you."

Tony tried to sound calm and friendly. He said, "You can relax. Really. I know you want to call your Uncle Ox. I know you want to warn him about the Bratva Medved and the crazy man who leads them."

"How do you know that?"

"A lot has happened since you were taken. I know all about you, and I know a lot about your uncle. In fact, he came to see me."

"Uncle Ox? When?"

"Last night." As Tony said it, he could barely believe his conversation with the Ox had been just a dozen hours previously. It felt like a dozen years. He said, "Foley ordered me to find you. That was unnecessary, of course. I would've moved Heaven and Earth to find you without your uncle's threats."

"Threats?"

"Yes. He pointed a gun at my sister's head and told me twenty of his biggest men were going to rape her. Then he described how he was going to cut me into pieces."

"Dear God."

"Yeah, pretty much my reaction, as well."

"So you found me. Thank you for that. I owe you my life."

Tony raised his eyebrows and nodded toward the gun.

Moira's face grew red, and she lowered the weapon. In a softer tone, she said, "Sorry. So did you call him? Did you tell him I'm safe?"

"No, Moira. Not yet."

"But why?"

"Because the timing of all this is really important. First, I need to know where he is. How long will it take him to get to Allihies?"

"Why? What are you planning?" The tension was back in her voice, and Tony could see her fingers tighten on the stock of the gun. In an act of bravery, stupidity, or blind faith—maybe a little of all three—Tony decided to go all-in.

"I'm helping the guard catch him. I'm helping the good guys put an end to his grip on the throats of the Irish people."

"What? You can't! Tony, he's my uncle. Please, if you care about me at all, you can't be part of hurting him."

"I'm sorry," Tony said. "The decision's made, and the wheels are in motion."

Moira nearly screamed. "He'll *kill* you! He'll kill your sister and your friends. He'll kill your parents, and your feckin' girlfriend!"

She continued to rant while Tony sat quietly and let her run out of steam. It didn't take long. The effects of her captivity had taken their toll.

When she finally sat back in the chair and let the tears roll, Tony said, "Listen to yourself, Moira. What you just said is exactly why we're doing this. Ox Foley is a murderer. He tortures and kills his enemies in the most horrific ways imaginable, and he murders the young people of Ireland with the poison he peddles on the streets. He forces innocent girls into prostitution and he steals hope from poor, working-class blokes who are just trying to feed their families. He must be stopped."

"But he's… No. You can't…"

"It all ends tonight," Tony said quietly. "We could use your help."

"My help? My *help*!"

He looked into her eyes. "Moira, it's time to choose. You have a chance to save yourself. To get out of that life. To go to school and have a real career and real relationships with ordinary people—people you can trust."

She shook her head as a cross between a croak and a laugh escaped her lips. "Don't be so feckin' naive. It won't happen, it can't happen, because the Ox won't let it happen. He's controlled everything, forever. There is no version of living where he's not in charge."

For the first time, Tony thought he might fail. Hearing her, he could understand how hard it would be for her to imagine another way of life. He set aside his doubts and tried again.

"Tonight, good people are going to stand up to your uncle. They're going to put an end to the Foley Gang. If you help, they have a better chance of succeeding. If you help, you have a chance to save yourself. If you help, there's also a chance to bring down the Russian bastards who put that scar on your neck."

"The Russians? What *are* you planning?"

Tony shook his head. "You have to choose, Moira." He stood and put his hand out. Moira pulled the gun closer, gripping it with both hands.

Tony smiled. "My pants, please. You keep the gun. I'm keeping the phone. If you choose to side with your uncle, shoot me and take it. I'll just be the first of many good people to die because you made the wrong choice."

***

They chose 3 p.m. to make the call. They figured if Foley was in Dublin, he would still have time to get to the coast tonight. If he was much closer, he probably would have enough patience to wait until nightfall to attack. Either way, 3 p.m. seemed the most logical time to light the fuse. *Just because it's logical doesn't make it right*, Tony reminded himself.

He was disappointed that Moira had not decided to help. Knowing where Foley was now would add a much-needed level of precision to their planning. It also would help to know if a shipment of drugs was coming in tonight. That could impact Foley's decision-making, as well. So far, she had spent the day in the guest room, coming out only to eat. Tony and Ryan were, in effect, her prison guards, charged with making sure she didn't leave the house or get access to a phone.

At the appointed hour, Tony sat at the kitchen table and removed the white card from his wallet. He took out his phone and entered the number from the card. Setting the phone in the center of the table, he put it on speaker mode so Ryan could hear.

"Speak!" It was Foley, charming as ever.

"It's me. Harrington."

"Ye best be callin' with wha' I'm waitin' ta hear."

"I am. I found her."

"Well, shite! Out with it. Where she be?"

Tony described the former copper baron's mansion and its precise location.

"Yer sure she be there?"

"Yes, sir. When I looked through the basement window on the east side, I saw her. She's strapped to a chair. Looks like she's in a bad way."

"Those feckin' hallions." Foley's voice was strained. It sounded like he was holding back tears, but somehow Tony couldn't picture that.

Tony said, "I wanted to help her, but you said to call and leave it to you."

"Feckin' right. I'm gonna make them…" he paused and asked, "What else did ye see? How many men? Weapons? Security?"

"Not a lot," Tony said. "A handful of cars plus the panel van in the lane, so maybe a dozen people inside. No cameras or motion detectors that I could see. No alarms were raised as I went up there and back, at least none that I could hear."

"Feckin' morons. Ye' di' okay, Mr. Harrington. Now go away an' forget ye ever saw me. Understand?"

"Yes, sir."

"An' Harrin'ton."

"Yes?"

"If I be down there an' she's no there, you and every person you love in yer life will be dead by summer." The call ended.

A quiet, feminine voice said, "Jesus."

Tony and Ryan turned in their chairs and saw Moira standing in the doorway to the kitchen. She walked up to the table, laid the shotgun across it, and said, "You're right. This must end. How can I help?"

Chapter 30

Saturday, May 30
Beara Peninsula, Ireland

Petrov was tired of talk. He wanted to act. Needed to *do* something. Instead, he sat at one end of the dining room table listening to Polshkov rant and watching three members of the Brotherhood as they stared at their hands and hoped their boss's rage would not turn violent. *Frightened kittens*, Petrov thought, a sneer forming on his lips.

When Polshkov demanded, for the third time, that the men explain to him how the woman had escaped, Petrov decided he'd had enough. He said, "They don't know. I don't know. This isn't helping."

Polshkov turned and stared at him, his features as hard as the face on the marble statue in the courtyard outside the window.

"You wish to speak, Arsendo?"

"Yes. The girl's gone. We don't know how. Obviously, she had help, and obviously it wasn't the Gardai. Screaming at the incompetent fools who allowed it to happen won't bring her back."

"So you're suggesting I do something differently? Something *better*?" The Bratva leader spat the words out through a snarl.

"I suggest *I* do something. Let me go out there and find her."

"You want to wander the countryside looking for an Irish girl? Wonderful idea. Perhaps you could stop at the guard station and ask if they've seen her. Or maybe she left a trail of bread crumbs. Or maybe you just want to leave so you don't have to get your hands dirty when Foley's men show up to take their revenge."

Petrov's face reddened, but his voice remained calm. "I'm not frightened of Foley or his men. If you need me for your little war, I'm happy to kill as many of them as you like. That still doesn't help you retrieve the girl."

"Why should it matter now? If she's back in the Ox's fold, we won't get her back. We've missed our chance."

"You forget," Petrov said, "she's seen your face. You told her your name. She can testify against you as the perpetrator of kidnapping and torture. You'll be a wanted man here, and if you're caught, you could be put away for a long time."

Polshkov snorted, but Petrov knew his words had struck home. If the Brotherhood was going to continue expanding its operation in Ireland, its leader needed to be free to travel here. Polshkov couldn't allow himself to become a recognizable felon, risking arrest every time he passed under the wrong surveillance camera.

His voice conceded nothing, but said, "So what do you suggest? Where would you start?"

"The girl was suffering physically, yes? I could check nearby hospitals and clinics. I could go to her employer and friends in Allihies and persuade them to help us." Petrov licked his lips. The idea stirred him. He pushed it out of his mind and said, "But first, I would find the man from the hotel, the one she was shacked up with when you took her. He will know how to find her. He may even be the one who helped her escape."

"Perhaps," Polshkov said.

Petrov could tell there was more there—something Polshkov was holding back about the American. It didn't matter. All that mattered was finding the girl. He cared nothing for Polshkov's problems. He cared about only two things. First, he must complete his assignment. His perfect record was essential to maintaining his reputation. In his business, reputation was everything. Secondly, he wanted the girl. He craved the kill. Hours of waiting and anticipating had elevated young Moira to an obsession. He must find her.

Petrov stood. "So it's settled. I'll gather my gear and go. Call me if Foley shows up with an army and you need my help."

The comment appeared to give Polshkov pause, and Petrov immediately regretted making the offer.

The Bratva leader said, "Wait. Let's think about the..."

His thought was interrupted by his phone. The ringtone was a grating blare, like a fire klaxon. Polshkov answered it immediately, saying only, "Yes?"

In moments, a smile erupted on his face and his entire countenance transformed from anger to excitement.

Petrov saw his opportunity and stepped away from the table to leave.

"Wait," Polshkov barked it like a military command. Into the phone he said, "One moment." He withdrew the phone from his mouth and said to his henchmen, "Paper and pen."

In seconds, both materialized on the table in front of him. To the caller, he said, "I'm ready." He jotted one short line on the paper and said, "I owe you. Name your price." He paused. "Ah, a very good choice. A night or a weekend?" Pause. "Of course. Use my villa at Krugloe. You'll like the view of the sea, and the neighbors are too far away to see or hear what you do. Shall we say this time next

Saturday?" Pause. "Excellent. She'll be waiting."

Returning the phone to his pocket, Polshkov clapped his hands.

Irritated, Petrov said, "You asked me to wait. Why? So I could listen to you fix up a friend?"

"Don't be an ass," Polshkov said, still smiling. "This is for you." He held out the paper with the single line he'd written.

Petrov frowned and took the paper, but didn't look at it. "Me? What is it?"

"It's your destination. A house in Kenmare. It's where the Ox's niece is hiding. *Now* you can go. And take someone with you."

Unwilling to express his astonishment or appreciation of Polshkov's accomplishment, Petrov simply nodded.

The Bratva leader said, "Just to be clear, let nothing stop you. The girl comes back here, dead or alive."

It was Petrov's turn to smile.

Chapter 31

Saturday, May 30
Bantry Bay, Beara Peninsula, Ireland

Heavy cloud cover was bringing the day to a close early. A light mist was in the air. Sam Kilborgen glanced at the screen on his single-sideband receiver. More modern and more capable weather forecasting tools were available, but Kilborgen never saw the sense in investing in them. He mostly relied on his barometer and his nose. The receiver was just a bow to convention. This evening, all three said it was likely to rain, but no serious storms were predicted. It would be a little rough out on the open water, but nothing he couldn't handle.

When he stepped down from the pilot's seat and headed for the aft deck, he once again saw a vehicle on the hillside, descending toward the dock. This was a late-model sedan, not a car he recognized. Kilborgen's stomach twisted, adding another knot he didn't need. He took a deep breath and positioned himself in front of the gangplank.

A young man, slender with dark hair, walked out onto the pier.

As he neared the boat, he asked, "Permission to come aboard?"

An American? What in the name of the saints? "What's yer business?" Kilborgen asked.

The American seemed to think about how to answer. Finally, he said, "I'm here to report on Moira, and to keep you out of prison."

Kilborgen gaped and took a step back. *What the feck?*

He composed himself and said, "Very well, then. Welcome aboard."

***

Kilborgen was just as Moira had described him—stocky with gray hair, a neatly trimmed beard, and gray eyes so light they were a half shade from being invisible against the white of his eyeballs. Even through the man's all-weather fishing garb, Tony could perceive his enormous biceps. Not a man you would want to cross.

Tony held out his hand as he introduced himself.

Kilborgen gave it one brief shake, then pulled back and said, "You mentioned Moira. What about her?"

"She's been found. She's safe."

"Thanks be for that," the fisherman said. "Where?"

Tony ignored the question and said, "She sent me here."

"She sent ye?"

"She said you're new at this—the smuggling. Said she could tell your heart wasn't in it. Said you'd welcome a chance to get out."

"Did she now?"

"She did. So I came to tell you today's your lucky day. The Gardai need your help. You want out? This would be a good time. Take advantage of being needed."

"First, Mr. Harrington, despite your Irish name, I don' know ye. I don' know why ye came to me. And if Moira sent ye, why she din' come herself?"

"I came to you because I know you're involved in the smuggling of hard drugs. I even know how you transport the contraband so you don't get caught. So let's not pretend you're innocent. In answer to your second question, Moira didn't come because she's hiding from the Russian bastards who took her and tortured her."

Kilborgen's eyes grew wide. "Russians? *Torture*?"

Tony nodded and said, "That's right. She suggested I come because she thought maybe, as an American, I could convince you I'm not some plant from Foley, or from the Russians. She thought maybe you'd believe me when I said you have a chance to get out."

"Which brings me to my secon' point. Ireland don' do plea deals. Don' give immunity in exchange for cooperation. None like ye see on American TV. Ain' no part of our justice system."

"Not officially," Tony agreed. "But the guard and the prosecutors decide every day about who to arrest and who to let pass. I have no authority to promise you anything, but I'm convinced that if you help us tonight, you'll be hailed as a hero, not a criminal."

"You drink whiskey?"

Tony wondered if he'd heard the man correctly. "Excuse me?"

"Come below an' have a nip wi' me. Tell me what ye want."

"Right."

***

Kilborgen downed his second shot of rye before agreeing to talk further. He'd insisted Tony drink with him. Rather than risk losing him, Tony finished his first shot and toyed with the second. As a light drinker, he knew his limits. He needed to stay sharp. He also didn't mind having a couple of minutes to gather his thoughts. Lynch and the authorities in Dublin had done a tremendous amount of preparation throughout the day. Tony needed to decide how much to share with Kilborgen, how much he could trust him.

"'Kay then," Kilborgen said, gesturing at Tony to speak.

"As I said on deck, we need your help. We want you committed to working with the guard, to dealing a serious blow to the smuggling of cocaine into Ireland. By doing so, you may save yourself, and you will absolutely save a lot of innocent kids."

"Yah, I get it. So what does 'committed' mean? What exactly are ye askin'?"

Tony took a deep breath and forged ahead. "For starters, we need the precise time and coordinates for your rendezvous with the cargo ship tonight."

"Yer askin' me to double-cross Ox Foley. Tha' be deadly foolish."

"If all goes well, you won't have to worry about Foley. But even if it doesn't, I think you'd rather die than spend twenty years in a prison cell."

"To be sure. There be more 'n one way o' dyin'. Ye need the info fer what then?"

"The Naval Service will meet the ship and commandeer it."

"The Colombians'll ne'er give 'er up."

"If they don't, the Navy's going to sink her. I'm guessing a torpedo across the bow will put an end to any resistance."

"An' while the blue coats be takin' on the suppliers, what'll I be doin'?"

"We need your boat on the northwest coast. A house there is being raided. The guard wants a contingent of officers to attack from the sea."

"The peelers got boats. The Coast Guard's got boats."

"Yes, patrol boats. Vessels that are easily recognizable. Your trawler has a much better chance of getting people close to shore without raising any alarms."

"The guard could grab any boat they need."

"I don't know about that," Tony said. "But if they just marched into a port and took a boat, it would raise a hell of a stink. People would be shouting about it from one end of the peninsula to the other. The risk of it reaching the wrong ears would be too great. You, on the other hand, will be discreet. Also, you have a large boat with twin engines. You're better able than most to deal with rough seas and a rocky coastline."

"Ye seem to know a lot about me," Kilborgen said.

"Moira told me a lot. I also saw you in action Wednesday morning."

"Shite! That's where I saw ye before. You were on the dock. Yer the one tha' shoved Moira into the water."

"It's all I could think to do. No way to know how many shooters were up there."

"Ye saved her life."

"You, too," Tony said. "You fished her out of the water and got her out of there."

"Don' be makin' me a hero. I was scared pure and ran away."

Tony smiled and looked at his watch. He said, "We don't have time to argue about it. If you're in, you need to leave. Getting from here to Ballydonegan Bay is going to take you several hours."

"Ballydonegan? What's there?"

"Your passengers. Inspector Lynch and several others will be waiting for you on the private dock in the north cove." Tony handed him the coordinates. "Lynch is a good man. Take care of him."

Kilborgen stood, put the bottle and two glasses in a rack by the sink, and said, "Ballydonegan. Shite! Yer right. I need t' go." He opened a drawer, took out a pencil and paper, and jotted some notes. He handed the paper to Tony. "There ye be. The time an' location for the Colombians."

"Thank you."

"You comin' wi' me?"

"Sorry," Tony said, standing. "I've got a car. What will take you hours to traverse around Crown Head will take me twenty minutes over land."

"Will I see ye there then?"

"No. My job is to look after Moira. I'm letting the professionals take care of the warring gangs of criminals."

"The peelers and me, ye mean," Kilborgen grumbled. "I'll be gettin' my ass shot off while yer slaggin' with Miss Dimples."

Tony grinned and shook the man's hand. "Don't get your ass shot off. It's my turn to buy the whiskey."

***

Once seated behind the wheel of the Renault, Tony texted the information about the Colombian ship to Lynch. As soon as he finished, his phone buzzed. He saw it was Ryan.

"Hey, what's…"

"They took her!"

Tony pulled the phone away from his ear. Ryan was screaming.

"Who? When?" Tony shouted.

"Those Bratva bastards! They have her!"

Tony started the car, put it in gear, and hit the gas. As he lurched up the narrow lane toward the main road, he said, "What happened?"

"I was in the loo. I heard Mrs. Lynch answer the door. She screamed, then Moira screamed. I ran into the hall, and they already had Moira out the door."

"So go after them!" Tony yelled. "Take her car! Flag down a car. Do *something*!"

"I can't. Fuck. I can't. Mrs. Lynch is hurt. A wound in her side is bleeding. They stabbed her. I have to help her."

Tony couldn't argue with that. He slammed his hand against the steering wheel. "Shit, shit, shit."

"I'm sorry. Hang on," Ryan said.

Tony turned onto pavement and stomped on the accelerator again. Ryan returned. Tony could tell his phone was now in speaker mode.

"I'm in her car. I'm headed to the hospital. You have to stop them. You know where they're going. I'm not sure where you are, but I bet you're at least as close as they are. Beat them there. Stop them before they get her back into that fortress. In a few hours, it could be a war zone."

Tony slowed, allowing the car to squeal around a narrow curve, then pushed his speed up again.

He shouted, "I'll try, but I don't even have a weapon. I left the shotgun with you and Moira."

Ryan said, "Actually, you do. Once Moira agreed to help us, I put my automatic in the car's glove box. It's fully loaded, a nine-millimeter with seventeen rounds."

"Well, that's something," Tony said. "What are they driving? What do they look like?"

"Same as before," Ryan said. "White panel van. Two dark-haired brutes."

Tony grimaced. *Probably the same bastards who took her from my room.* He slammed on the brakes, skidded around another curve, and hit the gas.

"What are you doing?" Ryan asked.

"Driving too fast," Tony said. "These roads wouldn't qualify as bike trails in Iowa. And did I mention the damn steering wheel is on the wrong side?"

He hit the brakes again, avoiding a lamb on the left side of the road. A quick glance told Tony it was a straggler. Moments earlier, he would have encountered a whole herd of sheep crossing his route. Ryan said, “Slow down a little. You can’t help Moira if you’re wrapped around a tree somewhere.”

“I hear you. I gotta go. I need two hands to negotiate these cow-paths.”

“That’s okay. I’m just pulling into the hospital drive. Good luck.”

Yeah, luck. Tony frowned and eased off, but not much. When he came to a stop sign, he paused long enough to put his destination into the phone’s GPS app. Getting lost also wouldn’t help. As soon as the virtual assistant told him which way to turn, he was back at full bore.

***

Immediately after the hospital staff secured Mrs. Lynch on a gurney, Ryan turned and left. A woman called after him, undoubtedly wanting to ask who she was, what had happened, and a hundred other questions. Ryan had no interest in answering any of them. More importantly, he had orders from the FSB to protect Moira and kill Polshkov. He couldn’t do either one from a hospital waiting room. He ran to the parking spot where he had left Mrs. Lynch’s Volkswagen Polo. He squeezed back into the tiny, two-door car, quickly checked the gas gauge, buckled in, and headed south toward the baroque mansion.

He wasn’t religious, but as he drove, he found himself pleading to whatever higher power might exist in the universe. *Please, please protect them*. Tony simply must succeed. Must survive. Must save Moira, again.

He’d never felt such desperation. He tried to slow his breathing so he wouldn’t hyperventilate, tried to loosen his grip on the steering wheel. After a few minutes, he realized he was hunched forward in the seat, as if willing his body to reach his destination sooner. None of it was helping. None of it *could* help. He knew this because it was all his fault. Moira was back in the Brotherhood's hands and Tony was racing toward a confrontation he couldn't win all because he, the hotshot Russian agent, had fucked up.

Chapter 32

Saturday, May 30
Beara Peninsula, Ireland

Tony crested a hill and peered through the near-darkness at a tiny village in the valley up ahead. "Village" was an overstatement; it was a wide spot in the road, with a pub, a gas station, a market, and a half dozen houses. The pub was the one Ryan, Rita, and he had visited during their sightseeing tour the previous Saturday. In other words, he'd arrived. Although it couldn't be seen from this stretch of road, Tony knew the manor sat on the bluff on the opposite side of the valley, facing the ocean to the west. In two minutes, he would be at the entrance to the lane that wound through the mountain pass to the house. Thanks to Ryan, he now knew which was the correct one.

What am I doing? he wondered. *I'm not prepared for this. I can't fight those two cretins on my own.* Subconsciously, he reached up and rubbed his temple where the Russian's boot had connected. *Either of those guys could break me in half like a twig. I'm gonna get killed. And for what?*

Ryan's "cowboy" comment resurfaced in his mind. *I'm not just trying to be the hero, am I? There must be more than my ego at work here.*

The litany of self-doubts and fears continued, but didn't slow him down. He pressed forward. The bottom line was, Moira had sought refuge with him. He simply could not leave her to suffer more, and perhaps worse, abuse at the hands of those goons.

He scanned the roads for as far as he could see to the northeast. There was no sign of the white van, no sign of any headlights at all. He raced down the hill and slowed only when he reached the correct turnoff. Immediately after making the turn, he skidded to a stop, took a deep breath, and prayed he wasn't too late.

Think. Think!

The lane had a stone wall along the left side, perhaps three-and-a-half feet tall, and a ditch abutting the other. The edge where the lane met the ditch was uneven, undoubtedly the result of rainwater erosion. Tony pulled the sedan to the far left, as if trying to be courteous to someone wanting to pass. However, he picked a spot where the ditch encroached farthest into the road's surface and stopped. While parked there, any vehicle with four wheels, especially a van, would be unable to pass. He turned off the engine and put the key in his pocket.

He reached down and popped the hood release, then got out and raised it. He returned to the car, reached in, and retrieved Ryan's gun, a Glock 17, from the glove box. Tony knew a little about guns. He ejected the mag and confirmed it was fully loaded, then snapped it back into place. He noted the weapon had no manual safety. Assuming he could trust the manufacturer's internal safety mechanisms, he tucked the pistol in his belt, nestled against his spine. Whether or not the automatic would be enough would depend upon the Russians. Because this was Ireland, they might not have any guns at all. As far as Tony knew, the two men had not displayed any firearms in either of their assaults on Moira. On the other hand, because they were Russian criminals, they could be carrying anything from handguns to assault rifles, or grenade launchers for that matter. Ryan somehow had procured a handgun in Ireland, so Tony had no doubt the Brotherhood could do as much or more.

He looked around and formulated a hint of a plan. He climbed over the stone fence and dropped down on the other side, then walked along it, back toward the intersection with the main road. He crouched down and waited. It occurred to him how outrageous it was that he was hoping two Russian enforcers would be coming soon.

Outrageous or not, he got his wish. Less than five minutes later, he heard a vehicle turn off the road, start up the lane, and stop. Two doors slammed. Footsteps. Then, from the direction of his parked Renault, he heard loud exclamations in a foreign language, almost certainly Russian. He risked a peek.

As he hoped, both men were standing near the car. Their curses were interrupted by occasional efforts to resolve their problem, such as checking the car for keys, and examining the ditch to confirm they couldn't risk driving off the edge of the road.

While they did this, Tony scurried along the remaining few feet of fencing to where it ended at the intersection. He peered around the end to confirm the men weren't coming back already, then sprinted to the rear of the van. Because the growing darkness could aid an escape, he thought momentarily about opening the back and removing Moira. However, it seemed likely the van door would activate an interior light, alerting the kidnappers. Also, Moira was almost certainly tied up. He didn't have the time or means to free her, and if he tried to carry her, the two brutes would chase him down in seconds.

Only one option remained, an option made easier by the fact the kidnappers had left the engine running. Tony quickly moved along the right side of the van, pulled open the driver's door, and climbed in. He threw the van into reverse and stomped on the gas, throwing up a cloud of gravel and dirt. When the rear tires hit the paved road behind him, the van lurched back. He slammed on the brake, pulled the shift lever to Drive, twisted the wheel to the right, and floored it again.

He could hear the two Russian men screaming, and could hear Moira squirming in the back, trying to talk through some kind of gag. He ignored it all and concentrated on driving, wanting to put as much distance as possible between the van and the Russians.

Ryan's Glock was digging into the skin at his tailbone. Tony reached back and pulled it free, setting it on the center console. He settled into his seat and began considering next steps. It was a glorious escape except for one detail. Moments after the van found a straight stretch of road and the ride became less tumultuous, Tony felt a cold metal surface pressing into his skull, just behind his left ear. A man's voice, low and accented, said, "Stop. Stop now, or you die."

Tony kept going, trying to buy himself time to think. It had not occurred to him that a third man would be in the van. Shit, shit, shit. He accelerated even more, reaching over 80 KPH. He couldn't do the math, but he thought that was about 50 miles per hour. He knew the gunman couldn't shoot him at that speed without risking serious, and perhaps fatal, injuries to himself.

The voice said, "You think you're smart." The pressure from the man's gun disappeared.

Tony's heart sank as he realized what was coming. He was right.

The voice snarled, "I am going to shoot the girl. I will start with her legs and move my way up. One shot every three seconds until you stop."

Tony withdrew his foot from the accelerator and let the van slow. He guessed they were two miles or so from the pair of kidnappers they'd left behind. He wanted to keep that distance growing.

"I said stop!" the man screamed.

Braking and pulling to the left side of the road, Tony let the left wheels stray onto the tiny strip of shoulder. Their speed slowed to 30, 20. Then, when the speedometer read 15, Tony slammed down on the brake pedal. The van lurched to a stop, throwing Tony against the steering wheel, and, he hoped, throwing the gunman onto the floor. He knew about the surprisingly violent effects of a sudden stop at as little as 10 miles per hour. He threw the shifter into Park and spun in the driver's seat. Dismayed but not surprised, he saw the Glock was gone. He assumed it had been thrown to the floor as the van screeched to a halt.

Knowing he couldn't take the time to search, he didn't pause for even one heartbeat. He clawed his way over the center console between the seatbacks, and fell into the rear compartment just as the man collected a pistol from the floor and turned to fire.

With only the dashboard lights illuminating the interior, Tony lashed out blindly. His left forearm connected with the man's hands, pushing them up, as his right fist found the man's face. He heard the satisfying crunch of cartilage. Simultaneously, the man screamed and the gun went off, blowing a hole through the roof of the vehicle. The sound in the enclosed space was deafening. Moira screamed into her gag and tried to squirm away. Tony kept scrambling toward the Russian, reaching up to grab the man's gun with his left hand and taking a second swing with his right.

However, the man was too quick. He twisted to his right, pulled the gun free, and rolled over on the van's metal floor. Tony's punch missed and hit the metal strut next to the side door. "Damn!" he bellowed as the pain shot through his hand, wrist, and arm. He turned in time to see the man pull himself to his knees, trying to get the gun aimed.

Tony lunged forward again and the two men locked arms, Tony's left hand forcing its way up to grip the weapon. He pushed the man into the corner and down, hoping his weight and leveraged position would prevent the attacker from regaining a line of fire. As a tactic, it worked fine, but Tony quickly realized he couldn't sustain it. The man was strong. Inch by inch, he pulled his arm down, overpowering Tony's muscles as they strained to hold him.

As Tony weakened, the man grinned. Tony sensed it more than saw it in the dark. The fury it ignited fueled a renewed effort to stop him. The man's progress slowed, but only momentarily.

"It's over," the man hissed. "You are going to die, and the girl is going back with me."

Tony only grunted, desperately trying to hold on.

The man said, "Killing her friends was a mistake. I don't make mistakes. I'm going to make this right. When my employers have what they need, I'm going to enjoy killing this one too."

Teeth gritted, face hot, breathing rapidly, Tony gripped, and pushed, and… lost.

The man broke free, turning to his right and springing forward. The action cast Tony aside, and he fell onto his back. The man, crouched under the van's roof, turned and swung the gun in Tony's direction. Instinctively, Tony raised his right leg and kicked hard. His shoe connected with the man's chest, knocking him backward. He landed on his back, on top of Moira.

Suddenly, her hands appeared above the man's head. They were secured with zip ties but had no trouble reaching over and down, and pulling back toward his neck. In an instant, Moira had her assailant in a stranglehold. She leaned back, grunting, her left forearm straining against his throat. The man choked and tried to turn the gun on her. Tony reached out and pulled it from his grasp.

The man didn't seem to notice. His hands flailed, groping at Moira's arms.

With the assailant's gun in hand, Tony sat back and said, "Good job. I got it!"

Moira didn't stop.

Tony said, "It's okay, Moira. I've got him covered."

Still, she didn't stop. If anything, she squeezed harder.

The man's eyes bulged and he clawed at her, then banged his hands on the van's floor.

"Moira? *Moira!*" Tony reached for her, but she kicked at him and strained harder to keep her arm locked against the man's throat.

Avoiding her kicks, Tony pushed himself up next to her and began pulling at her arms. She shook her head wildly and yelled something indistinguishable into her gag.

Tony realized he was going to have to do something drastic, perhaps even strike her, to get her to stop. Before he acted, the man suddenly lurched, stopped struggling, and went limp. Tony turned and looked at him in shock, then turned to Moira. She still was gripping the Russian. Tears poured down her cheeks.

Tony bent down and put his ear to the man's chest. He sat up and said, "You can let go. He's dead."

Another ten seconds ticked by before Moira finally eased her grip, more from exhaustion, it appeared to Tony, than from any decision to quit.

Tony pulled the body off her, searched it, and found a folding knife in a trouser pocket. He opened it, cut Moira's ties, and removed the gag.

She immediately lunged forward and threw her arms around him, sobbing into his chest.

He had no idea what to say, so he let her cry for several seconds. Then he gripped her shoulders and pushed her back. "There are others, and they'll be coming. We have to go."

Moira nodded.

When Tony turned toward the front, he counted four people approaching the van. He said, "We've attracted a crowd. Probably from a nearby farm. Cover him up with whatever you can find and lie still back there."

He climbed back over the center console and into the driver's seat. He looked straight ahead and didn't acknowledge any of the stares or shouted questions as he put the van in gear and drove away.

***

Ryan slowed and turned into the lane leading to the former copper baron's mansion. He stopped. The rented Renault, the car Tony had been driving, was parked in the lane, blocking passage. The hood was up and the driver's door was open.

"Dermo," he cursed in Russian. "That can't be good."

He backed out of the lane and went looking for another path he could use to get partway to the house. As he drove, he took out his phone. Tony answered on the third ring. *Hallelujah.* "Where are you?" Ryan asked.

Tony said, "Not exactly sure. Driving around southern Ireland with an exhausted waitress and a dead body."

"Indeed? I take it the waitress is alive and well?"

"Alive, yes, and moderately traumatized, but no more than I am."

"Wonderful to hear," Ryan said. A chuckle escaped his lips, and he added, "…that she's alive, not that you're both traumatized."

"How about you?"

Ryan said, "I'm not lost, but I am searching. It seems my partner has blocked the lane I intended to use to get to the scene of tonight's action."

"Lynch told us to stay away from there."

"Yes, I believe he did," Ryan sighed. "And I'd love to obey.

Sadly, I have orders from a higher power."

Tony's voice rose. "Jesus, Ryan, you can't go in there. It's going to be a hellhole."

"Relax. I fully intend to be finished and out of there before the excitement begins."

"But I have your gun."

"You have a gun."

"Good grief. How many… Never mind. Even if you succeed, Lynch will shoot you himself when he finds out."

"Just wish me luck, Tony. Which reminds me, I need to tell you two important things, in case this all goes south."

"Ah, man."

"Just listen. The first thing is, the Russians found us at Mrs. Lynch's place because of me."

"*You?*" Tony sounded genuinely shocked.

"I called the FSB and gave a report. I told them where we were. I should have guessed that Polshkov would have someone on the inside. His mole obviously reported it all back to the Brotherhood."

"That makes sense," Tony said. "But if it's true, it means Polshkov knows all about you. He knows who you are. He knows you're coming. You can't win under those circumstances."

"I have to try," Ryan said, "Which brings me to my second point. If I don't make it, tell Rita how much I love her. She is the one truly good thing in my life."

"Ryan, please don't do this. Let the Gardai take care of Polshkov."

"I stand corrected," Ryan said, ignoring Tony. "You're the other good thing in my life. Take care of yourself and Moira, and Rita, of course. I'll see you tomorrow." The call ended.

For the second time that day, Tony found himself banging the palm of his hand against the steering wheel.

***

Less than a minute later, Tony's phone buzzed again. It was Lynch.

"Where are you?" The inspector sounded angry.

Tony thought it wise to adopt a more somber tone than he had with Ryan.

"I'm on a highway somewhere north of ground zero, but south of Kenmare. Moira's with me. The Russians took her again, but I managed to get her back. She killed one of her captors."

Silence. When Lynch finally spoke, his voice was more even-tempered. "Is she okay?"

"I think so. We've barely spoken. I'm driving the Russians' van, trying to put some distance between us and them. I'd welcome any suggestions about where to go."

"Keep going. By the time you get to Kenmare, I'll think of something. So what happened?"

Tony described to him everything that had occurred since arriving at Kilborgen's boat.

Lynch's voice was strained, and loud. "So why am I hearing about this now? Moira's kidnapped and my mother's injured. My *mother* for shite's sake! And you don't bother to call me?"

"I've kinda had my hands full."

"Bullshit!" the inspector said. "You could've alerted me in thirty seconds or less. *Should* have alerted me."

"You're right. I'm sorry. Is this the first you've heard about your mom?"

"No. The hospital called me. Someone there knew her."

"Is she okay?"

"Hurting, and hopping mad, but she'll live."

"Thank God for that."

"I've got an officer headed there to stand guard. The loss of manpower is the last thing I needed tonight, not to mention the worry." He paused, then said, "How did they find you? How in the hell did the Brotherhood know Moira was in my mother's home?"

Tony knew he couldn't tell him the truth about Ryan, so he simply said, "I don't know. I didn't talk to anyone, not even Rita or Darcy."

The inspector sighed loud enough to be heard over the phone, and said, "A worry for another day. Tonight, we have, as you Americans like to say, bigger fish to fry."

Before hanging up, Lynch suggested to Tony a plan for hiding in plain sight.

Tony thanked him, wished him luck, and ended the call.

***

When they arrived in Kenmare, their first stop was not one Lynch had suggested. They returned to his mother's house. They knew it wouldn't be safe to stay there but thought it worth the risk to grab some things they needed. They gathered up blankets, pillows, bottles of water, and small portions of food and loaded them in the van. Digging around in some kitchen drawers, Tony found a few simple tools and stuffed them in a second grocery sack. In the utility closet, he found a flashlight and a spare set of batteries. He added them to the bag. They used the bathroom, made sure everything was turned off, locked up, and left. Tony's final act before going out the door was to grab the shotgun.

They drove across town to a car dealership Lynch had suggested. As the inspector had predicted, a line of trucks occupied the back row of the dealership's lot. Tony backed the van into an empty spot and turned off the engine.

He got out and walked down the row of trucks. Two small vans and one large lorry were among them. As hoped, the back doors of the lorry were not locked. The required padlock was missing. Since the interior was just a big, empty box, it made sense that no one bothered to lock it.

Tony returned to the van in which they'd arrived, stuck his head inside, and said, "How would you like to not sleep next to a corpse tonight?"

Moira's eyes grew wide enough to be seen in the dark. "Yes, please."

He climbed in and used one of the borrowed blankets to cover the dead man. Then he grabbed the sack with the food in one hand, the tools in the other, and said, "Bring the bedding and follow me."

Outside, he locked the van and led her to the lorry. He opened the back doors and helped her up into the box. Once inside, he pulled the doors closed, reached into the tool bag, removed the flashlight, and turned it on. He propped it up so it shone on the white ceiling of the box, creating an ambient glow that allowed them to maneuver.

Tony encouraged Moira to arrange her blankets and pillow at the front of the box, letting him camp nearest the doors. They put the food and water in the center and sat cross-legged on opposite sides. As Moira handed out napkins and snacks, she said, "I'm nervous about the doors."

"Oh?"

"If someone wanders past and locks them from the outside, we could die in here before anyone found us."

"Don't worry," Tony said. "My phone still has enough juice to get us to morning. And even if it fails, we have a shotgun."

Moira smiled. "Yeah, there's that."

"You okay?" he asked.

She shrugged. "I guess. I didn't know I was capable of such a… a…"

"It's okay," Tony said. "He was planning to kill you. We humans are wired to flee or fight, and fleeing wasn't an option."

She looked at him. "I don't regret it. I'm glad he's dead. Does that make you think less of me?"

"No," Tony said, and meant it. "After what you've been through, it's completely understandable."

She took a bite of cheese and washed it down with water. She looked hard at Tony and said, "You realize you've saved my life three times."

Tony shook his head. "Pretty sure you only have one life."

"You know what I mean. Shoving me off the dock, rescuing me out of that chamber of horrors, and hijacking the van. That's three. In each case, you risked your life to help me."

Tony shrugged, unsure what to say. He bit off the end of a sausage link and looked in the bag for a cracker to accompany it.

"How can I ever repay you?"

"That's not necess…"

"I know how I *want* to repay you."

Tony looked up. Moira's dimples were on full display.

"Moira, you know I can't…"

"I'd never tell," she said, her voice dropping half an octave. "No one would ever know."

Tony could feel himself getting aroused. It was tempting. Moira was attractive in all the ways that mattered to him: smart and brave, sexy and fun, good-hearted and, despite all that had happened, upbeat. And there was no question it would feel good. His mind instantly conjured up images of her naked, entwined in his arms and legs, exploring… Would it hurt to escape all this madness for an hour?

He surprised himself when he said, "I'm sorry, Moira, but *I* would know. What kind of man would I be if I broke my promise to the woman I love?"

"Well, shite, you'd be the kind of man who doesn't reject an Irish lass in her time of need." She pushed her lower lip into a pout.

Tony assumed she was teasing but couldn't be sure.

"Please believe me," he said. "This is not rejection. I desperately want to say yes. I simply can't."

"I think you're afraid," she said. "It's ironic. You're not afraid of snipers or drug smugglers, but you're afraid of Darcy Gillson."

"Maybe," Tony said. "I still can't." He couldn't admit to her that she had it wrong. He wasn't afraid of Darcy. He was afraid of Moira. If he partook in that sweet elixir and loved it, then what?

They finished their meager meal in silence.

Moira stood, stretched, and stepped over to her blankets. She began unbuttoning her blouse.

Tony turned his back. It was the hardest thing he'd ever done in his life.

From behind him, he heard her say, "If you change your mind, you know where to find me. I'll be over here in these blankets, sleeping in my underwear, waiting to give you the best jagging of your life."

Tony groaned, lay down on his bedding, and reached for the flashlight. Clicking it off, he said, "Good night, Moira. Sleep well."

Chapter 33

Sunday, May 31
Beara Peninsula, Ireland

At 1 a.m., Tony's phone vibrated in his pocket, waking him. He reached in and shut off the alarm. Lying quietly in the dark, he listened for, and heard, Moira's deep breathing. He felt for Ryan's Glock on the floor and re-tucked it into his belt. He stood and picked up the shotgun and flashlight. He stepped over next to Moira and lay them both within her reach. If anyone came through the doors after he was gone, she would have a reasonable chance to defend herself.

Exiting the lorry's box, he walked down the row of vehicles and climbed into the Russians' van. He didn't like the idea of driving around with a dead body for a companion, but he had no choice. He started the van and drove out of the lot. Less than an hour later, he arrived at the entrance to the lane accessing the copper baron's estate. He drove past slowly, noting the Renault was still parked next to the stone wall. He drove the van the half mile down the highway to the roadside pub and parked it in the lot near the rear of the building. Keenly aware of the corpse in the back, he checked to ensure it was covered by the blanket. He climbed out of the vehicle, locked it, and hid the key under a rock a few steps away. Then he walked back to the rental car, keeping a lookout for anyone who might have been posted to wait for the car's owner to return. The lane and surrounding area appeared to be deserted.

When he reached the car, he closed the hood, climbed in, and backed out of the lane. He knew the Gardai were coming, and he didn't want the vehicle to impede their operation.

He debated what to do next. He had no plan and wasn't sure why he had come. He simply had known he couldn't sit in the safety of a truck in Kenmare when Ryan and a lot of other good people were risking their lives here. He might not be able to help, but at least he wouldn't feel as if he'd abandoned them.

He assumed the Gardai were nearby. They probably were watching him now. He turned the car onto the first path he came to that was wide enough to accommodate it, drove about a hundred yards, and parked in a tall stand of weeds. When he stepped out, he scanned the surrounding area but saw no one.

As he had done on his first visit to the estate, he decided to walk. This time, he headed northwest, toward the ocean. He knew Lynch was with the contingent of officers arriving on Kilborgen's boat. Approaching the house from near the coastline might help Tony hook up with them. Again, he wasn't sure for what purpose. He just assumed if he was going to be here, it would be better to be with someone who knew he was one of the good guys.

When he was near enough, he looked out to sea and spotted a trawler churning through the whitecaps toward the shore. He only saw it in the darkness because it was running with full lights on, presumably to maintain the ruse that it was an ordinary fishing vessel.

Tony assumed it was Kilborgen delivering his cargo of special forces. Why else would someone be crazy enough to approach the rocky shore at night in rough seas?

As he scrambled to get nearer, Tony needed to remain frustratingly far inland and high above the water because of the jagged bluffs forming the coast. There was no beach down below, no place for a casual stroll. In addition, the irregular shape of the landscape prevented him from keeping the trawler in sight.

He kept moving. Each time he caught sight of the boat, it was nearer the shore and north of his position, in the direction of the old mansion. *Do they have a destination, or are they just taking their chances with the rocks?* Tony had trouble believing the latter. *There must be a cove with a protected dock.*

Suddenly, his stupidity hit him. He turned his back to the house, to avoid being seen, knelt, and pulled out his phone. Google Earth would show him exactly what was there. Except it wouldn't. His phone was dead. He knew he shouldn't be surprised, but knowing it made sense did nothing to quell the anger that erupted from his soul. A little forethought would have prevented this, he knew. *You effing twit!*

He shoved the phone into his pocket and resumed walking.

Through the trees and rocks, the house was now visible more often than not. Tony slowed his pace, bent low, and began picking his route more carefully. He also risked moving closer to the edge of the bluff, determined to see where Kilborgen was headed with his passengers. When he encountered a boulder as big as his garage back in Iowa, he picked a path around it. When he reemerged to a spot with a view of the cliffs, he saw movement on the next outcropping to the north. Two men with rifles hurried to the edge and began to position themselves facing the water.

"Not again," Tony groaned to himself. The men were less than fifty yards away, but a huge chasm separated them from Tony. To walk around the split in the rocks and confront the men up close would take time and would require him to traverse a long stretch of barren rock where he would be completely exposed. However, if Tony didn't act, it was obvious these snipers were going to shoot at Kilborgen's boat.

Not knowing what else to do, Tony pulled the Glock from his belt, pointed it at the men, and screamed, "*Freeze!*" As he said it, he wondered if he could be heard over the sound of waves crashing into the rock face, or if the Russians had watched enough American movies to understand what "freeze" meant.

Whether or not they understood him, it was obvious they heard him shout. The gunman nearest him jumped up and swung his rifle around.

Tony dropped to the ground on his belly and began crawling backward as a shot ricocheted off the giant boulder behind him. A second round buried itself in the dirt beside his shoulder. Tony kept pushing back, never taking his eyes from the shooter.

Suddenly, the man jerked and fell onto his back. The second sniper fired toward the sea, and Tony realized what had happened. A garda sharpshooter on the boat had fired at the bluff, hitting the first sniper. The second sniper responded by firing on the boat.

Tony raised himself up on one knee and fired a single shot at the gunman on the bluff. Not surprisingly, he missed completely, but the shot got the man's attention. He turned to aim at Tony, then collapsed and lay still. Whoever was firing from the boat was one hell of a shot. *Two kill shots from a bouncing boat deck. Holy sh…* Tony decided to stay down so he would not be mistaken for another sniper.

Minutes later, the sky exploded.

***

Tony watched in amazement as flares went up, a helicopter landed near the house, bullhorns blasted, and shots rang out. He stood and ran north, not toward the house, but toward the spot where Kilborgen's boat must have docked.

Sure enough, when he reached the edge of the bluff directly west of the mansion, he found a staircase carved in the rock, leading down to the water. At the bottom, he found a cove protected from the worst of the waves. A large concrete dock extended out from the staircase into deep water. Kilborgen's boat was moored there.

The dock also extended to his right, running parallel to the rock face. It seemed to dead-end where the bluff turned out toward the sea. Curious, Tony walked along that portion. When he reached the bluff, he realized the concrete path actually led to an opening, hidden by the odd angles of the stone outcroppings. He didn't step inside, thinking it unwise without a source of light. Cursing himself again for letting his phone battery die, he turned and walked out to Kilborgen's boat.

He found the fisherman pacing on the aft deck.

"Aye, Mr. Harrington. Though' ye said I don' be seeing ye tonight."

"What can I say? I couldn't stay away."

"Quite the show underway up thar."

"Yes. I hope it's going well."

"If not, ye be in the right place. As ye know, I be ready to run away, should ye need."

"Happy to go with you," Tony said, smiling. Gesturing toward the cliff, he said, "There's a cave or something back there."

"Ya. The inspector said it looks to be another way up. Under the ground. Can ye imagine?"

Tony thought about it and realized he could. A mining baron would have the money, the technology, and the manpower to carve a tunnel from the house to the dock. "Perfect setup for smuggling," he said.

"Er fer simply gettin' to yer boats without bravin' the Irish weather," Kilborgen pointed out.

Tony nodded and smiled. "Or for smuggling."

The gunfire and other noise quickly subsided. Tony hoped that was a good sign. He asked Kilborgen if he happened to have a charger cord for an iPhone.

"Aye. Seems a couple o' my crew ne'er live without their screens." He went to the galley, rummaged through a drawer, and produced the cord, gesturing to an outlet above the galley's counter.

As soon as the phone was plugged in, it lit up with messages. Doug asking for an update, Rita asking if he was okay, and Darcy copying him on her text to Lynch and wishing him sweet dreams. A message from his mother made him smile. She hoped he was having a peaceful, relaxing vacation in Ireland, and chided him for not sending pictures. *Sure Mom, which corpse do you want to see?* As he finished glancing through the texts, not responding to any, a new message popped up from Lynch.

We're secure here. Knowing you, you're not far away. Where?

Tony texted back, *On Kilborgen's boat.*

Of course. Wait there.

Tony didn't respond. He left his phone charging on the galley counter and found a padded bench to lie on. In less than a minute, he was asleep.

Chapter 34

Sunday, May 31
Beara Peninsula, Ireland

Tony woke and glanced at his watch. He'd been out for about forty minutes. He sat up and saw Inspector Lynch sitting on the bench opposite him, sipping on a cup of tea or coffee.

"Sorry," Tony said.

Lynch waived away his concern.

Tony said, "So you're good?"

"Better than good. Twenty-eight arrests. Ten Russians and eighteen members of Foley's crowd. More than four hundred pounds of high-grade cocaine confiscated from the house. And one Colombian ship in custody with another huge amount drugs yet to be assessed."

"Casualties?"

"Three gunshot wounds, all suffered by Foley's people. One death."

Tony raised an eyebrow.

Lynch said, "Darius Polshkov. One single shot to the forehead."

"Might be for the best," Tony said, "considering what we've heard about him."

"Did you do it?" Lynch asked calmly, almost offhandedly, as he peered over the rim of his mug.

"*What?*"

"Our men didn't do it. Polshkov was dead when we got here. Did you kill him?"

"Don't be ridiculous. How would I manage that?"

"Someone did. Let me see your gun."

"My…?"

"The Glock tucked in your belt. The illegal firearm you're carrying. Let me see it."

Tony took it out and handed it over. As Lynch took it, Tony noticed the inspector was wearing gloves. He lifted the gun to his nose.

"It's been fired."

Tony could feel his face warming. "Only once. I tried to distract a sniper so he wouldn't fire on your boat."

"That was you up on the bluff?"

"Yes. I spotted two men with rifles getting into position to fire. I shouted, and one fired at me. Then he went down. I assume your man killed him. Then the second gunman fired down toward the trawler, so I fired the Glock to distract him. When he turned to return fire, he also went down. It goes without saying, your marksman deserves an award."

"She has several," Lynch said. Setting the Glock on the seat beside him, he looked at Tony. Finally, he said, "Thank you. If we hadn't been alerted to the men on the bluff above us, tonight's casualty list might look a lot different."

"Glad I was able to help."

"So if you didn't kill Polshkov, who did?"

"No clue," Tony said, conjuring up his most innocent face. "Maybe one of his men was tired of working for a lunatic. Took advantage of the chaos to be done with him."

"Maybe," Lynch said, sounding unconvinced.

"And Foley?"

Lynch frowned. "That's the one thing that went arseways. We didn't find him. His men played dumb. Said no one by that name came with them."

Tony thought about Foley's vow to get Moira, and to get the Russians who took her. He said, "I don't believe it. He's here. Maybe he killed Polshkov. I assume you've searched the house and grounds."

"The ERU teams are going through everything for the second time. I think he's gone, or else he never came."

"ERU?"

"That's our Emergency Response Unit," Lynch said. "It's like your SWAT teams."

Tony glanced to the side, distracted by movement on the dock. Men were emerging from the entrance to the underground staircase. The first three men were dressed in black fatigues and had their hands in the air. Behind them was an officer wearing full riot gear, urging them forward with the barrel of his assault rifle.

Lynch followed Tony's gaze and said, "I thought we had everyone in custody. The guard must have found these three hiding in the underground." He turned to Kilborgen. "You okay transporting some prisoners back to Castletown?"

The fisherman shrugged. "Long as they be trussed proper, I don' mind."

Lynch shouted to the officer. "Good job! Bring 'em on out here."

Tony watched the group approach, assessing each of the prisoners. He assumed he would be asked to assist as the inspector and the ERU officer got the men settled and cuffed or perhaps tied with ropes. Thinking about the difficulties of those tasks made Tony wonder how one officer had managed to corral all three gangsters. Even with an assault rifle, it would be dicey work.

I wonder...

Tony stood and looked more carefully. The murky predawn skies made it hard to see details. He turned to Kilborgen. "Binoculars?"

"Just here," he said, stepping into the cabin and returning with a pair.

"What is it?" Lynch asked.

"Hmm, maybe nothing." Tony lifted and focused the binoculars. The three captives were all white males. They appeared to be young and reasonably fit. Nothing about them appeared to be amiss, although Tony had to admit he didn't actually know how a member of a drug cartel should look. He wished he could get a clear view of the garda. Without taking his gaze from the group, he asked Lynch, "Is it normal for an officer to stand so close to his captives? Isn't that dangerous?"

"Bad craic," Lynch said. "He should know better."

Then, for an instant, a gap opened between two of the prisoners, and Tony could see the officer's eyes. He dropped the binoculars and screamed, "Down!"

On the dock, the officer lunged forward, knocking two of the captives into the water. He raised the weapon and pulled the trigger.

At the same moment, Tony dived for the deck, scooping the Glock off the vinyl seat. A series of bullets ripped through the boat. When the onslaught paused, Tony looked over the gunwale and saw Foley, still dressed in ERU gear, charging the boat.

Tony rolled up on his knees, aimed, and shot him in the face. The Irish gang leader spun, fell hard to the dock, and rolled over the edge into the water. Weighted down by the equipment he wore, Foley dropped out of sight quickly.

Tony heard someone groan behind him. Lynch shouted, "Our captain's hit. Get those two who went in the water."

Tony jumped up, stepped to the side of the boat, and ordered the two men treading water to climb up the ladder onto the aft deck. They didn't argue. The water here was probably 50 degrees Fahrenheit. Once on board, Tony kept the Glock trained on them. Lynch tossed a pair of handcuffs out onto the deck. Tony kicked them over to the men. "Each of you put an arm through that steel winch mount and cuff yourselves together."

Once they'd done as he demanded, Tony left the Glock on the seat, walked over to the men, and made sure the cuffs were tight. The men were secure. There was no way around or over the mount. He quickly searched them for weapons, then he turned his attention to Kilborgen. He was lying in the doorway to the cabin. Blood dripped from under his coat.

Tony knelt and began to ask how he was.

Kilborgen said, "Ye coulda gave me a lil' more notice. I don' move so fast."

"Sorry," Tony said. "What can I do?"

"Ye can tell the peeler here ta stop cuttin' my coat. I'm cold, an' tha' thing cost a wee fortune."

"He just wants to expose your wound so he can bandage it. Hate to have you bleed all that whiskey out onto your deck."

"Ooh, funny," Kilborgen said, "but shoudn' ye be looking fer the other guy? There were three o' them on the dock with the shooter."

Tony shook his head. "Foley killed the other man when he fired at the boat. His body's on the dock. You should be grateful. He took some of the slugs meant for you."

"Ya, I be feelin' feckin' grateful, to be sure. Ow!"

"Sorry," Lynch said.

"Is that my whiskey ye be pourin' on my side?"

Lynch smiled and nodded.

Tony got up, found some clean towels in the galley, and brought them to Lynch.

The inspector thanked him and continued dressing and wrapping the wound. He said, “Looks like one round caught his side. Tore up some flesh and probably broke a rib, but never penetrated the torso.” He looked at his patient. “You’re a lucky man, Captain Kilborgen.”

“Ya, did I mention I be feelin’ feckin’ lucky ’bout now? Put some o’ that whiskey in a glass for me, ’fore I order ye off my boat.”

***

When Kilborgen was safely tucked into his cabin, and the ERU officers were back on board, Tony bid Inspector Lynch a good morning. The sky in the east was beginning to lighten. Sunrise was not far off.

“You don’t want to ride with us?”

Tony chuckled and said, “No, I’ll let you take the boat full of bullet holes out into the open sea.”

Lynch grinned.

Tony added, “On a serious note, I can’t wait around while you fish Foley’s body out of the water. I still need to retrieve my rental car, and help a waitress get back to her apartment. Oh, and I have a shitload of stuff I need to return to your mother’s house.”

Lynch looked at him and shook his head. “I don’t want to know. Of course, I’ll need to see both you and Moira at the guard station in Castletown. Tomorrow?”

“Tomorrow’s fine. In the meantime, you’ll find the goon she killed in the back of the Russians’ van. It’s parked at the pub down the road.” Tony told him how to find the key, then added, “By the way, as we fought in the van, this guy admitted to killing the two students in the cable car."

Lynch's eyes widened, and he dropped heavily to the bench behind him. "I hope it's true. It would be good to close that horrible episode." He looked up at the sky and ran a hand through his hair. "Jesus, Mary, and Joseph, this case is going to take me a year to sort out, and five years' worth of paperwork."

Tony smiled, shook the inspector's hand, and stepped out onto the dock.

***

A text on his phone said, *Meet me*. The number was anonymous, but Tony was pretty sure who it was from and what it meant.

He climbed up the rock staircase to the top of the bluff and hiked to the outcropping of rock where he and Ryan had previously taken turns pointing guns at each other. When he arrived, he found Ryan sitting cross-legged on the ground, leaning back against the rock face.

"Asleep?" Tony asked.

"No. I could hear you coming from a hundred meters out."

"I wasn't trying to be quiet. The guard is wrapping up here. Most of them are leaving."

"Success?"

"You first. Did you kill Polshkov?"

One quick nod said he did.

Tony said, "How did you manage it?"

Ryan shrugged. "I speak Russian. I'm wearing dark clothes. It wasn't that hard to get close to him. I told the guard outside his room that I was relieving him for a twenty-minute break. The dipshit was happy to hear it. He took off like a Sarmat missile, no questions asked. Then, I grabbed a comforter from the couch in the hall, wrapped it around my automatic, and walked into Polshkov's room.

He looked up from a writing desk, and I put a round in his brain. The blanket muffled the shot, so no one came running. I left. I'm making it sound easy, but don't get the idea that it was, or that I liked it. Now, tell me about the operation. Did the guard succeed?"

Tony told him what Lynch had said, then described what had happened in the cove.

Ryan stared, then said, "You're unbelievable. Are you sure you don't work for the CIA?"

"You forget. I don't work for anybody."

"I'll trade your problem for mine." As he spoke, he reached down and began tracing patterns in the dirt with his right index finger.

Tony lowered himself to his haunches and said, "Obviously, we have to talk about this."

Ryan nodded.

"First, you should know that I've taken some precautions for myself. I've written about you, put it in a sealed electronic file, and sent it to three people I trust to keep it locked up, unless something happens to me."

Ryan looked at him.

Tony said, "I'm not just saying this. I really did it."

Ryan smiled. It was a flat, woeful smile that never reached his eyes. He said, "I'm glad you did. Honestly. It will discourage the FSB from coming after you."

"That was the idea. Now what about you?"

"Yes, well, that's the question, isn't it? I want to go back to Chicago and resume my life."

"You know that can't happen. I can't knowingly let a Russian agent live among us. Your next assignment could be something genuinely harmful to our country."

"Right." He sighed deeply. "So what are my options, besides putting a gun in my mouth and pulling the trigger?"

"Don't even think that. You know better than I do that you have two choices. Return to Russia or go to the CIA and offer to be a double agent. Go to work for us."

"It's tempting," Ryan said. "If I was able to stay with Rita, I might consider it."

Tony shook his head.

Ryan continued, "You're right, of course. I can't be with Rita, can't expose her to the risks. Not if I truly love her. Besides, as I've told you, I'm a patriot. I love my country. I took an oath to protect her. I can't betray that oath."

"Then you have to go."

"You won't stand in my way?"

"Not if you give me your word you'll go there and stay there. I don't want to be on vacation in California someday and find you basking in the sun on the beach in Malibu."

"Okay," Ryan said. "You have it. Now, what will you tell Rita?"

"You'll have to do it," Tony said. "You're a much better liar than I am. Tell her you've met someone else, that you've decided to stay with her in Europe. Tell her you're sorry, but convince her it's over. Convince her there's nothing she can do to change it."

"She's going to be hurt," Ryan said. "I don't think that's just my ego talking. I think she loves me."

"I know she does, but it's the only way," Tony said. "She has to believe you're gone for good, if she's going to have any chance to move on with her life."

Ryan wiped tears from the corners of his eyes. He stood and held out his hand. As Tony took it, Ryan pulled him into a bear hug. Into his ear, he said, "Goodbye, Tony. I hope you find what you're looking for."

As Ryan disappeared down the mountainside, Tony turned and walked the other way. When he reached the cliff at the ocean's edge, he turned to watch the sunrise. Ryan's parting words haunted him.

Am I really so lost? Is it really so obvious, even to a man who's just walked away from everything? The thought was more than depressing; it was frightening. *Who in the hell am I?*

Chapter 35

Thursday, June 11
Dublin, Ireland

Tony decided walking had been a bad idea. The sun was shining, and it was hot—the first uncomfortably warm day he'd experienced in Ireland. He reached up and wiped sweat from his forehead. The beads of moisture on the back of his hand reminded him of Darcy. He loved the sight of sweat on her skin. The thought made his pulse quicken and his heart ache. He missed her terribly. Fortunately, he didn't have long to wait. She was scheduled to land at Dublin Airport in time for dinner.

During the past ten days, while Darcy had been shooting at Pinewood, Tony and Rita had been busy exploring their family's roots in County Cork. Rita had been devastated by Ryan's sudden breakup, so Tony had stayed at her side every day, helping her cope and keeping her occupied.

Fortunately, she seemed genuinely interested in learning more about the Harringtons in Ireland. She willingly accompanied him on trips to old churches, cemeteries, and public archives, and suggested a couple of side trips to villages mentioned in the old documents they found. She reached the point where she wasn't crying every night and had less trouble putting on a smile during the day. Tony thought she'd moved through the stages of grief quickly and had arrived at acceptance. He'd grown confident she would be okay. In any case, Rita had returned to Chicago the previous day. Tony had stayed in Dublin, where he and Darcy had agreed to meet.

Now, Tony was walking to a restaurant and bar at the south edge of Phoenix Park, a couple of miles from his hotel. Lynch had suggested it, probably because it was near the Gardai headquarters which, oddly, at least in Tony's view, was located inside the park. Reaching the restaurant had required more time and sweat than Tony had anticipated due to Dublin's maze of streets around odd-shaped blocks, and obstructions like the River Liffey and multiple train tracks. By the time Tony arrived, he was ten minutes late for their appointed lunch. He was glad to see Lynch hurrying in the door, obviously running behind as well.

Tony had requested they meet, hoping to bring closure to several aspects of the events on the Beara Peninsula. Once the two were settled at a table, Tony could see Lynch was in a good mood. He hoped that would help to loosen his tongue.

Before Tony could even ask, Lynch said, "I assume you'll be interested to know that it's official. The two students who died in the cable car were murdered by Polshkov's man, the one Moira strangled in the van."

"No surprise there," Tony said, "but what do you mean by 'official'?"

"The folding knife he was carrying had traces of blood in the opening mechanism. DNA testing proved it was Lauren O'Grady's."

"So Moira killed the man who had tried to kill her. I call that poetic justice."

"His name is, uh… was, Arsendo Petrov. He was a well-known assassin often employed by the Bratva. Interpol is more than happy to know they can stop searching for him."

"Wow, Moira…"

"Moira is lucky to be alive," Lynch interrupted. "And so are you. This guy was as skilled as he was cold-blooded. The British estimate that he killed more than a dozen people in England alone. He was one of those who loved killing, relished it… and the more challenging, the better."

Tony swallowed hard. "Like inside a cable car suspended above the sea."

The inspector nodded and said, "It makes me wonder how she did it. How did a twenty-something waitress manage to kill one of the deadliest men on two continents?"

Tony's brow creased. "I thought you knew. I can tell you how…"

Lynch held up a hand. "I've read your statements. I know what happened in the van. It just seems so… unlikely. A woman—a girl, really—whose hands are tied, and is still recovering from her ordeal in that basement, has the presence of mind and the strength to overcome him. Doesn't it make you wonder?"

Of course it does. "No," Tony said, unable to break his habit of protecting her. "It was mostly dumb luck. As he, this Petrov, fought with me, he literally fell into her lap. She reacted instinctively, and fear fueled her strength. In the back of that van, the adrenaline was flowing like Guinness at a bachelor party, I promise you."

"Hmph. I suppose," the inspector said. Then, trying to maintain a stern, official face, but somehow falling short, he said, "There's another interesting twist."

"Oh?"

"Your fingerprints are also on the knife. In fact, they're the most prominent prints we found."

"*My* prints?" Tony was astounded, but only for an instant. He quickly recovered and said, "Of course they were. After Petrov died, I used his knife to cut the zip ties that bound Moira's hands and feet."

Lynch nodded. "She told us that. If she hadn't, we might be having this conversation in a jail cell instead of a pub."

Tony shook his head. "Don't you ever get tired of trying to paint me as a murderer?"

"Nope," Lynch said, and laughed.

They both paused and turned as a waiter approached. Lynch ordered bangers and mash, and Tony asked for the house burger. He was ready for something that might resemble American food.

When the waiter departed, Tony said, "With the killer dead, I guess we'll never know exactly how he committed the crime."

Lynch grunted his agreement. Tony didn't know the inspector was unwilling to admit that members of the Gardai Water Unit had found a wingsuit washed up on the rocks at the edge of Dursey Sound. Tony's original speculation, that the killer had done a BASE jump from the cable car to the water below, had been correct.

Oblivious to Lynch's secret, Tony moved on. "What about the other guy at the cable car station? The one who called himself Rob?"

"He was one of the people we arrested during the raid on the house. His real name is something Russian I can't pronounce."

"So what happens to all these people?"

"The Russians? Good question. We're sorting that out. I'm pretty sure the guy we call Rob will be held for trial here. He was directly involved in the murders of Lauren and Michael. We're disinclined to let him leave, and the families of those kids want some justice. As for the others, I think most will be deported."

"And Foley's people?"

"Again, it's a mixed bag. Some are wanted for specific past crimes, so they'll go to trial. Not surprisingly, everyone who went to the house that night to get Polshkov was carrying a firearm. Of course, most of them didn't have licenses. At the very least, they'll face charges for that. A couple were foolish enough to threaten or fire at ERU officers, so that will add to their woes. There may be additional charges related to the drugs if we can get a couple of them to rat out the others.

"Which reminds me," Lynch added, "the bloke you kicked in the head on the street in Dublin…"

"Yes?" Tony reached back and rubbed his skull, where a slight ridge could still be felt beneath his hair.

"His name is Desmond. They call him Desi. He was one of those arrested. After a couple of hours in lockup, he sang like a bird."

"And?"

"And the three of them worked for Foley. They came after you because a Bratva man told them you were coming to kill Moira."

"What?" Tony's eyes went wide.

"Desmond didn't admit to this next part, but I'm guessing the guy they heard it from was one of Polshkov's men, a guy named Rurik Alekhin. He was found dead in Ireland, presumably tortured and killed by Foley. The guy probably named you in an attempt to save himself."

"Named me? But how?" Almost as soon as the words left his mouth, Tony realized both the how and the why. "Oh, shit."

Lynch gave his head a bob, indicating he knew what was coming.

"My involvement last winter in stopping the Russian terrorist attack."

"Bingo." Lynch said. "Some nasty people in Russia consider you an enemy. One of them was the guy Foley had under the knife. So he gave Foley your name, thinking it was a fine idea to have one enemy of Russia do them the favor of killing the other."

"Well, they got their wish, just in the opposite way they wanted."

"A lovely outcome," Lynch agreed, "if it weren't for all the blood and stuff."

Anxious to change the subject, Tony asked, "So what's the bottom line on the drug trade?"

"It's nice to have a big win," Lynch said, "but we're not foolish enough to think it's going away. Most of the Foley gang is still intact. We're sure they'll pick up the pieces and keep going. If they don't, a rival gang will step in quickly enough. The only truly good news is that the Russians appear to be backing off. Polshkov was the one pushing their expansion in Ireland. Now that he's gone, talk of a drug war has dissipated."

Their drinks arrived. Tony, still parched from his walk, took several swallows of his Coke. Lynch had iced tea.

Tony leaned forward and asked, "Any decision about Mr. Kilborgen? Is he okay?"

"You mean physically? Yes, he's recovering nicely. The doctor told him he couldn't go out on the boat for another couple of weeks, but I'd bet a month's pay he's already at it."

"I'm glad, but I was asking about his legal status. Is he in trouble?"

"Relax," Lynch said. "The prosecutor and the chief agree with you. Kilborgen risked his life to help us and ended up taking a bullet in his side and a bunch more in his boat as a reward. We think he's paid his dues. If he keeps his nose clean, no pun intended, he'll be fine."

"That's good," Tony said, sitting back to allow the waiter to set his food on the table. He took a bite and nodded his approval.

"It's okay?" Lynch asked.

"Some weird sauce on it, and more onion than I prefer, but I have to admit, I like it."

"We'll coax that Irish heritage to the surface eventually."

Tony grinned and took another bite.

The inspector did the same, then said, "By the way, I have a question for you."

"Oh?"

"How did Kilborgen transport the cocaine without leaving any traces on his boat? I asked him and he laughed and said to ask you. I think his exact words were, 'Yer sleeveen American boyo thinks 'e knows.'"

"Sleeveen?"

"Loosely translated, it means con man."

"That seems a bit harsh considering I may have saved his life."

"You put him in that position to begin with, so don't be expecting any gratitude from the captain."

"Fair enough."

"Now stop ducking the question," Lynch said, "and tell me how he did it."

Tony wiped his mouth with a napkin, took a drink of soda, and said, "I can't be sure, of course, but it seems obvious to me that the bags were the key."

"The bags?"

"When I was on the dock that morning, when the drugs were being unloaded, I could see they were carried in wide, shallow bags, instead of bound in traditional bales. It would be a lot of trouble to package the drugs like that, so there had to be a reason. Then I looked at the winch at the back of the fishing trawler, and it dawned on me."

"He somehow winched the bags of cocaine up inside his nets!" the inspector said loudly, then looked around to see if anyone was listening.

Tony smiled and nodded. "He probably modified the nets to

accommodate the bags. If you examine the nets, you should be able to confirm whether I'm a genius or not."

"You're not," Lynch said dryly, "but Kilborgen might be. Think about it. The perfect setup. The drugs never touch the decks, so there's no residue to find on anything. If he gets approached at sea by the Coast Guard or Gardai Water Unit, he just lowers the nets before they can get to him. The drugs are gone and the seawater washes any traces off the nets. We never would have caught him if Moira hadn't given him up."

"I think she did that to protect him. She wanted him to have a way out before it was too late." Even as he said it, he realized he once again was lifting up the beautiful Ms. Kennington. *Those are some powerful dimples*, he thought, grinning to himself.

The inspector said, "In any case, it's valuable for us to know about it. We need to watch for similar setups in the future."

"So big wins all around," Tony said. "Let's say Gardai thirty-six, bad guys nil. However you score it, I'd say it's about the best you could've hoped. Congratulations."

"Thanks, but it's hard to relax and feel like I can close the case. Two big mysteries remain unsolved."

Tony nodded, suppressing a groan and trying to maintain an impassive expression. He knew what was coming.

The inspector said, "I'd love to know who shot Polshkov, and I'm even more curious about who killed the sniper on the bluff. If it wasn't you, and I've reluctantly concluded that it wasn't, then it feels like there's another operative lurking in the background. Any thoughts about that?"

Tony kept his eyes focused on his food and shook his head. "No clue. There were a lot of despicable characters involved in this from both gangs. It could have been any one or more of them. As you said before, you may never know unless someone decides to sing."

Tony dared to look up at Lynch as the inspector sighed and said, "Just one last question. Where did you get the Glock?"

Tony smiled. He had anticipated the question and had concocted a reasonable lie the authorities would not be able to disprove. He said, "You mean the Glock I fired twice? Once to save you from a sniper and once to save you from the Ox's assault rifle?"

Lynch looked pained as he acknowledged this with a nod.

Tony said, "I took it from the guy in the van, um… Petrov, right? When I searched him for a knife to cut Moira's bonds, I found a second handgun in his rear pocket. Considering all that had happened, I thought it would be smart to hang onto it."

"Not smart, and not legal in Ireland," Lynch reminded him. "But as you said, it saved our arses. Also, we checked the ballistics and it wasn't the gun that killed Polshkov, so I suppose I won't haul you off to jail." He leaned back in his chair and spoke quietly, as if to himself. "I just wish I knew…"

Tony decided it would be wise to redirect the conversation. He said, "You didn't ask for my advice, but I'll give you a little I heard often from my Aunt Hill."

"Aunt Hill? Seriously?"

"Sister Mary Hilary Harrington, a proud Irish nun. She said the secret to happiness is to focus on what you have, and not on what you don't have."

"Not particularly original," Lynch said.

"No, but very profound, and worth remembering in this case. The cable car murders are solved, an international assassin and two major drug lords are dead, huge quantities of illegal drugs are off the streets, a major drug war has been averted, and more than two dozen criminals are locked up. I'm guessing that wins as big as these are rare. You have much to celebrate."

"All true," Lynch said, not looking like he meant it. Then,

surprising Tony, he said, "As much as I hate to admit it, you deserve a big slab of the credit. We appreciate what you did."

"Thanks," Tony said. "I got a nice letter from the chief superintendent saying the same, followed by a lot of words that basically invited me to go away and not try to be 'helpful' again."

Lynch chuckled. "I wonder who drafted that letter for him?"

***

After lunch, Tony had two important tasks to complete. First, his call to Doug Tenney was overdue. His friend would be curious and worried about Tony's recent activities. If Doug was paying any attention at all to the news from Ireland, he would know about the murders, drug busts, and arrests. He would assume Tony had been in the middle of at least some of it and would want to know all the gory details. In addition, Tony had made some decisions about his future. He wanted his friend's advice before doing anything rash.

Second on Tony's to-do list was shopping. He needed gifts for his family and friends, mementos of his trip. There was a perfect store on Grafton Street, near his hotel, that he especially wanted to visit. He turned in that direction. As he walked, he pulled out his phone and told it to call Doug.

Chapter 36

Friday, June 12
Dublin, Ireland

The garden behind the House of Mercy was even more beautiful in mid-June. Tony wondered if it was the summer sun or the fact he was holding Darcy's hand that brought the flowers into full bloom. Either way, it was a perfect afternoon.

Darcy had arrived in Dublin on schedule the night before. Her film had wrapped, and she'd met him at the Fitzwilliam Hotel. It had been a perfect night of great sex followed by pasta at Zizzi on Grafton Street followed by even better sex. As Tony thought about it, he corrected himself. With Darcy, it wasn't sex; it was lovemaking. He loved Darcy Gillson.

Now, on a Friday afternoon, he was excited to show her around the Mercy landmark that had meant so much to his Aunt Hill.

They were alone in the garden and Tony suggested they sit on one of the wrought iron benches. When they were settled, he turned to her and said, "I know you've been worried about me."

Smiling, she said, "I can't imagine why. Just because you've been fighting drug lords and snipers and…"

"That's not what I meant."

Darcy apparently caught the seriousness of his tone. Her smile vanished, and she waited quietly.

Tony said, "Leaving the *Town Crier* was harder on me than I dreamed possible. My view of myself—my whole identity—was wrapped up in being a journalist."

"You still can be," Darcy said earnestly, squeezing his hand.

"I know," Tony said. "I've thought about that. We could move to a bigger city, or I could work remotely from Orney. I could even write for a virtual publication online."

Darcy was smiling again.

Tony said, "However, I've realized I was wrong."

"Wrong?"

"Wrong about what I missed. Think about it. While at the *Crier*, I was constantly in trouble with Ben for overstepping my bounds as a journalist, for jumping into the fray, for taking action instead of being content to just write about crime. In fact, by the end of my time there, the writing of the news was becoming a nuisance. I wanted to be out there *doing*."

Darcy nodded. Five trips to visit Tony in hospitals in two years had certainly proven the truth of what he was saying.

He continued, "You told me yourself not long ago that you knew I would always opt to take action, that it was my nature to be the hero."

"Yes," Darcy said quietly, looking down. "Your time in Ireland has done nothing the dispel that notion."

"Exactly," he said. He reached out with his free hand and lifted her chin. "I've realized, Darcy, that I'm not a journalist, I'm an activist. It's not the best word for it, but it's what I am. More to the point, it's what I want to be. I want you to be okay with that. I want you to stick with me as I do these things."

"What things? I don't even know what that means. Are you joining the FBI or what?"

"Probably not," Tony said. "I'm not especially good at following the rules."

She acknowledged that but prodded him to answer the "or what" question.

"I suppose it will take the form of private detective. Get a license and hang a shingle so people can find me. Then see what comes my way. I'm confident I can do this. I've proven to myself that I have at least the rudimentary skills necessary to take on evil and win."

Darcy looked away. Although she barely moved, Tony sensed her unease.

He waited, trying to give her time to process the idea and respond. The silence grew unbearable. Finally, he said, "You're skeptical. I get that. You're worried I'll fail. It's..."

She turned to look at him and shook her head. A tear leaked down her cheek.

Tony stopped and swallowed hard. When he spoke, his voice was softer. "Please don't cry. Just tell me honestly, can you, will you, stay with me if I pursue this? If you say no, I'll set it aside and find something else. I told you before, nothing is more important to me than this relationship. That hasn't changed."

"There you go again," she said, forcing a smile. "Being all noble." She sniffled and reached into her purse for a tissue. A moment later, she turned back to him and said, "I'm not worried about your success. There's no doubt in my mind you'll do great things for people who need you. I worry about your safety."

Tony started to speak, but she put a finger to his lips.

She said, "It's me, Tony. *Me*. I'm not sure I'm brave enough.

Every time I get one of those calls telling me you've been hurt, it's like my heart gets ripped from my chest."

He braved a smile. "I guess I'll just have to make sure I don't get hurt."

She shook her head. "Let me finish. I'm not sure I'm brave enough, but I'm willing to try. If this is what you really want, if this will make you happy, then yes, I'll stand by you."

It was Tony's turn to brush back tears. He pulled Darcy close and kissed her deeply. As they separated, she grinned and whispered, "Down, boy. I'm not sure the nuns want us necking in their garden."

"It's okay," Tony said. "I told them there might be a little of that."

"You told them…?"

Tony stood, turned to face her, and dropped to one knee. Pulling a box from his pocket, he held it up and said, "Darcy Gillson, you are my partner, my best friend, and the love of my life. Will you do me the great honor of becoming my wife?"

Chapter 37

Tuesday, June 23
Dursey Island, Ireland

Moira Kennington pulled her jacket closed and zipped it up. Even in late June, it was chilly out here on the westernmost tip of Dursey Island. The breeze kept her hair in a dance around her face, and the clear skies allowed the temperature to drop quickly as the sun touched the ocean on the western horizon.

She had surprised herself by deciding to ride the cable car out to the island. Although she wasn't normally squeamish, the memory of Michael and Lauren's blood-soaked bodies was still vivid in her mind. Despite all the things she had witnessed as Ox Foley's niece, the cable car murders were intensely disturbing. She supposed it was due, in part, to the fact the two students were innocents, and even more so, to the fact the female body on the floor of the car was supposed to be her.

She had come back to Allihies to pack up her remaining

possessions and say goodbye to Connie and others who had been good to her. She enjoyed the village and would make a point of returning for visits, but she knew her future wasn't here.

Thoughts of the future reminded her of Tony Harrington. In recent days the celebrity news had been filled with reports of actress Darcy Gillson's engagement to an out-of-work journalist from Iowa. While the pundits scoffed at and even ridiculed the mismatch, Moira knew Darcy was a lucky woman. Tony was an exceptional man. In Moira's mind, the offer still stood. If Tony and Darcy ever split, she would love to have him back in her life.

However, she knew a future with Tony was very unlikely, not only because of his circumstances, but because of hers. A lot had happened in the past three weeks. For starters, the authorities had officially cleared her of any wrongdoing in the death of her captor. Considering she had been kidnapped from a private home and tied up in the back of a van, it hadn't been hard to make a case that she had acted in self-defense. Tony, *dear Tony*, had submitted a written statement in support of the finding.

The chief superintendent of the guard had sent her a letter of commendation for assisting in the largest cocaine bust in Irish history and in the demise of Lennox Foley. Thinking of the letter made her smile, but not because the chief had been insensitive to her relationship to Foley. He had, in fact, noted that it must have been especially difficult for her to help the Gardai, considering Foley had been her uncle. The funny part was it hadn't been difficult at all.

When hiding at Mrs. Lynch's house, after her escape from the Russians, Moira had spent the day thinking about her future and all its possibilities. Tony had been right, in a way. Getting rid of Ox Foley had created an opportunity for her to have a new life—just not the one Tony had envisioned.

She had handed over the shotgun and had gone all-in with Ox's pursuers when she had realized his arrest or death would leave a giant void in his criminal enterprise. All the people and mechanisms would survive him, and the money would still flow. All they needed was a leader. In the confusion and uncertainty that followed Foley's death, others would vie for, even fight for, a chance to take his place.

However, Moira had realized the person most likely to succeed her uncle would be the one who had been his flesh and blood. Members of the gang would be most likely to support the person who was the Ox's favorite protégé, who already knew all his key people, who was privy to all his secrets, who was smart and capable, and who was tested and proven to be a willing and able killer. In the end, she had been right. In just three weeks, all the essential players had fallen in line. One particularly stubborn foe had simply fallen.

Now, Moira strode boldly to the end of Dursey Island, and stood alone at the top of the westernmost cliff of Dursey Point. It is said that whoever stands there is the last person in Europe to see the sun set. It seemed the perfect place to bring closure to her old life and begin anew as the wealthy, powerful, and fearsome leader of the Foley Gang.

Afterword

I've been planning to write a novel about Tony Harrington's trip to Ireland ever since my third novel was published. In *The Third Side of Murder*, Tony travels with his Italian mother to her hometown on the Amalfi Coast of Italy. I found it immensely challenging and entertaining to write about a relatively normal Iowa man encountering evil in exotic places.

Harrington, of course, is an Irish name, so it seemed natural—even inevitable—that Tony would eventually travel to the home of his paternal ancestors. I began writing this novel in 2023, but soon realized it would be difficult, if not impossible, to do it justice without visiting Ireland myself. So, Jane and I packed our bags and took an eight-day trip through the magnificent places described in the story.

We literally mapped out the trip I later created for Tony, Rita, and Ryan, going from Dublin to Cork to the town of Allihies on the Beara Peninsula. With the exception of some light rain, we loved everything about it. The food, the scenery, the music, the accommodations, and the Irish people were all wonderful in equal measures.

I'm eager to return.

While this is a work of fiction, and all the people and events are creations of my imagination, you may be interested to know a few key things are true.

First, Allihies is a real place and I urge you to visit. There really is a beach, and just a few miles down the road, a cable car really will carry you across the sea to Dursey Island.

Sadly, another fact is the burgeoning problem of drug abuse. When talking with residents of Ireland, they suggested that cocaine smuggling should be at the heart of a novel set there.

On a much happier note, the story of Catherine McAuley is also true. She lived in Dublin in the 1800s and is recognized as a major historical figure. Before the Irish converted to using the Euro, their five-pound notes featured an artist's portrait of Mother McAuley. The founding of the House of Mercy, and later, the Religious Sisters of Mercy, as related here is true albeit far too abbreviated in this telling. If you'd like to know more about this extraordinary person and her followers, you can find a great deal of information online and in several published histories. One of the most complete is *The Path of Mercy* by Mary C. Sullivan, RSM. Copyright 2012, The Catholic University Press of America.

If you haven't been to Ireland, I urge you to go. If you have been fortunate to have visited there, I'm confident you share my desire to return. In the meantime, I hope this tale filled the void, at least for a little while. Thanks for joining Tony and me on the ride.

Acknowledgments

As always, the completion of this novel would not have been possible without the tremendous support of my family, friends, and everyone involved in editing, proofing, designing, and publishing it. I am grateful beyond words for every one of them.

In the case of this book, I have some very special people to thank. Phil and Janice Harrington are longtime friends who gave generously of their time and knowledge of Ireland. As an aside, the fact Tony is named Harrington is completely coincidental. I created Tony in the 1980s, when I first dabbled in writing a novel. I met Phil and Janice and their wonderful family twenty years later.

They also helped this novel by introducing me to some of the people living in Allihies, including David Dudley, one of the operators of the Dursey Cable Car. David provided valuable insights and suggestions, as did several others from the village.

Insights into commercial fishing and its vessels were provided by another longtime friend, Cory Nelson, who works for a financial institution involved in the industry.

Please know all these people answered every question and provided outstanding information. Any errors are mine alone and any liberties taken with the facts were the results of my decisions to do so to enhance the story.

I also am honored to thank the Sisters of Mercy who founded, built, and served in the health care systems which employed me for over thirty years. I was privileged to work with and for many of these remarkable women. I feel hopelessly inadequate in expressing how much it meant to me to be a part of their ministries. I can only hope they know how much I appreciate and admire them.

Lastly, I want to thank the booksellers and readers who support authors and their work. I have been blessed with enthusiastic support from Tony's fans (I've always said he's much more popular than I'll ever be). Each time I walk into a bookstore and see my novels on the shelf, it creates a special thrill. Even better is receiving an email or message from a reader who enjoyed one or more of the books. I'm happy to say I get these regularly, and they are always appreciated.

I'd love to hear from you too. Write to me, and I'll do my best to respond.

In the meantime, keep reading and recommending books, and know you have my very sincere appreciation and best wishes.

Joseph LeValley, 2025
joe@josephlevalley.com

Enjoy Joseph LeValley's other Mysteries/Thrillers

featuring Tony Harrington

Critics and Readers Love Them!

- **James Rollins, NYT #1 Bestselling Author:** "More people need to be reading LeValley. Like right now."
- **Publishers Weekly:** "Fans of reporter sleuths...will be pleased."
- **U.S. Review of Books:** "Don't miss it!" — RECOMMENDED
- **Midwest Book Reviews:** "Nearly impossible to put down."
- **Online Book Club:** "Heartily recommend."
- **Danielle Feinberg, Pixar Studios:** "A gripping, page turner!"
- **Max Allan Collins, Bestselling Author of *Road to Perdition*:** "LeValley is one of the best writers of suspense around. Don't miss his latest thriller!"

Get Your Copies Today!

Joseph LeValley's books are available from your local bookstore, Barnes & Noble, Amazon, other online sellers, or from the author directly at **josephlevalley.com.**

Check the website for more information about books, public appearances, and much more!